BATHED IN MOONLIGHT

STACIA KAYWOOD

To finding love in the moonlight
Stacia Kaywood

Copyright (C) 2022 Stacia Kaywood

Layout design and Copyright (C) 2022 by Next Chapter

Published 2022 by Next Chapter

Edited by Graham (Fading Street Services)

Cover art by Lordan June Pinote

This book is a work of fiction. Names, characters, places, and incidents are the product of the author's imagination or are used fictitiously. Any resemblance to actual events, locales, or persons, living or dead, is purely coincidental.

All rights reserved. No part of this book may be reproduced or transmitted in any form or by any means, electronic or mechanical, including photocopying, recording, or by any information storage and retrieval system, without the author's permission.

For my children, you are my inspiration and greatest joy. Never stop reaching for your dreams. But perhaps, L, animatronic dinosaur parks might be better than live ones.

For my mother, thank you for believing in me.

Bee, thank you for answering the hundreds of phone calls, questions, and your encouragement.

CHAPTER ONE

April 1945

As the first rays of sunlight filtered through the lace curtains, Greta Müller blinked open her eyes and took inventory of how many mornings began this exact same way. *548 – has it actually been that many days? Impossible, but no. If today was the 10th of April, then it has, in fact, been 548 days.* She groaned, flipped over, and tugged the quilt up over her head. "Maybe today will be different!" she whispered in anticipation. But, then again, different had all sorts of variations. Maybe today will be a touch different. Not bad "different," definitely not that. Just different.

Maybe Ezra would not run into the room within the next five minutes, and she could get some extra sleep. Or maybe Liesel would stop in for a visit and bring real coffee. Or the war could end. She laughed. If she could simply wish for anything, it would be to wake up in her old bed in Berlin to a world where the war had never started! But that was not to be, so instead, she waited.

She counted the seconds: one... two... three, and there it was. Ezra's soft patter along the hardwood floor, a poke on her shoulder, the sharp intake of air as he checked to make sure Greta was still there.

Stifling a groan, she rolled over with a wide smile on her lips. "I am up, Ezra." Throwing off the quilt, she reached towards the ceiling, stretching her muscles after a night of rest. "Ready for another exciting day?"

His deep brown eyes sparkled with amusement, and he nodded his head, his dark locks tumbling across his forehead. Turning on his heel, he ran back out the door. *Ah, so there's my answer – definitely not different today.* Thus, the morning would begin as it always did in their home, nestled away from the world.

The house was a perfect cozy hideaway, with woods on one side and an open field on the other. It had two small bedrooms, each with a comfortable bed and downy quilt. The kitchen and living room suited their needs: a fireplace to keep them warm and a table where they could fill their bellies from their limited pantry. However, the most important feature about this home wasn't what could be seen, but rather what was hidden below. It was for this reason Liesel sent Greta and Ezra to stay here and not with her.

"I insist, Greta. You and Ezra cannot live here with me. It would only be a matter of time before someone started asking questions. Stay at my old home near the woods. No one goes near there. I'll tell everyone I've leased it to my niece. And since I have so many, no one will question it." Liesel patted Greta's hand. "Trust me."

The next day, they moved in, and Liesel revealed its secret. "Wilhelm didn't like leaving me behind. He worried about the long cold winters and insisted on building a root cellar right here." She pointed down to a burgundy and gold handwoven rug in the center of the living room. Liesel lifted the rug, pointing to the floorboards. "I know it doesn't seem like much, but see that notch there?" She pointed at a knothole in the wood. "It's actually a handle." Greta leveraged her hand through the knot and tugged. To her surprise a few floorboards lifted up. It was a trap door. Underneath, a simple rung ladder led down to a dirt room. The walls were reinforced by wooden slats and shelves holding a few jars.

"Liesel, this is perfect."

"Yes. You and Ezra can hide if need be. And we can stock the shelves, so you have food to last."

Together, Greta and Liesel devised a method for rolling the rug back over the floor using strings threaded through the floorboards. This house, with its perfect hiding spot, was exactly what they hoped for.

Beginning her morning calisthenics, an odd tingling sensation crept up her spine. *Perhaps today will be different after all.* Except this feeling caused her stomach to lurch forward and beads of sweat to gather at the nape of her neck. "Oh, please, nothing bad! Not now, after all this time," she cried out.

Inching across the room to the window, she peered out at the line of trees edging their yard. She heard the faint chirp of birds, saw the trees swaying in a breeze. Everything appeared as it always did. Yet, the feeling persisted. She waved her arms, trying to shake it off.

"You are letting the isolation get to you, Greta! Hearing things that aren't there." She quickly dressed and went to the kitchen to prepare their meager breakfast.

Ezra rolled his train across the floor, the squeaking of its wheels the only sound. Greta longed for the day when he would speak again, when she could hear him utter the barest of words. But it had been nearly two years since that fateful day and absolutely nothing – just silence.

As she gathered ingredients to make breakfast, the eerie feeling intruded on the pleasant morning once again; her shoulders tensed, her ears heated. This time something was different. "What was that?" she asked Ezra, rubbing down the tiny hairs prickling in fear along her arms.

He stood perfectly still, alert like a hunted deer. His eyes grew round. A faint noise rose from the woods behind the house... *Hide!* the voice in her head screamed, forcing Greta into action.

"Go! Now!" Greta cried out, as they both ran to the center of the living room, wrenching up the secret door in the floor. Down they scurried into their cramped hiding space, hunching against the wooden slats. Greta replaced the hidden door and yanked the string, moving the rug back in place over the opening.

Gunfire! The rat-a-tat-tat grew louder, as the fighting drew closer. Ezra leaned into Greta's arms. She held him tightly, whispering words of comfort into his ear. "They will move past us quickly, Ezra. Have faith." As the sounds strengthened in intensity, Greta's fervent prayers became silent words whispered upon lips that soon stilled as they waited with bated breath.

The gunfire thundered around them. Voices passed by, then faded in retreat. Greta hitched herself up closer to the floor, trying to distinguish the sounds coming from above. Ezra shrank into a small ball against the dirt floor, covering his ears with his tiny fists. *He's been through so much, please, God. Let this be over quickly.*

There was a jumbled mix of shouting and gunfire. A bullet whizzed above their heads. Porcelain shattered. Another bullet broke a window. Bullets zipped through the room above them. Greta situated herself next to Ezra, holding him close to ease his tremors.

She cooed softly into his ear, "It will be over soon, Ezra, I promise." Silent tears soaked the knees of his tan short pants as he wrapped his arms around bent legs, clutching them to his body. The encounter brought back terrible memories, memories of the place they fled.

"We will wait here a while to be sure they leave. Keep quiet for now." She hummed lightly into his ear, cradling him as she continued the lullaby. She held onto a fervent hope for the day he would feel safe again, when he would no longer hide from monsters who haunted his nightmares. As quickly as the fighting came, it left with an unnatural silence following in its wake.

Long minutes passed. The cuckoo chirped the hour. Still they stayed in the security of their hiding spot. Ezra stopped crying. They would wait until the cuckoo chirped once again. Then it should be safe for them to emerge and go on with their day as if nothing had happened.

Bang! The door slamming against the wall shattered the silence. Footsteps! Both Greta's and Ezra's hearts pounded with abject fear as they listened to the cacophony above. Someone walked heavily – one foot thudded, the next slid behind, step, drag, step, drag, step, drag. The tattoo of leaden boots echoed through their hiding place, each step punctuating the silence. Whoever entered the house collapsed onto the sofa above them.

Ezra instantly went rigid. They were both too frightened to move, holding in their breath as if the mere act of breathing would give them away. *Who is it?* The springs in the sofa squeaked. A gut-wrenching moan. The sofa shifted, a small scrape against the floor. A heavy thud and prolonged groan... and then he was silent. *Is it a soldier? An American?* She swallowed hard. *Or could he be German?*

The man coughed, moaned. She needed him out of her

house. He could not stay here; someone would be searching for him, surely. And if he were found with them, if the Germans found Ezra? What would happen then? The war was fast approaching its end. It has to be if there was fighting this far inside of Germany. She could not risk anyone discovering the truth, not now.

She whispered to Ezra, "Stay quiet." Gently, she rolled back the rug and pushed the floorboards up just enough to peek through an opening. Seeing no immediate threat, she carefully concealed Ezra and moved from her hiding place.

CHAPTER TWO

Resting his head against the back of a sofa, Captain Jimmy O'Brien tried to figure out what had gone so terribly wrong. One moment he was leading his small patrol of men through a wooded area, the next thing he knew, they were ambushed from the rear and front at the same time. The encounter quickly descended into chaos, but some quick thinking and convenient cover helped his patrol regain the upper hand. All, except for Jimmy.

The situation was totally FUBAR. He remembered the sensation of falling, a bullet piercing his shoulder, hitting the ground hard. Hearing the gunfire fade into the distance, he raised his head, seeing no one. He was helplessly alone. Rising from the mist in the meadow before him was a house, it called out to him. Help. He had to get help. At some point his men would return and take him back to their camp. For now he could only hope he had found the aid he needed.

Bracing against the sofa, he attempted to push himself back to a standing position, but it was no use. Pain shot through his shoulder, dizziness followed, his vision tunneled.

Warm, sticky blood pooled along the gash in his thigh. *This is it. You have no choice, Jimmy, you must get up. There's no one here to help you.* But try as he might, he could not force himself to rise. He prayed for a miracle.

The creak of floorboards drew his attention. He tried to force his eyes open, but they stubbornly refused. He heard a faint clearing of a throat and a sharp intake of breath.

"Ach, du Lieber!" a soft female voice exclaimed. Whoever it was inched closer to him and fingered the name on his uniform. "English, yes?" When he didn't respond, she softly prodded around his shoulder, then his thigh.

Did an angel of mercy come to my aid or is it an agent of my death? As she leaned closer to him, he caught the faint scent of lilacs and clean linen. Such a pleasant smell, with death lurking around the corner.

All too quickly, she left his side. Her absence left him cold. Jimmy released a frustrated moan. He wanted the warmth her proximity gave him, to smell her heavenly perfume. He called out to her, but the sound choked in his dry throat.

A clink, slosh, thunk next to him told Jimmy of the angel's return. Her warm breath washed over his face as she placed her small hand against his chest. He felt her unbutton his shirt and her fingers explore the wound at his shoulder. "Here, let me take off your shirt." Her sweet voice was lightly accented. He allowed her to tug the sleeves away from his shoulders and down his arms. Ever so gently, she pulled him forward while she removed his uniform.

"Hold still, please. This will be over quickly, as long as you do not move." She spoke barely above a whisper, her voice a soothing balm. He felt the sharp edge of a blade, a tug, and then a shooting pain through his shoulder.

His eyes shot open from the pain as he gripped her hand with all the strength he had left. A triumphant smile greeted him, and she held the bullet out for inspection. His heart stopped beating as he took in the vision before him. Buttery blonde hair fell around her face. Blue-green eyes of a clear summer's day. A pixie face with delicate features. She was beautiful.

"It's over. Here." She dropped the bullet into his outstretched hand. "It is out. Now, I need to sew up the wound, as it is too large to bandage. I will try not to hurt you." His eyes darted from her to the blade to the bullet and back again. She repeated her promise, a placating hand resting above his heart.

I did it! Greta could scarcely believe her first aid worked, and the bullet was out. She had been terrified by his lethargy and the pallor of his skin, but the moment his eyes flew open, she breathed a sigh of relief. He should live, thank goodness.

He was too stunning to die; it would be too tragic, such a waste. His eyes, she had never seen such a color, two perfect pools of melted chocolate. And the rest of him! She felt like she was touching a Greek statue with perfectly defined muscles, firm jaw, and broad shoulders. But he was a real man, with a sprinkling of dark hair curling around the neckline of his undershirt, the sight of which caused her stomach to bubble rather pleasantly. It had been far too long since she last saw a man, let alone one so perfectly proportioned. *Focus, Greta!*

She applied pressure to the wound with a bandage, which helped staunch the bleeding. "Can you manage to put pressure here? I need to inspect more of you." He placed his hand on the padding and remained still for the rest of the examination.

Next was his leg, where his hand clamped the fabric over a growing pool of crimson. Greta admired his long fingers, imagining how they could feel cradling her cheek, stroking her skin. She lifted his hand from his leg, resisting the urge to hold it for a moment, and instead inspected the wound. It was very deep. She needed a better view of his injury, but cutting open the leg of his pants was not an option, as he would have nothing to wear. There was no other way. Tentatively she reached for his belt and button fly. In a flash, his hand grabbed hers, his eyes flew open, glassy and confused.

A flush crept across her face, as she gestured to the injury. "I am sorry, but I need better access to the wound. There is no other way. Your pants, they must go."

For a moment, he studied her face. She gave a wry smile and waved her fingers over his leg. He reluctantly nodded, but indicated he would take over the task of disrobing. Motioning to her to turn her head around, he began removing his clothing. She could hear the slide of the buckle, the rustle of his pants. The intimate sounds caused a blush to bloom over her chest as she tried not to envision what he might look like underneath. She folded and refolded the towel in her hand, concentrating on anything but the fact he was taking off his clothes.

Jimmy cleared his throat, and she turned around. A rag now covered his lap down to the wound. She moved his hand back to his shoulder and instructed him to hold the bandage again as it was still oozing a bit of blood.

He grimaced as she touched the skin near the tear on his exposed thigh. The wound was gruesome, his flesh red and swollen around a gash, running the entire length of his thigh. It was deep, possibly even to the bone, in need of stitches to keep out any infection.

"I will be back. I need to retrieve a needle and thread. Keep pressure on your shoulder and," she placed his hand on a folded rag on his thigh, "if you can, rest as much weight as possible here." Keeping his head back and eyes closed, his Adam's apple bobbed as he swallowed deeply.

In the kitchen, a pot of water simmered on the stove. She disinfected her needle. After washing her hands in water as hot as she could stand, she fished out the needle, gathered a few supplies, and returned to the living room to see her patient.

"Here, drink this and take a few of these." She handed him a glass of water and some aspirin tablets. He swallowed the pills and drank the water down in thirsty gulps.

Finally, feeling like he could open his eyes without becoming dizzy, Jimmy took in his makeshift hospital and the woman before him. The room was small, modestly decorated with lace curtains and a cuckoo clock on the mantel.

As for her, she was worth admiring a bit closer. He resisted the urge to sweep his fingers across the dusting of freckles covering the bridge of her nose. He wanted to feel her silky skin against his own.

His bewitching angel motioned to the kitchen. "I need a few more things." She held her hand against his forehead. The touch was soothing as he leaned his cheek against the palm of her hand. She left again, leaving behind an odd coldness in her wake.

A floorboard creaked. He spied a curious face peeking up at him. Jimmy flashed a weary half-smile. "Well, hello there, little fella," he rasped, as the boy carefully crept to his side.

"Your mom is taking care of me," Jimmy said, pointing with his head behind him, but the boy said nothing in response.

Up onto the sofa Ezra climbed, plopping next to Jimmy, and beginning to inspect him with childlike curiosity. He reached for the shirt, which still rested on the arm of the sofa. His tiny fingers traced over the diamond patch for the 4th Infantry Division.

"Those are the green ivy leaves of my unit," Jimmy explained. "Our nickname is Iron Horse." Then Ezra's fingers outlined his name patch. "O'Brien, that's my name. You can call me Jimmy." He lifted his hand off his wounded thigh, shakily extending it in greeting. The boy gripped his index finger in a shake before Jimmy lowered it back onto padding.

Ezra reached out to hold Jimmy's face, clasping it in his little hands, turning it from left to right. Then he rubbed his palm over the salt and pepper stubble along Jimmy's cheeks and chin. "Believe it or not, kid, my beard used to be all brown before the war. This war has made me an old man." He laughed, and Ezra returned a small smile.

Her arms full, Greta returned and stumbled backwards with a startled cry in German, "Ezra, what are you doing here?"

"Oh, he's no problem, ma'am. It's nice to see kids." Jimmy leaned back, the action causing more pain than he intended, and his dizziness returned.

"You're not Irish?" She startled with brief surprise, as his voice reflected a distinctively American accent, not the Irish one she expected.

Jimmy opened one eye, concentrating on what she was saying. "No, ma'am, American through and through. Is that a problem?"

"I am sorry, I noticed the name on your uniform, and it confused me." She sat down near his leg, rubbing his skin with soap and water. It stung and he shifted slightly. "I sometimes forget Americans have Irish names too." She gestured to the towel she held. "This will hurt, but it is necessary. I have no way of getting you to a doctor or the Americans. And we certainly can't risk an infection."

"Were you hoping I was British?" he asked, wanting to distract himself from the discomfort of her ministrations.

She shrugged, as she threaded the needle. "I know not which of the Allies were in the area, I am just relieved you are not a German." Pulling on the thread and needle, she began to sew up the wound. Moving the needle gently in and out, the action brought the ragged edges of the skin together. He shifted and gritted his teeth.

Jimmy winced as she stitched further. "Agh!" His hand clamped down on his thigh, trying to squeeze the pain away.

"I'm sorry," she lamented with pity in her eyes. "I don't have anything stronger for the pain." Her brow furrowed and her teeth worried at her bottom lip as she concentrated on keeping the stitches straight and even.

Jimmy focused on her face. The pixie nose, wondering how she could breathe through one so dainty. Not like his somewhat large but ordinary beak. Such a delicate creature, this German woman. Why did she prefer the company of an American, versus her own countrymen? She was a puzzle, but a beautiful one. "I am very grateful to you." He sucked in his breath as she prodded around a particularly tender spot. "Don't worry, they will come looking for me."

Jimmy liked this close proximity, having her so close he could smell her freshly laundered clothing. He could study her idiosyncrasies, the way she tilted her head from side to side when the stitching was difficult. The faintest hum of approval when the process went smoothly.

"Mister O'Brien, can you move your other hand, please? I need to sew up your shoulder now." She leaned in toward him as she reinspected this shoulder wound.

As she pressed closer, an ache grew within him. A need to touch and feel a woman again. *Oh my God! What is wrong with me?* He felt a mad compulsion to bury his face there, right against her milky white skin, resting his weary head against the pillowy softness, and sinking into blissful surrender.

She yanked a touch too hard on the thread, breaking through his lustful musings. "Oh, I am terribly sorry, I don't mean to hurt you."

Finally, she finished the stitches and began to clean him

off. The wet rag was comforting against his skin. He studied her, the way she tilted her head from side to side. She kept chewing on her lip as she tenderly put the cloth onto his skin, gently rubbing the same spot over and over again. *What was she thinking?* The boy popped into view again, drawing his attention reluctantly away.

"What is your son's name?" he asked.

Greta jumped slightly, appearing as guilty as he felt. "My son?" She looked at him quizzically. He pointed behind her. "Oh, Ezra. He's Ezra." Her voice trailed off. Warmly, she smiled down at the boy, and he regarded her with wide, excited eyes. Ezra chewed on a piece of bread, his cheeks rosy and full.

"I think, for now, you should rest for a while." She laid the back of her hand across his forehead, then spoke in German. "Ezra, please find a blanket for the American."

He ran from the room, then returned proudly holding up a quilt. Jimmy reached for the blanket. "Danke," though it sounded more like *dane-key*.

She tucked the quilt around him, careful of his injuries. "Is this good? Are you comfortable?"

"Absolutely, couldn't have gotten better care than I did here. Especially from a lady as pretty as yourself." A faint blush spread across her cheeks. "My name is O'Brien, Captain James O'Brien. But I prefer Jimmy."

"I am Greta Müller. It is so nice to meet you, Jimmy." She placed her hand on his, giving it a squeeze. The tender sign of affection filled Jimmy with fervor, as he fought the urge to haul her closer to him, to let his mouth show how truly grateful he was.

CHAPTER THREE

Careful not to disturb her patient, Greta picked up the uniform from the arm of the sofa and went to the kitchen. There she mended the holes and tried to wash it the best she could. It would never again be a proper uniform, but at least she could return him to his unit in a somewhat presentable state.

With Ezra's help, she cleaned up the mess left behind from the firefight. She replaced the curtains with sheets, swept up the broken vase, and hammered a weathered board over the broken window. The armchair had suffered the indignity of a large rip in the fabric, but there was nothing she could do to fix it now.

Ezra and Greta both had the same thought. "Poor Liesel, this was her husband's favorite chair." She pointed to the stuffing falling onto the floor. "I won't tell her if you won't." She winked at Ezra who gave a silent laugh.

Jimmy watched the way that Greta and Ezra interacted with each other with rapt curiosity. There was something strange in the way the two of them behaved, not as mother and son, but rather with a distance between the two. Jimmy noted the stark differences in their appearance. Greta was fair, with blonde hair and blue-green eyes, while Ezra had dark brown hair and eyes. Perhaps Ezra favored more of his father, but something nagged him. The longer he lay there, the more the situation puzzled him. There were secrets in this house, and he wanted to know the answers.

Ezra quickly became Jimmy's guardian in Greta's absence. Every time she left the room, Ezra would stand on his tiptoes and inspect Jimmy himself. After a while, Jimmy began to talk with the curious boy, but he never received an audible response. Nonetheless, Jimmy continued to talk, and Ezra listened intently, sometimes gifting the soldier with a bright smile or laughing silently. Jimmy was never sure if his new friend actually understood him or was reacting to the tone in his voice. Nevertheless, he enjoyed the company, as it took his mind away from the throbbing pain.

Regaling Ezra with a story about his driver, Corporal Tony Ricci, Jimmy received a startling surprise. "So there was Tony, covered from head to toe in flour saluting the General, like this." Jimmy executed a perfect imitation. From the other side of the room, he heard a soft giggle. The sound startled Jimmy, lowering his hand as he peeked over at his tiny friend. "Did you just laugh, Ezra?" The cheerful boy nodded and ran over to Jimmy, handing him a storybook.

"You want me to read this?" As he scanned the pages, Ezra stopped him and pointed to a particular story. "I don't know, Ezra. I haven't read any German since high school, so it will probably be pretty bad!"

Smoothing out the pages, Jimmy attempted to read. "*Es war einmal*, once upon a time. Is this a fairy tale?" Ezra flipped a few pages, showing Jimmy the illustration of Little Red Riding Hood. "I see." He cleared his throat. "*Es war einmal eine kleine süße Dirne, die hatte jedermann lieb.*" A snort came from Ezra. Jimmy raised his eyebrow. "I told you my accent was bad. OK, where was I? Oh yeah." Jimmy cleared his throat, his distinctive nasal accent impossible to hide. "*Der sie nur ansah, am allerliebsten aber ihre Großmutter, die wusste gar nicht, was sie alles dem Kinde geben sollte.*" Ezra could no longer hide his mirth and broke out in giggles.

His laughter was infectious, and Jimmy joined in. "It was bad, huh, little fella?" Ezra wiped a tear from his eye, nodding. Tousling his hair, Jimmy leaned back against the back of the sofa. "I'm tired now, I think I better rest for a minute."

Greta returned, taking in the sight of Ezra's delighted face. "Are we having fun?"

"Yes, I think he was making fun of me, Greta. He wanted me to read, but my German wasn't up to his standards." Jimmy rested his good arm behind his head.

"Oh, it wasn't?"

"No, he laughed at me," he said with a touch of self-mockery.

The smile faded from Greta's face. "Pardon? He laughed?"

"Yes," he looked puzzled. "Doesn't he laugh?" The mystery deepened. The more questions answered, the more questions he had. Who was this beautiful, enigmatic woman in front of him, and who was this child obviously desperate for company?

"No," her answer was barely audible, her eyes glistening with unshed tears.

"Why doesn't he laugh?" That was the question he wanted to know the answer to the most. A darkness lurked in the shadows of the room, and he was determined to find the source.

She waved his question away and whispered something to Ezra. He picked up his book and train. Then, dragging his feet, he left the room.

"Your color has improved." She inspected the bandages, satisfied since the bleeding had stopped.

Hearing the cuckoo chirp four times, Jimmy looked over at the clock. "I see it's later than I thought." His voice was a rich baritone. "I think, perhaps, my men must still be chasing the soldiers. It seems unlikely they will find me anytime soon. Can I stay here, would it be all right?"

"Absolutely, we would be happy to have you here with us. I made soup and baked bread for a light supper."

"Anything you can offer would be most appreciated."

Greta smoothed out her plain cotton dress. "I think it would be better for you to use my bed. I am afraid this sofa is not the best place for resting." Jimmy started to protest, but she cut him off. "You will not say no."

He pushed himself up but fell back. The movement sent pain shooting through his spent muscles and his head throbbed in protest. "I would like to put my clothes back on." A light flush crept up his cheeks.

"They are currently drying. Do not worry, I will not look," she teased, as he smiled wanly. Greta cleared the path from the living room to the bedroom. Trying to avert her eyes from the sight of Jimmy clad in nothing but his undergarments, she helped ease him up from the sofa.

"Here," she wrapped her arm around his waist, draping his arm over the opposite shoulder, "give me your weight and I will help you into the bedroom." Working together, shifting his weight, they hobbled from the sofa to the bedroom. He favored his injured leg, limping gingerly alongside Greta.

He lowered himself onto the bed, groaning painfully. "The hard part is over," she said to reassure him. She fluffed a pillow, placing it under his head and covered him with a downy quilt. "Rest, it is the only thing you should do right now, but do not sleep. With your injuries, I would like for you to stay awake for a while longer to make sure it is nothing more serious." Greta smoothed his hair over his brow, and he relaxed in response to her touch. "I will be in the next room, call out if you need anything."

"I will," Jimmy assured her. At the door, she turned and contemplated him one last time. The sight of her furrowed brow, her consternation, left Jimmy with an inexplicable feeling of contentment. He felt his eyelids growing heavy. He shifted his position, trying not to sleep. He relished the comfort of a regular bed after far too many nights on a cot with only a woolen blanket for cover. It was all he could do to stay awake.

He snorted and realized with a start he had fallen asleep. Greta stood at the door, her tiny shadow snickering. "Dinner's ready." She helped him sit up in bed. "I made vegetable soup. I thought it would help you regain strength. Then you should probably sleep."

Ezra ran into the kitchen. A few moments later he returned with his bowl. Cradling it on his lap, he took a spot on the floor near the bed and began eating. Jimmy leaned over the edge of the bed. "Is it good, little fella?"

Ezra nodded in response and took a big spoonful. "Seems he likes your cooking." Jimmy sat upright, as Greta slid a chair near the edge of the bed. She held the bowl for Jimmy, helping him eat.

"I'm glad Ezra isn't a picky eater. What we have is rather limited, but he seems to like it all." She spooned more of the soup for Jimmy. It was simple, made of bone broth and a few vegetables, mostly cabbage. It was meager, but the warmth and taste were comforting and helped to further settle his stomach.

He made silly faces over at Ezra, who erupted into peals of laughter. Every time he peered in Ezra's direction, he saw the boy straining to make eye contact. Again, a funny face, then laughter.

"Enough you two, time for bed." Ezra was reluctant to leave the room. He ran up to Jimmy and threw his arms around him. Drawing him close, Jimmy kissed the mop of brown hair covering his head. Greta let out an audible gasp. Her voice wavered when she said, "I will be back in a moment. Help yourself to more food if you want."

Jimmy sipped another spoonful; however, the queasiness from earlier returned. He closed his eyes as he waited for Greta. When she was near, everything came into focus. He didn't understand these feelings and how she was able to stir them up. But there they were, emotions he didn't want to name, boiling so close to the surface. He ran his good hand over his face and blew out the breath he held. *What's happening to me?*

Greta returned to the bedroom, shutting the door behind her with a faint click. Jimmy tried to stand, but his leg could not bear any weight at all, and he crashed back down onto the bed. Greta ran forward. "Here, let me help you."

"You know, I am still not wearing pants," he said grimly, as she placed herself under his good arm to support him.

She smirked. "Well, we can't very well do anything about that now. Your clothes are still wet. Where are you wanting to go?"

"Er, the bathroom would be nice," he said, uncomfortably.

"It is ten steps this way." She showed him to a small room nestled between the kitchen and bedroom.

As she closed the door behind him, Jimmy gripped the sink with his hand and stared at his reflection in the mirror. The person staring back was not the man he remembered. Gone was the carefree smirk and perfectly quaffed hair. Instead lines now bracketed his eyes, his hair was in desperate need of a cut, and the long, jagged scar running across his left cheek served as a constant reminder that he'd changed, never to be that man again. He splashed water on his face and took a steadying breath.

Greta returned to the bedroom and righted the bedclothes. She had enough time to clean up the dishes before she heard him call out to her.

"I am ready now," his voice muffled through the wood door.

She opened it as he braced himself against the wall. "Use me as support again." He draped his uninjured arm around her and limped with her back to the bed.

As he lay down, she covered him with the quilt, tucking it around him. She placed her cool hand against his forehead, feeling his skin and noticing it was now warm and dry. He relaxed, comforted by sweet ministrations.

"Stay." He reached out to her and clasped her delicate wrist with his hand. It was dwarfed by his strong fist. Conflicted, her head shifted from him to the doorway and back again. "Please, stay. It has been so long since I've talked with a woman." Sighing, she sat down on the chair. "Tell me about yourself. Where are you from?"

It had been over a year and a half since she had last spoken with a man, any man. She felt utterly inept. Looking into the depths of his chocolatey eyes, she relented and decided it would do her no harm to talk to him a bit. "Berlin, and you?"

"Reading, Pennsylvania." He flashed his charming smile, and her breath caught in her throat. "How do you know English?"

"I learned it in school." She relaxed slightly as she shifted in her chair. "I am very good at language learning. I speak Polish and Danish as well. I was working translating documents when everything started, before I..." She stopped suddenly; she was revealing too much. Would her job from the past put her in danger with the Americans? Would she be considered a criminal, or could she answer these questions freely?

"Before what?" he asked.

"It is nothing." She shook her head. She did not wish to talk about her past and changed the subject. "You are so kind to Ezra. I've never seen him so happy."

"It isn't nothing, Greta, and that boy needs kindness. You both do." Their eyes locked as they tried to break through the barriers they both had erected. She crossed her legs and rested her elbows on her knees. He reached across the quilt for her hand, but she jerked back, pushing the long sleeves further down her arms. "What are you hiding?"

Everything, she wanted to say. "It isn't safe to tell you, not now."

"You can trust me, Greta."

"Can I, Jimmy? Can I trust a man who was sent here to kill me?" She was absolutely torn by the need to finally unburden herself to this enticing man sitting before her, yet terrified to reveal the secrets she had long held. Hers, Ezra's. How could she trust a stranger with the truths that had long prevented Ezra from speaking?

"I wasn't sent here to kill women and children, Greta." His voice hardened. "I have no desire to kill anyone, least of all innocent people."

"Am I innocent?" she whispered.

After a long moment, Jimmy answered, "As innocent as I am." So many shared feelings existed within those few words. "Where's Ezra's father?"

"I don't know." She shifted again, stating the fact without elaboration. Each time he asked these questions, the ones she wanted to answer so desperately, she felt more restless.

"Don't you worry about your husband?"

"My husband? I have no..." She stopped suddenly.

"No husband," Jimmy finished her sentence. Greta stood quickly, walking over to the toys Ezra left in her room. "Who's Ezra, Greta?" She bent down to collect them.

"I think you'd better get some sleep." She started for the door, but stopped as she heard Jimmy groan. Turning around, she saw how he tried to get up and follow her. "Lie back down, please." She dropped the items from her hand and returned to his side, tucking him back under the covers.

"Greta, I can help you," he pleaded with her.

Why this man wanted to help her, she had no idea. What frightened her more was how desperately she wanted to accept. "Jimmy, you need to save your strength." Again, she avoided answering him, but his words froze her.

"He looks nothing like you. Greta, tell me."

Would others notice the same thing? How long can we continue pretending? She shook her head as she clasped her hand over her mouth, forcing herself to keep quiet. "I can't," she pleaded with him.

His eyes burned through her very soul, but she had to persist; she had to keep their secrets hidden for a while longer. She could see how sleep weighed heavily on his eyelids. He wanted to resist but could no longer fight it. "Sleep, Jimmy, please."

Reluctantly, he nodded as sleep finally took hold. She watched his body relax, his breathing slowed. If only she could sit with him and finally unburden herself. To explain all that had happened. But no, it still wasn't safe. Something about his manner spoke of a desperation she too could understand. There was no doubt in her mind he needed her, and perhaps, if she was truly honest with herself, she needed him a little as well.

CHAPTER FOUR

Jimmy blinked once, twice as his eyelids struggled to lift over his scratchy eyes. Pain radiated through his shoulder and thigh, preventing him from being able to stretch out his long limbs, leaving him feeling coiled and tight. His throat was parched, and he only had a dim recollection of where he was. The memories of yesterday replayed in a hazy blur. Sluggishly, his senses began to work and put the pieces of this fuzzy puzzle together. The quilted blanket. The pale-yellow walls. The noises from beyond the door. And then there was the scent on his pillow, a field of lilacs.

Not my tent. Not the Army camp. He relaxed against the headboard and thought of Greta. Her ethereal vision haunted his dreams like no woman before. Erotic dreams. But more than that, what he most remembered was her smile. The way her entire face lit from within, eyes sparkling, lips wide, her lilting laugh. The image burned into his mind, the vision he awoke to.

Jimmy heard the soft pitter-patter of Ezra's feet and felt the boy's fingers poke against the quilt. Smiling, Jimmy turned over. "Good morning." Jimmy yawned. Wide-eyed, Ezra inspected the patient, then ran away as quickly as he entered, a brown head bobbing past the doorway.

Seconds later there she was, leaning against the doorframe. Her eyes were somehow brighter than he remembered, the smile deeper, more genuine. She reminded him of the Irish faeries from his grandmother's bedtime stories.

"Good afternoon, Captain." She then spoke in German to Ezra – Jimmy understood the word *Wasser*, she must be asking about a glass of water. She rested her cool hand across his forehead. "No fever. I think rest was exactly what you needed."

It was ironic she claimed he had no fever. He, however, felt engulfed in flames. Each of her caresses caused his blood to surge, his pulse to race. When she brushed away the hair that had fallen over his forehead, he nearly came undone.

Ezra returned, handing him a glass of water. The liquid soothed his dehydrated throat. Fishing around the pocket of her tidy blue apron, Greta pulled out a small bottle with the label Bayer. She dropped two tablets into his palm. "Here, this should help with the pain."

He swallowed the pain reliever with a large gulp of water, emptying the glass. "How long have I been asleep?" he asked, his voice still rough from a long rest.

"I've lost count, at least fifteen hours," Greta responded while examining the stitches on his shoulder.

Fifteen hours and he still felt exhausted. Once this war was over, he was going to sleep for a month. "Danke," he said to Ezra, holding up the glass. The boy seized the chance to be helpful and fetched more water for Jimmy.

"I am afraid my stitching is not the best. You will probably have several scars." She trailed her fingers down his arm. Jimmy closed his eyes, falling under her spell.

Her scent filled his lungs. It hung in the air, on his

bedclothes. It even clung to his undershirt. "No worries, I already have lots of scars. Grew up rough." He pointed to a long one on the side of his face. It ran the length from his left eyebrow through his cheek. "See? A few more won't hurt me."

He watched as she reached out her index finger, tracing along the puckered white scar. Her blue-green eyes seared through the walls he built around his heart. "What are you thinking about, Greta?"

"Your scar, it reminds me of a Schmisse."

The way she tilted her head, biting her bottom lips sent waves of desire coursing through Jimmy. The need to feel her next to him, to touch her velvety lips against his boiled raging need throughout his body. *I must kiss her.* "What is a Schmisse?"

"A dueling scar. At university, men would give each other these scars while fencing. It was a badge of honor, showing how a man would be a good husband, how he was brave." She stopped tracing the scar and reached over to straighten his bedding. "My father has one. But their popularity waned, and the Nazis outlawed them." She shrugged and smiled up at him.

"So, you like it?" He winked at her, and she blushed. He loved having that effect on her, seeing her face flush a perfect shade of carnation pink.

Greta took note of the room, seeing that Ezra had left again, she answered the question. "On most men, no." She lowered her voice. "But on you, I do not know. It adds a certain quality to you. A little dangerous, yes? But perhaps, no." She dropped her head. Her fingers worried the hem of her apron. "I sound daft, I am sorry."

Is she feeling this attraction too? He cleared his throat. "No, not daft." Shaking his head, he attempted to clear his thoughts. "Can you help me up again?"

Dropping the apron, she motioned to him to scoot to the

side of the bed. Then having him lean his body weight against her, he was able to shift himself off the bed. Together, they hobbled to the bathroom.

Noticing how Ezra was distracted with his trains, Jimmy seized the opportunity to draw her inside the tiny room and, using his body, to press her against the door. He could hold back no longer.

"I am sorry, I just have to." He hesitated for a moment, giving her a chance to refuse. But as her eyes met his and her tongue darted out to wet her bottom lip, there was no more hesitation. He lowered his mouth over hers. His lips parted, tasting a hint of mint. She tilted her head back, lifting against him. Her scent filled the tiny room, and he could no longer hold back the flames burning within. His tongue swept inside, relishing the taste of her.

Greta ran her fingers along the nape of his neck and up through his hair, gently tugging it. Her fingers gripped the back of his head as they continued, their tongues tangling. His body hardened as they lazily explored each other with touch. His hands slid down, one stopping at the small of her back, the other gripping her buttocks tightly. He molded her against him, she mewled in delight. The sound caused his arousal to surge, but he was too injured, and this was not the place for a dalliance, no matter how much he desired it. With great effort, he separated from her.

"I need to stop," he said, resting his chin on top of her head. She gave a slight nod, words failing her completely. Stepping back, he admired the effect the kiss had. Her hair was mussed, her cheeks flushed, her berry-stained lips swollen. A seductive and knowing smile crept across his mouth.

"Um," Jimmy finally said and indicated to the toilet.

"Oh, right, yes. Let me leave." She breathed a heavy sigh. Then she fumbled with the door, hitting herself in the forehead as it opened. Releasing an embarrassed giggle, she turned to him, rubbing it. He guffawed and leaned in, brushing his lips against the reddening spot. Then she fell through the door onto the floor. She couldn't stop the nervous laughter following them both as he shut the door behind her.

Ach, du Lieber! What a complete fool I have made of myself. Ezra came over to her, his eyebrow hitched with a silent question. "I am all right, just tripped over my feet." She picked herself up and lightly tapped his head. "Don't worry about me, I am fine." Smoothing over her dress, she attempted to righten her appearance.

What happened? There was something about Jimmy. He made her stomach flip, and all sense left her brain. Never before has she felt that way about a man, let alone seen a man as utterly striking as he was. The way his deliciously chocolate eyes raked up and down her body caused her to heat from within. And his smirk! How his mouth curled up in the corner! And lips, full and firm.

But the scar on his left cheek, so much like the Schmisse. She hated the scar on her father's face. Then there was the horrible one of Heinrich's. She shuddered. But with Jimmy, when she reached out to touch it, a flash of vulnerability appeared. It was all but the briefest of moments, nevertheless, she caught it. He needed her.

The sounds of vehicles approaching broke through Greta's haze. She and Ezra froze. Since Jimmy arrived, she let down her guard and now they were caught unaware. The vehicles were coming closer. Then one passed by the door, stopping in the yard. Another followed. There was no time to hide the captain; his injuries prohibited any quick movements. Panic burned through her body. "Stay here, don't move," she called to Jimmy through the door.

She sent Ezra hurriedly into his hiding spot. Then, opening

the door to the bathroom, she threw in Jimmy's clothing that had dried overnight in the kitchen. She heard Jimmy curse and fall against the door, but there was no time to help him get dressed. Taking a moment to calm herself and collect her thoughts, she straightened her appearance. With a deep breath, she peered out the decorative window by the front door. The beveled glass prevented her from seeing exactly what type of vehicle it was. If they were German, perhaps a cunning explanation would convince them everything was as it should be, nothing was amiss. *Please let them be Americans!*

She could see two – no, three men. They exited the vehicle and surveyed the area. Rifles up, they scanned the yard. One man broke away and approached the door. She saw his handgun at his side, ready if needed. As he knocked on the door, Greta sucked in her breath. *Breathe, just breathe.* She opened the door and took it all in. The Americans had arrived.

CHAPTER FIVE

"Oh, thank goodness. You are Americans. Please, please come in." The man in front of her furrowed his brow. He was not expecting this welcoming greeting, nor an English-speaking woman. "I assume you are looking for Captain O'Brien, yes?" The man nodded. "The captain is inside. He is injured and will need help."

"Jones," he called back to one of the men behind him, "bring the medic. Ricci and Heffernan, keep watch."

She held the door open. One soldier took a spot near the entrance; the other positioned himself in the kitchen, effectively preventing any possible surprise attack. "He is in the bathroom. Let me get him for you."

She paused, studying the man in front of her. He was only a few inches taller than Greta. His hair cropped short against his scalp, his thick brows drawn together. His face full of creases, the kind one gets after countless days and sleepless nights, leading men through the type of hell only war can bring.

"Yes, ma'am." He inclined his head in a polite acknowledgment.

She knocked on the door lightly. "Jimmy, it's American soldiers. You are safe."

She heard him groan. "Sort of, couldn't get my uniform on."

Greta opened the door. He stood in his boxer shorts and unbuttoned uniform top. He seemed so defeated, Greta fought the urge to hold onto him.

"It hurts too much to button it and forget about the pants." He motioned to them on the floor.

"Perhaps, we should let them see the wounds first." She picked up his pants, draping them over her shoulder. "Lean into me." She wrapped her arm around his waist, he rested his long arm across her shoulder. "I have you, Jimmy."

As they entered the living room, Jimmy attempted to straighten up at attention. He saluted. "Major." His feet were unsteady, and he wobbled. Greta was at his elbow before he fell over.

The major returned the salute and quickly said, "At ease. Medic, see to Captain O'Brien."

A lean, redheaded man ran towards them. "I've got him, ma'am," taking the weight of Jimmy off of her. They limped together towards the sofa.

"Hi there, Kowalski," Jimmy greeted the medic, who began a quick assessment.

Greta called down to Ezra in German, "It is fine now. It is safe to come out."

They all stared as the rug rolled back and the floorboards rose up from the spot that the major occupied not a moment earlier. Out came a little boy. He rushed over to Jimmy, watching the medic inspect the wounds carefully.

Ezra leaned into Jimmy's side as the medic asked, "Who sewed you up?"

"Greta. I think she might be responsible for keeping me

alive until you all found me today." He tilted his head back, gazing up at Greta. He gifted her a sly wink, reminding her of their recent dalliance in the bathroom.

"It was nothing." She blushed slightly, tugging at the sleeve of her dress.

"It was not nothing. We thank you for taking care of our man." Some of the sternness faded from the major's voice as he reassured her. "Not every German would have done what you did. In fact, many would have let him die."

"I hardly can call myself a German anymore, sir." She rested her hand lightly on Ezra's shoulder.

The major nodded and asked the medic, "Can we move him, Sergeant?"

"Yes, sir, we're not far from the aid station. We need to get him Penicillin to stave off any infection. I am afraid there is serious muscle damage to his leg and shoulder. We may have to put him into surgery. May I ask, ma'am, how did you clean his wounds?"

"I used clean towels and boiling water. I am afraid I did not have anything else to really use. I also boiled my instruments before sewing him up. I sincerely hope it was enough."

The sergeant followed Jimmy's gaze, noticing where the captain was staring. The sergeant cleared his throat, trying to bring his comrade back to the present situation.

"Sergeant Kowalski, Private Jones, help the Captain to the jeep." The major walked outside. Before leaving, he turned again to Greta. "If there is ever something you need, you only have to ask. We are forever in your debt." He bowed slightly and left.

"Hey, guys, can you give me a little help here?" Jimmy held out his uniform and Kowalski and Jones helped him to put it on. He grimaced as the fabric slid up his leg and let out an audible yelp when they buttoned his shirt.

Greta jumped straight up. "Oh, wait!" She ran to the mantelpiece and picked up a small jar, dropping its contents into her hand. "Your bullet." She stood before him and placed it into his palm. "I thought you might like it as a souvenir – er, well, something, anyway."

The bullet undulated in Jimmy's palm. Placing it in his pocket, he reached out to Greta and clasped her hand in his. "Hey, guys, can you give me a second?" he called over his shoulder. The men obliged by moving toward the door, acting incredibly interested in something outside the window. "I can't leave without a proper goodbye."

Greta shook her head. "No, no, not goodbye, auf Wiedersehen. It's better." He raised his eyebrow. "It means until I see you again. Goodbye is much too final."

He leaned down to her, his face merely inches from hers. "Auf Wiedersehen, Fräulein." His breath wafted across her lips. He closed the distance between them, their mouths fusing together. A soft moan escaped Greta as he gripped her shoulders, bringing her closer.

A faint "uh-hum" broke the moment, and the kiss was over. Much too quickly for Greta's tastes. She heard Ezra snicker. "Auf Wiedersehen," she sighed breathlessly.

Jimmy motioned for Ezra to come closer. "Listen, little fella. Take care of Greta while I am gone." He gave the boy a hug and then tousled his hair. "I'll be back soon."

The soldiers came to Jimmy's side, helping him toward the door. At the threshold, Jimmy turned, his lip quirked at the corner in a sexy grin. "Oh, and, Greta, I mean it, I will be back."

CHAPTER SIX

A few days later, another surprise visitor appeared at Greta's door. The two quick raps followed by four longer knocks signaled to Greta and Ezra that Liesel had come for a visit. Before they could answer, the door opened to the sound of a cheery voice calling out, "Guten Tag!"

Ezra ran into Liesel's open arms. He collided with her, and she let out a small "oomph" as she struggled to stay fully upright. "Hello, my darling friend. I have brought you a honey cake and some bratwurst." She lifted her heavy basket for him to inspect.

"I am so happy to see you." Greta motioned for Liesel to come into the kitchen. "Please, sit down."

"Max butchered a pig. It had met an untimely end thanks to a recent scrimmage near his farm. He gave me a bit of sausage, so naturally I must share it with two of my favorite people. Also, I wanted to check on you after the commotion from the other day, but I needed to make sure the soldiers left the area before stopping by. I didn't want to draw attention to you." Liesel began unpacking the contents of the basket. It contained a few jars of canned fruits and vegetables, two small honey cakes, a few bratwursts, and a couple of books. "Now, Ezra, when cleaning Johann's room, I came across something special." With a flourish, she withdrew a small wooden box, presenting it to the boy.

Ezra pried open the lid, his eyes opening wide. He removed each of the finely painted tin soldiers out of the box one by one.

"Oh, Liesel. These are so precious. Are you sure you want to give them away?" Greta nodded, as Ezra held up each of the soldiers for her inspection.

"Oh, heavens, yes. Johann would have wanted his things to go to someone who would enjoy them as much as he did," Liesel twittered with joy.

Ezra set the soldiers up on the floor near the sofa and pretended to stage a battle between the red and blue uniforms.

Greta heated the kettle on the stove and made tea for her and Liesel. They sipped their beverages as they watched Ezra playing on the rug.

"I wanted to stop by earlier but was afraid the soldiers were still in the area. I saw several vehicles approach your house, but they seemed to leave quickly."

Greta took a long sip. "They were Americans. One of their soldiers was injured and I took care of him."

Liesel tilted her head to the side. "Interesting. So the Americans are surrounding our village. That's good news." She smiled lovingly at Ezra. "And what of this soldier? Did he make it?"

"Oh yes, we were able to treat Jimmy's wounds and keep him safe." Greta could feel her cheeks glowing red.

Liesel gave her a knowing look. "His name is Jimmy, intriguing." Her pale blue eyes sparkled. "And what of this mysterious soldier? Describe him for me."

Greta tried to hide her blush, but this only furthered Liesel's curiosity.

"Oh, I see." Liesel turned to the boy. "Perhaps now would be a good time to speak little Ezra. Tell Auntie Liesel all about this mysterious stranger who has Greta blushing so."

Ezra giggled. He shook his head and went back to playing.

Liesel startled at the sound of the laughter. "Did I hear Ezra?"

"It's a recent development. The American, he somehow got our boy to laugh again."

Liesel swiped away a tear. "Tell me more about this man."

"He was here for a brief time. I am sure I will never see him again," Greta said, her voice cracking.

"Perhaps," Liesel sounded far less assured. "And perhaps he will be back again soon. This handsome," Greta's blush deepened, "American soldier. And what did he say about Ezra?"

Greta dropped her head and released a heavy sigh. "He knew Liesel, somehow he knew Ezra was not my son."

Liesel shifted in her seat, leaning over the table, and lowering her voice. "Do we need to change your location? Do we need to find another hiding place?"

"I think we are safe as long as it is Americans who question. They would not harm a child."

"I feel you are correct in that assessment, my dear. But the minute you no longer feel safe, you come to me. Do you understand? I have ways of hiding you again."

Greta gripped Liesel's soft, plump hand. "I know. I wish there was a way to repay your kindness."

"Bah! No need to cry. I've always liked you, Greta. Always approved of my nephew, Fritz's, infatuation with you, my dear. He would want me to do everything I could to protect you and, protecting Ezra, well that's God's plan." Liesel pointed to the basket of food. "Now I expect this to be empty when I return in a few days."

Ezra ran to the basket and chose a honey cake. He threw his thin arms around Liesel's waist and let her kiss his head. With a mouthful of the treat, he returned to his game on the rug.

At the door, Liesel turned to Greta once more. "Be careful, Greta. I'm good at feeding tummies and providing safe houses. Broken hearts are too hard to fix."

Greta kissed her friend on the cheek. "I will be." As she watched her friend make her way across the field stretching between their properties, Greta wondered how prophetic Liesel's words might be. Could it be that Jimmy would return? Her heart raced in anticipation. The memory of their kiss occupied her nightly dreams and filled her with a hope she had not felt for a very long time. Perhaps there was something good left in this world after all.

CHAPTER SEVEN

The jeep's brakes emitted a loud screech and Jimmy winced. "So much for a quiet surprise," he muttered to his driver, Corporal Tony Ricci.

Jimmy took a deep breath and rubbed his sweating palms on his pants legs. Greta, he dreamed of this moment, of seeing her again, since that fateful day weeks ago. The anticipation, the excitement, the nervousness. His stomach was tangled in anxious knots. Without thinking about his injured leg, he jumped from the jeep, landing too hard. He grabbed at the side of the vehicle as his knee buckled.

"Careful there, Captain." Tony placed a firm hand on Jimmy's shoulder. "We just got ya upright."

Jimmy's recovery had been challenging. In fact, he still had a long way to go before everything completely healed. After being taken to the field hospital, he went through surgery to repair the bullet damage to his shoulder and thigh. Neither would ever be the same. Time in the hospital revealed more extensive injuries to his knee and ribs. He was lucky he found Greta. Left alone, he would have perished.

Very little of that day remained a part of his memory. Bits and pieces, like photographs taped together, filled in a few blanks. Jimmy remembered leaving the Army encampment and being in the woods. The sofa. The soft bed. Ezra's laughter. And Greta. He could never forget her beautiful face, her smile, and the kiss.

Jimmy shook out his leg, willing the pain away. "Yeah, yeah. I'm fine." He pushed himself off the vehicle, gathering his gifts for Ezra and Greta. "Thanks for bringing me, Corporal."

"You don't think we scared them?" Tony motioned to the silent house.

"Surely she already heard that the war is over." Tony glanced over at his friend. This might not go as well as Jimmy planned. In all of his excitement at finally being allowed out of the camp, he hadn't counted on how secluded Greta and Ezra were. That they might not be aware of Jodl's surrender to the Allies. He lifted his hand and gave a firm knock, calling out as he did. There was no answer.

Tony smirked and elbowed Jimmy. "Try the door."

He turned the knob slowly. The door opened, the creaking hinges the only sound. In front of him was the neat living room of his faint recollections. There was no other sign of them. Jimmy called out again. "Hey, Greta. You can come out now."

He heard a muffled reply. "Jimmy? Is that really you?" The rug rolled back, and the floorboards pushed up. Before he could catch his breath, she was up the ladder, throwing herself into his arms. "Mein Gott! You are a sight, all healed!"

Ezra peered around the sofa, his eyes bright and wide as he waved to Jimmy. Feeling a bit braver, he ran to him, throwing his arms around Jimmy's legs.

"Hey there, little fella." He kneeled so he was eye to eye with Ezra. "I've brought you something." He lifted a small package. "It's a chocolate candy bar."

Ezra's brown eyes widened, letting out a soft rush of air on a silent "oooohhh." Waving the chocolate to Greta for approval, she mouthed "yes" to him. Then he scurried off to the sofa, tearing into his special treat. Both Jimmy and Greta watched as he tore off chunks and popped them into his mouth. Closing his eyes, he let the chocolate melt over his tongue before swallowing.

"Greta, this is Tony." He pointed to his friend. Tony was as tall as Jimmy but leaner. He removed his hat and extended his hand.

"Nice to meet ya. Lovely home y'all have here." His slow drawl was musical.

"Thank you." She clasped his hand. "Any friend of Jimmy's is welcome here. Over there," she pointed to the sofa, "is Ezra."

Tony waved at the boy with chocolate spread across his face. "Hiya, Ezra!" The boy waved a chocolate-covered hand.

"Tony, your accent is delightful. I can't place it. Are you from Pennsylvania, like Jimmy?"

He laughed, then spoke again in his rich drawl. "Nah, ma'am. I'm from Texas, Dallas to be precise."

"Oh, the funny-shaped state?"

Tony grimaced.

Jimmy laughed and clapped Tony on the shoulder. "Oh, Greta. Don't tease a Texan about their state. They are a bit, um shall we say, proud of it."

Tony gave Jimmy a disgruntled glare. "Yes, ma'am, we are a might proud and don't like to call it funny." He winked at her and smiled brightly.

"Oh, please forgive me. I meant unusual, not funny. Mist, English has too many words; German is more precise."

"Greta, why did you say mist? It isn't raining."

"Um," her cheeks flushed brightly. "It's German."

Jimmy prodded further. The delightful shade of red she

was turning was too much to resist. He had to know what she said. "And what does it mean?"

She stared at the floor. "Manure," she squeaked.

Jimmy threw back his head and guffawed. Tony gave her a commiserating smile.

"No harm, all's forgiven. Can't stay mad at a pretty li'l lady like yourself. We Texans pride ourselves on manners. Not like these stiff Pennsylvania boys, who like causin' trouble." He glowered at Jimmy for a moment, then plopped down next to Ezra on the sofa.

"I have something for you." Jimmy's rich, velvety voice sent shivers down her spine. He extended his hand, holding a simple bouquet of flowers.

"Oh, these are lovely!" she exclaimed. "Lilacs are my favorite." Holding the purple blooms to her nose, she inhaled their sweet, powdery aroma.

"I know. After I left here, every time I smelled lilacs, I thought of you."

"Why are you here?" She threaded her fingers through Jimmy's, her smile setting his mind ablaze. "Are you better?"

Her blue-green gaze caused his pulse to flutter, his skin heating. The very sight of her filled him with longing. She was the elixir to cure him. "Well, as it so happens, we thought you might want to know that the war is over." His hand settled against the small of her back, pressing her further against him.

She squealed and covered her mouth, a bright pink flushing her cheeks. "Honestly?" she choked out in disbelief. "After all this time, it's finally over?"

"We did it!" Tony thrust his chest out in pride. "It's over!"

"And Hitler?" she whispered to both of them, almost afraid to ask.

"Dead, killed himself in the Führer bunker. Goebbels, too."

Greta rested her head against his shoulder, softly crying.

Jimmy wrapped his arm around her waist, using her to steady the dizzy rush of emotions her tears caused.

Ezra jumped up from the sofa and threw his arms around Greta. She spoke softly to him in German. "Verstehst du? Der Krieg ist zu Ende!" He nodded, his smile stretching wide across his face. Then he quickly ran to his room and returned a moment later carrying his large book.

"What a relief," she sighed. "And the others?"

"There is quite the mess to clean up. Still tryin' to figure out who we have and who escaped. But don't fret none. We'll get 'em," Tony explained.

Ezra flopped back down next to Tony. "Hey, li'l man, whatcha got there?" Ezra lifted his favorite storybook up, then crawled over next to him, pointing to his favorite stories.

"You have healed nicely," Greta said, turning over to Jimmy and lightly stroking his arm. Her voice was mild and soothing, the touch electrifying.

Jimmy looked her over with a yearning to have her completely to himself. She was everything he remembered. Her buttery locks were swept away from her face, clipped with a tarnished barrette. Her dress was worn, the pattern faded after many washes with homemade soap. But none of this detracted from her overall beauty. He wanted to reach out and feel the gentle glide of her satiny skin under his rough and calloused hands. Count all the freckles dusting her nose. And her eyes were the most startling shade of blue-green. They reminded him of his favorite lake in Pennsylvania.

He broke his heated perusal and motioned to his injured leg. "I will have a limp for a while, and I can't lift my arm fully. But hey, I am here because of you." His voice changed, becoming thick and smoky. "I do have a couple of scars, too. If you're lucky, I might show them to you." He winked, his lip curling into a slow smirk causing a liquid heat to pool in Greta's stomach.

She shuddered at his dark promise and then stretched up, lightly bussing her lips against his cheek. "It is so very nice to see you again." Her body pressed against him. "It has been too long."

Tenderly, he clasped her hand in his and pressed his lips to the palm. He could not stop touching her. He wanted to memorize every part of her, to taste her lips, to feel the curves of her body against him. Moving his hand along her forearm, he nudged the sleeve of her dress. Greta inhaled sharply and drew back her hand.

Her reaction to his touch gave him pause. Perhaps he read her wrong all along. He started to pull away, but then in the briefest of moments, he saw it as she tugged her sleeve back down.

She wasn't repulsed by his touch. She was hiding something. There on her forearm were six blue numbers, amateurly tattooed. "Greta?" He pointed to her arm. "What's that?"

"It's nothing, nothing at all." She yanked at the sleeve again and pasted a weak smile onto her face.

"No, it's not nothing." He reached for her arm again, but she tucked it behind her back.

"Please, Jimmy. Not today. I don't want to talk about it now."

"Soon then. I don't like secrets, Greta." His jaw tightened. Why was he being so demanding? He wasn't serious about her, how could this relationship be anything more than a brief affair? Yet, as he thought those words, he did not fully believe them. The attraction he felt was more. She was more. One thing he knew. Those numbers had a dark significance; something horrible happened to his Greta and nothing would stop him from finding out what it was. *His Greta?* When did he start thinking of her as *his?*

"Hey, Captain," Tony's voice broke through his confused tumble of thoughts.

Jimmy pressed his lips to her hand. "Give me a moment, Greta." He walked over to Tony. The two men spoke for a brief moment and then he returned. "We need to head back, but I was wondering if you would like to join us tonight. We are having a little celebration for VE Day, and it won't be the same without you both there."

"VE Day?" She wrinkled her nose in confusion.

"Victory in Europe Day! It's time to celebrate!" His charming smile caused a flush to burn from her chest to her cheeks.

"Oh, what a thought! The end!" She wistfully sighed, then her eyes rounded with horror at the sight of her pitiful dress. "I can't go out like this!" The dress showed its age, thin in places, the hem ragged. "It is terrible. Rags."

He shook his head. "Nah, you look radiant. Beautiful in every way." His eyes raked over her body, taking in every last curve of her figure. His slow perusal caused her skin to prickle, as if she stood too closely to a lightning strike. To steady herself, she placed her hand on the back of the chair. His eyes met hers, his pupils dilated, as he knew the exact effect he had on her. "Come on, you two, you don't want to miss this party, I promise."

"One moment, please," she pleaded softly.

Jimmy nodded and she scurried into the bedroom. Tony and Ezra headed outside. Quicker than he expected, Greta returned. She donned a simple crimson cotton dress, brown heels, her shapely legs bare. His voice rumbled with barely veiled desire. "I was wrong."

She tilted her head to the side. "Wrong? How were you wrong?"

He took a step closer. Reaching out, drawing her against him. "Each time I see you, you become more beautiful. How is that possible?"

She averted her gaze, not wanting to meet his eyes. "You flatter me."

"I mean it." With his fingers, he lifted her chin, forcing their eyes to meet. "You take my breath away, Greta."

CHAPTER EIGHT

The drive to the Army encampment was short. A few twists and turns, then they arrived. Tony stopped the jeep and helped Ezra down. Jimmy reached out his hand. As Greta took it, *zap* – a bit of blue arced between them.

"Electric," he laughed.

"It must be a sign," she teased, but the electricity she felt between them strengthened by the minute. She felt that same blue spark burning through her every time Jimmy was near.

"Do ya mind if I show Ezra 'round?" Tony held onto the boy's hand, talking with him. "If ya don't mind me askin', how old is he?"

"Ezra just turned five." Ezra excitedly held up his hand, waving the same number of fingers. "And he would love to tour the camp with you. He hasn't been outside in far too long." She turned to the boy and asked him in German if he would like to join Tony. He bobbed his head up and down.

Ezra showed Tony his chocolate bar and tried to offer him some, but Tony shook his head. "Nah, li'l man, you eat all the chocolate." Ezra broke off another piece of chocolate, letting it melt in his mouth. They continued, walking off together, Tony chattering in Ezra's ear. "How about I show ya the mess tent, where we eat? Or maybe I can show ya where we like to play baseball. Do ya like to play sports?" He laughed at Ezra, chocolate in both corners of his mouth. "I guess ya don't understand English, but you'll know the word chocolate soon enough."

"Schokolade," came a tiny voice.

"Yeah, li'l man. Schokolade. You want some more?" Tony asked as Ezra skipped along next to him, holding onto his hand.

Greta gasped. One word, that was all Ezra said. Her hand to her heart, she could not believe it. After all this time, the word he finally chose to say was *chocolate*. It was tantamount to an infant speaking his first words, but more. It was a sign of deep healing, of hope.

So caught up in the moment, she didn't even notice which hand clutched her heart. She felt Jimmy's thumb on her forearm, and panic tore at her. As she tried to snatch her hand away, he stopped the movement. Gently, he continued running his fingers along the blue numbers.

"Greta," he said, his voice thick as he lifted her forearm.

"No," she muttered, shaking her head, refusing to reveal this part of her. Her heart was pounding in fear.

"All right, we can talk about it later." He gently pressed his lips against her nose. "I have to warn you. Normally we aren't allowed to speak with Germans. But Major Clarkson agreed to an exception, what with you taking care of me and all. He wanted to say thank you." They walked together, knuckles bumping with each step.

"Of course I wanted to help you. I am still so glad it was you and not a German. It would have been hard to help a German."

"Why?" He stopped walking and turned to her. "Why wouldn't you want to help your own countrymen?"

Greta fought back a wave of nausea. "I am a woman without a country, I belong nowhere."

Jimmy held her hand to his chest. "You belong here." The intensity of his stare filled her with a burning heat.

She let out a faint sigh and allowed him to lead her through the camp. He showed her the mess hall and where his tent was. Flooded with curiosity, she took in the sight of the Americans. After years of being surrounded by people without enough food, ravaged by war, starvation, and fear, these men before her appeared otherworldly. Their wide, bright smiles, rounded faces, and swagger fascinated her. Each man possessed an air of self-assuredness she had not seen in years.

Then there was Jimmy. Every few minutes, she found herself staring up at the man walking beside her. His sable hair slightly curled around his ears and the nape of his neck. His chin was strong with a slight cleft, adding to his rugged appeal. The rolled sleeves of his uniform revealed thickly muscled arms. He was tall, broad-shouldered, and every bit as charming as she remembered. *It should be a crime for a man to look so good.* She released an indelicate snort and covered her face in embarrassment.

Jimmy hitched his brow and bumped his arm against hers. "You all right over there?"

"Absolutely fine." She squinted up at Jimmy, shading her eyes from the sun. "Everyone seems so healthy."

He shifted to block the sunlight, his towering figure casting a shadow over her face. "All these attractive men. Can't get enough of us, can you?" She lightly punched his shoulder. "We must appear very different from what you are used to seeing."

"Yes, better. Americans are so different from Germans. Like

movie stars, each and every one of you." She smiled at him tenderly. "I am so glad this war is over, so glad the Allies won."

"Whose side were you on? I thought you worked as a translator?" He studied her reaction intently.

Their eyes met for a brief moment before she turned and pointed to a group of soldiers sitting around an upright piano. One man tapped out a rhythm on top, while the rest sang along with the man playing the keys.

Desperate to change the subject, she asked, "You have a piano?" She felt genuinely surprised to see such an instrument in a place of war.

With his hand resting along the small of her back, Jimmy guided her near the group. They were singing a rowdy rendition of a popular song she knew well in German. However, they were singing it in English.

"Lili Marlene? I'm surprised you know it."

"When Marlene Dietrich came to the United States, she recorded an English version. It is very popular with the troops." Nudging her with his shoulder, he encouraged her to sing along.

She shook her head with a blush. "No, not here. But why is it painted green? I don't think I've ever seen an instrument that color."

"Funny story about the piano, it was one of many that were airdropped during our campaigns. We call them Victory Verticals and they are made by an American company - Steinway. I'm guessing like everything else, it was painted to blend in. Olive drab, we call it."

"Pianos airdropped during battle? That's almost as silly as Christmas trees being sent by train to the trenches during the Great War."

Jimmy and Greta left the group after they started singing a song with more bawdy lyrics. "Perhaps. But music is important to us. It's a bit of normalcy we've missed when surrounded by all of this for so long." He swept his arms in a circle, indicating the busy army encampment surrounding them.

"My father said something similar about the Christmas trees. Said it was like having a little piece of home with him, if only for a moment."

The conversation lulled with Jimmy lost in thought. They meandered through the vast network of buildings and tents. "What's over there?" She motioned to a cluster of trees, where a three-story stone building rose above the foliage.

The question roused Jimmy from his thoughts. He crooked his finger with a sensual promise. "Come and find out."

After a short walk, they arrived at a set of wooden stairs leading up the side of the building. "I have an office here, would you like to see it?" His deepening voice spoke of forbidden pleasure, something Greta longed to experience. With a nod of her head, she followed him inside.

CHAPTER NINE

Holding Greta by the hand, Jimmy gently tugged her up a narrow staircase, to a small room on the second floor. It was sparsely furnished with an ancient, scarred desk and one wooden chair. "My old office," he explained. "I wanted to be alone with you, before the party begins."

She turned to say something, but the thought was immediately chased away by what she saw, hidden within the chocolatey depths of his eyes. A smoldering passion burned away every one of Greta's thoughts. It was pure, unbridled lust, but there was something different in him, different from *him*. She shook her head. *No, not today, do not think of him today!*

"Greta." She loved how he said her name, drawing out every letter along his tongue, savoring each syllable. "Kiss me, Greta," he moaned, crushing her against him, their mouths meeting hungrily.

She leaned into him, wanting to feel every inch of him against her. *His lips, his plump, delicious lips.* Wrapping her arms around his neck, they melted together. Their tongues tangled in a primitive dance. He lifted her up, pressing her back against the wall. Her legs wrapped tightly around his waist, holding him against her most intimate place. "Jimmy," she mewled, an invitation to continue his sensual onslaught.

He slid his mouth down her neck, nipping at her skin. Goose pimples erupted over her arms. She quivered with need, wanting his heat to surround her. She could feel his sinewy muscles flex against her smooth body, smell his unique musk flooding her senses. "More," she pleaded, "please more."

He answered with an eager groan, lifting the hem of her dress around her hips. His hands grew urgent as he began to unbutton her dress. First one, then two buttons flicked open. His fingers skimmed across and then under her garment, his rough calluses tickling. She sucked in her breath. "Yes!" she exclaimed, as his thumb skated across her nipple, rolling it between two fingers.

"I want you, I need to be inside you," he groaned into her ear, continuing to tear her dress open.

Coming to her senses, she pressed lightly on his chest, breathless. "No, not here. Not like this," she pleaded quietly.

He stopped, his sigh heavy against her shoulder. In frustration he pressed his hardness against her. "Oh, Greta, please, I need you," he all but begged.

She shook her head, not wanting to end the moment, but knowing it was for the best. "No, this isn't a good idea."

Dropping his head, he sighed and reluctantly let her slide down the wall and stand up. His jaw clenched. "All right, my Angel, as you wish." He had to collect himself first. He stared into her eyes, wishing she would submit.

When she did not relent, he stepped back. He reached down, rebuttoning her dress with shaky hands. He could not look away, not just yet. Her lips were swollen, thoroughly ravaged by his kisses. A small love bite blossomed on her neck.

"There is a bathroom directly across from here, you can finish straightening up there."

As she left, Jimmy hit his head against the wall and let out a low groan. He was hoping for a brief dalliance with Greta, celebrating the end of the war in style. Tony had helped arrange the encounter, distracting Ezra, so they could have the time alone. He needed this moment. Needed her out of his system. One time, it was all he needed and then she would be a pleasant memory, not the current obsession plaguing him day and night.

But he had to stop. When a woman said "no," it's the end, but his disappointment radiated through him. His engorged length throbbed in the agony of unreleased desire. The obsession deepened.

Jimmy leaned against the wall, counting to himself, attempting to regain his composure. He couldn't remember the last time he kissed a woman with such fevered longing. If he was truthful, the answer would be *never*. He never felt such raging passion for someone. Naturally, he had experience with women, but nobody like her. She ignited a firestorm within him he could not control, did not want to control. And she stopped him, which was worse than a bucket of freezing ice water poured down his back.

She was right to break away and put an end to it before it went too far. This wasn't the place, not here in his boring old office. She needed a bed, flowers, candles, all the romance of a passionate night together. They needed the chance to lie in each other's arms, for him to whisper his innermost thoughts tenderly into her ear, and maybe some dirty ones too.

Lightly, he tapped his forehead against the wall. Frustrated and wanting more, he let out one small groan and then straightened up, waiting for her return, trying to turn his thoughts away from the lithe body he had held.

He knew that this relationship held no future. What kind of future could there be between an American and a German after such a hard-fought war? No, he knew better than to let his emotions get a hold of him, but he wanted her. He needed to feel himself fully embedded within her.

Ever since the day they met, she occupied his daily thoughts. Her warm smile, her honeyed voice, her curves, perfect sumptuous curves. The thought of possessing her haunted his dreams, he was so close. But then she stopped it, stopped it far too quickly for any satisfaction. Jimmy counted the ceiling tiles, hoping to settle down his throbbing erection.

CHAPTER TEN

Letting go reluctantly, Greta turned out of the room and walked directly into the bathroom, stumbling on the way in. After splashing cold water on her face, she finally looked up at herself in the mirror. *Oh, Greta, no, that was bad.* She paused and repinned her hair. *Oh, but so good!*

Her mortification over her wanton behavior eased. A few giggles escaped in relief as she remembered the building was empty, *Thank goodness.* It was their moment, their all-consuming need. Her lips still tingled, the memory of his kisses lingering. His heady masculine scent: a perfect mix of bay rum, clove, and musk clung to her dress. She inhaled deeply, the blended aroma warming her through. She opened the door and quietly walked into the office. Their eyes met expectantly.

"More beautiful than before," he muttered, as he reached out his hand.

Keeping back slightly, she purposefully left distance between them. She did not trust herself, did not trust that she would be able to break away again. She watched as his fingers twitched, then reluctantly let his hand drop. "I guess we should head back now."

His face was awash with forlorn disappointment. She leaned against his shoulder, placing a small kiss along his beautifully sculpted cheek. His slightly salt-and-pepper stubble tickled. His eyes closed as he rested his head in her palm. Quietly, she asked, "How old are you?"

"Is the gray in the beard worrying you, you think I am an old man?" He arched his brow.

"No," she laughed, "not worrying, only admiring. I am 22." She inched closer, his breath catching in his throat.

"Still so young." He erased the distance between them, nestling his nose against her neck. He softly kissed her shoulder. "I am 30. I am an old man, Greta."

She stifled a small chuckle. "Old? Old at 30?" She shook her head, her tone light. "You aren't old." She leaned into him. "You are distinctive, mature," pausing, "breathtaking, so stunning." They kissed, hard. Ardently, she broke away from him and fell against his chest. "Can we stay here forever?"

"Greta? What are you doing? Why did you start again, just to stop?"

She mumbled with confusion. "What? I thought..."

"You thought what? What game are you playing?" His voice hardened.

"I thought we were enjoying each other's company?" Her eyes danced back and forth, wondering why his tone had taken such a rough edge.

"I don't understand. We start kissing, you stop and leave. Then you come back to me, wanting more, only to stop again? You're a tease, Greta."

"I thought... I wanted to kiss you, that's all. Nothing sexual, a simple kiss."

"Do you have any idea what you are doing to me?" Frustrated, he balled his fists at his side, trying to recollect his thoughts. To stifle the hunger surging through him.

"What *I* am doing to you?" Her tone was accusatory; she didn't understand this change in him.

"Can't you feel how much I want you, how much I need you?" He pleaded to her. "It's been so long since I have felt a woman, I need the release."

"Um." She didn't completely understand what he meant. She had felt his arousal, but she knew this was neither the time nor place for what she wanted. "Jimmy, is this really where you want to do this? I mean, do you love me?"

"Love?" He choked on the word. "Oh, Greta." He attempted to brush a lock of hair from her face. The pity on his face sickened her. "This is something to do for now. We only have so much time and then I'm gone."

"Oh." Her small hand fisted his uniform shirt. "I didn't think of it like that."

His hand slid down her back, then clutched her rounded bottom firmly. He whispered against her ear, "Until then, we could have a lot of fun."

His heated voice sent shivers down her spine. Greta resisted the temptation to fall back against him. "So this is nothing more than an affair?"

He shrugged his shoulders. "I can't promise forever. Hell, I can't promise more than a week. So, no, this is something to pass the time."

Her voice was so faint, he leaned closer to hear. "And if we had time, what would it be then?"

He looked pained. "This can't be more, Greta. How can it? You're a..." He stopped.

"I am a what?" She fought to keep the acid from rising in her throat. "I am what, Jimmy?"

"A German."

She slapped him across the face. He stood there, slowly turning to her. Rage was boiling within him, but when his eyes met hers, it fizzled. The ice pooling in the blue-green depths cooled his ire. He knew he had gone too far.

Her bottom lip quivered slightly, her fists clenched at her side. "A German! I am no German!" With that indignant exclamation, she ran out the door. It slammed against the wall, the tears poured from her face.

Instantly, Jimmy regretted everything. He could not believe how the moment he dreamed of for weeks deteriorated so quickly. The hope for a delightful tryst evaporated and a sickening feeling overtook him. The significance of the moment hit him like a dump truck. He'd lost her. This stunning, enigmatic woman who saved his life was gone. He swallowed hard and shook his head. *What have I done? I am such an ass!*

Greta had no idea where she was going. She ran down the stairs and as far away from Jimmy as she could. She found a place behind a tent, out of the view of those nearby to finally catch her breath. A waterfall of tears poured from her eyes as she meekly attempted to regain her composure. The chance of a relationship between them was at best a dream, but declaring this was merely a moment of heated desire, with Greta serving to sate his lust, was an explosion of heartache she never knew before.

She straightened up, smoothing out her dress. She weakly rose to her feet. She needed to find Ezra and leave. There was no reason to stay now, to celebrate. Onward she walked through the camp. So many soldiers everywhere. Several played games. Others composed letters. A few smoked cigarettes. She felt all of their eyes boring into her as she passed. A loathed German woman walking among noble liberators. She held her head high, refusing to look anywhere but straight ahead.

Greta found Tony and Ezra watching a baseball game. A large group of soldiers played the game in an open field, and even more sat around watching. Ezra was on a small bench, his thin legs swinging back and forth, intently focused on the action in front of him. Every now and then he would stop, yank gently on Tony's sleeve and point. Leaning over slightly, Tony would explain a bit more of the game using exaggerated gestures.

Reluctantly, Greta approached, standing on the other side of Tony. He raised his head in surprise, noting that Jimmy was not there with her, but said nothing. "Tony, will you please take Ezra and I home now?"

He nodded. "Sure thing. Let's go, li'l buddy." Tony lifted Ezra to the ground. "Don't worry. We can watch a game another day."

Ezra was crestfallen, his toes dragging through the dirt as they walked back to the jeep. Every so often he would turn around to catch a glimpse of the game. Then he turned back around, let out a long-suffering sigh, and kicked a rock in front of them.

Greta was heartbroken. She didn't want to ruin Ezra's day, but how could she stay? She felt like the worst kind of person, so utterly selfish. She would make it up to Ezra. Perhaps a visit to Liesel would be just the thing to bring back a smile.

The journey home was a blur, she blinked, and they were sitting in the jeep in front of her house. Tony placed his hand over hers. "Stay a moment, please." He helped Ezra out of the jeep. "Li'l man, you run along inside." He motioned to the door, but Ezra threw his arms around Tony's legs. "Alright, a quick hug then." He scooped up his pint-sized friend, giving him a tight squeeze, before putting him down.

Ezra ran to the house. Turning around, he waved goodbye to Tony and then scurried inside.

Greta plucked at the hem of her sleeve. She couldn't face Tony. She was afraid of what she might see. Would Tony be angry, could he possibly even hate her?

"Greta," he patted her hand. As she turned her head, she was surprised to be greeted by a pair of sympathetic, hazel eyes. "Captain O'Brien, Jimmy, he's afraid."

"Of what, Tony? I'm no threat to him."

"You are the most dangerous kind of threat." She pulled back, but he gripped her hand tighter. "Darlin', he's done nothin' but talk about you since the day you met. He has been plannin' this li'l outin' for weeks."

"I don't understand."

He inhaled deeply. "No, I don't think ya will yet, but give it time. Trust me. Do me a favor?"

"Anything, Tony." She managed a slight grin.

"Give him another chance? He's a good guy, I promise ya that. He's worth it, Greta."

She slowly nodded and climbed out of the jeep. Waving goodbye to Tony, she entered the house and fought the urge to throw herself onto the bed and weep. Instead, she helped Ezra bathe, read him another fairy tale, and tucked him in for the night.

Tony's words and the events of the day swirled around, her thoughts a tumbled mess. Long after Ezra had fallen asleep and the night had grown quiet, she walked outside for a breath of fresh air. The cool air calmed the dizzying tangle in her brain. Staring up at the expansive night sky, she counted the stars like she and her mother used to do. Since the war was over, it was time to begin anew. A shooting star blazed quickly, long enough for Greta to close her eyes and wish for an answer to the question burning deep within her. *What am I to do now?*

CHAPTER ELEVEN

Jimmy laced his fingers behind his head, staring up at the olive drab tent. He replayed the events of the day over and over again, cringing at his reaction to Greta. He was mortified by his behavior and ill treatment of someone who deserved no less than to be treated like the goddess she was. How did something so right go so completely wrong?

He heard someone shuffle into the tent and sit down across from him. "I dropped Greta and Ezra off." It was Tony.

"Thank you." Jimmy continued to stare up at the roof of the tent, watching a spider spin its web.

"Ezra was disappointed to miss the end of the baseball game." Tony lit a cigarette and leaned over to offer one to Jimmy.

"Yeah, sorry about that." He shook his head no, continuing to watch the spider sliding up and down the silky thread.

"Greta barely said a word." Tony puffed on his cigarette while fidgeting with the laces of his boot. "Definitely was upset about somethin'." Jimmy glared at his driver, he didn't want to talk about it.

The two men had formed a bond over the past year and a half, becoming confidants and brothers in arms. They had fought alongside each other since Utah Beach. They helped liberate Paris, pushed the Germans back in the dense Ardennes Forest, and even liberated the camp at Haunstetten. They had been through far too much not to trust each other explicitly, rely on each other's advice and companionship. They kept the proprieties of the officer and enlisted man relationship. That, however, did not stop Tony from telling Jimmy just how wrong he had been.

Tony took a long drag of his cigarette, knocking the ash into a makeshift ashtray. "Thing of it is, you've been doing nothin' but talk about this gal nonstop for weeks. You came up with this plan to get her alone, and best I can figure by your scowl and general surliness, you didn't get the action you were cravin'. So spill."

"Lay off, man." Jimmy flipped to his side, hoping to dismiss Tony's good intentions.

"Nothing' doin'." Tony nudged Jimmy in the back with his foot. "Don't go into a decline, talk to me."

Jimmy growled and threw his pillow at Tony. "You really are insufferable, you know that, don't you?"

Tony smirked. "Ah, but the ladies find me irresistible." He waggled his brows to annoy his friend.

Jimmy raked his hands over his face. "I screwed up, bad, Tony. We were alone and things were getting hot and heavy. And then she backed away. Instead of being a gentleman, I insulted her."

"I see you've got a nice handprint there on your cheek."

Jimmy rubbed at his stinging skin. "Kinda deserved it."

"Yeah, she's no able Grable. She's got substance."

"I'm coming to realize that." At first, Jimmy only hoped to find someone to assuage the fire burning within him, but Greta was not that type of a woman. She was more than a dance between the sheets. They sat in silence, Jimmy hoping for any advice to help him fix this situation. "Think she'll give me another chance?"

"Don't know, but you damn well better try." Tony stood up and walked to the door. "She's been hidin' somethin' for far too long. Give her a chance to open up to you. Jimmy, she's worth the trouble."

And she was. Jimmy came to the same conclusion five minutes after she had left him with a raging erection. Previously, Jimmy relied on his charm to ooze past a girl's defenses, watching them fall so willingly at his feet. Greta was nothing like these conquests, the shallow and meaningless relationships he depended on. She was strong, determined, intelligent; he needed her like a starving man. But how was he ever going to show her, to prove she meant so much more after everything went so devastatingly wrong?

CHAPTER TWELVE

After yesterday's disaster, Greta knew it was time to alter their routine. Ezra needed a change of scenery. Fresh air and stretching the legs were the order of the day.

Waiting for Ezra to tie his shoes, Greta revealed their destination. "We're going to Aunt Liesel's. Won't that be fun?" He nodded his head enthusiastically and then jumped up to his feet. "I know she isn't really your aunt or mine, but she insists on the name. And well, it suits, don't you think? She is part of our special family."

Ezra tucked his fist under his chin and looked pensive out over the yard. After a thoughtful sigh as if he finally worked it all out, he grinned up at Greta.

"Aunt Liesel it is. Our little family." Greta gave him a small hug.

The perfume-laden spring breeze played with the hem of Greta's dress as she wandered along, humming a favorite tune.

Running ahead of her, Ezra kicked a stone, watching it spiral along the path. The warm rays of sunlight warmed their faces as they embraced their newly found freedom. All too quickly, the stroll ended as they arrived at Liesel's home.

It was a splendid and welcoming sight. Large windows flanked the heavy wooden door, each with a flower box boasting an array of colorful blooms. Red and yellow curtains hung in the window, a friendly invitation to any who happened by.

Greta knocked gently, Ezra shifted excitedly from his left to right foot. The door opened, revealing a disheveled Liesel, her wheat blonde hair coming loose from the braid around her head, her apron covered with a thin layer of flour.

"Greta!" Liesel threw her plump arms around her. "And Ezra! I knew you would come and see me! Come, come! I am making Spätzle."

"Spätzle, isn't that Fritz's favorite meal?"

Liesel patted Ezra's cheek and motioned for them to come inside, following her to the well-appointed kitchen at the back. Liesel added dough to the pot boiling on the stove. "I am nearly finished. Here," she handed Greta a plate, "give that boy a few spoonfuls. He needs to eat."

Ezra plopped onto a ladderback chair at the table, shoveling in buttery egg noodles. Liesel was always feeding Ezra, demanding he eat more and more. It was because of her love and care that his cheeks had grown rounder, his body less bony, and a few more inches added to his height.

"Oh, he reminds me of my Johann at the same age." She pinched Ezra's cheeks. "You will grow to be a big, strong man like my son." She stared out the window, releasing a slow and steady sigh. Then she smoothed her dress over her wide, round hips. "Well, I'm finished. We will eat the rest later. Come, let's sit down for a while."

In the living room, the furniture was tidy and comfortable with age. The cushions of the two small sofas were the same pattern as the curtains. A large cuckoo clock hung over the mantle, ticking away the time. On the small table at Greta's elbow, several photographs were lovingly displayed in silver frames. Two caught her eye in particular. Each showed a man in uniform, both with devastatingly handsome faces, their mouths quirked with the exact same smile.

"I see you looking at their pictures again." Liesel grinned and wagged her finger. Two pools of unshed tears filled her cornflower eyes.

"It is remarkable. They both have the exact same smile."

Liesel dabbed at her eyes with a linen handkerchief. "They never met, you know. Wilhelm was sent to France before we ever knew I was pregnant. He named Johann, did I tell you that story?" Greta shook her head, she heard it so many times, but it always brought Liesel joy to tell it again. "Sent me a letter the day he received the news and said if he was a boy, I was to name him Johann."

"And if it was a girl?"

"Charlotte, after his mom. But as you know, it was a boy. And what a good-looking boy he was." Liesel reached out for the portrait of her son, tracing over his treasured face. "I can't believe I lost them both in France. Twenty-four years apart." Greta wrapped her arms around Liesel's shoulders. There really were no words of comfort to give. Instead, she allowed the silence to carry away the sorrow. "I should hate the French, but no. It's war I hate. War: all the needless suffering and loss of life."

The door opened, a voice of Greta's youth intruded on the moment. "Aunt Liesel, I'm finished for the afternoon. Is lunch ready?"

He stumbled as he walked in, favoring one leg as he moved through the room. "Greta, is that Greta Müller?" He clumsily reached out to her, embracing her. "I have dreamed of this moment so often."

"Fritz Schröder! Can it actually be you?" She allowed him to spin her around, as she studied his gaunt face. It was the face she remembered so lovingly, a cherished friend and former love. The piercing cornflower eyes, so similar to his aunt's. Golden hair slicked back. But his face had changed, hardened. It no longer held a carefree spirit. There was something haunted lying within the depths of his eyes. Eyes that were once so soft and tender had grown cold and pained.

"Oh, Ezra! I think we have some Lebkuchen in the kitchen. Come with me." Liesel patted Greta's shoulder. "Such a nice surprise, Fritz came to me a few weeks ago. He wanted to help me with the farm. What a dear, sweet nephew." She kissed his cheek and shuffled Ezra through the door, sure to spoil him with more food and hugs.

"Oh, Greta, I have searched and searched for you. What happened, where did you go?" The anguish in Fritz's voice tore at Greta's heart. She knew he was speaking about that day, almost two years ago, when she disappeared from their engagement party.

"Poland," she choked out, resting her head against his sturdy shoulder. She could scarcely utter the words. Only one person knew of her story, and she had kept her secret safe. Liesel, the aunt of her former fiancée, the woman who saved both Greta and Ezra's lives.

"Poland!" He was understandably confused. "But what… how?"

"Your cousin." No more elaboration was given. She grew distant, the conversation giving rise to feelings she long ago buried.

"Let's sit down. I want to know how you came here to my Aunt Liesel." Greta nodded and offered her arm to Fritz. He shifted heavily against her, gladly accepting the assistance. They limped over to the closest sofa. He took her hand in his, tenderly rubbing his thumb over the back of her hand.

Fritz had aged greatly over the past few years. His skin was no longer soft white, but tanned and rough from prolonged exposure to the sun. His clothing used to always be pristine, but now he was covered in a layer of dirt after laboring outside. His rolled-up shirtsleeves revealed thick, puckering scars along his forearm.

She was very curious about what happened to him. Before she was forced from Berlin, he had been a successful translator working at Wehrmacht headquarters. But it was evident now that he had seen more than his share of the war.

"What happened to your arm?" Greta pointed to the angry, white scars.

He smoothed his palm over them, attempting to erase their existence. "At the Battle of the Korsun–Cherkassy Pocket, the tank I was in sustained major damage. My whole right side was burned from the neck down, most of the damage was sustained in my leg." He smoothed the fabric of his pants. "The injury kept me out of the rest of the war."

"Oh, Fritz, how did you end up in Poland?" She did not understand how he could have possibly been fighting on the Eastern Front.

He let out a snort of disgust. "Retaliation, I'm sure." Fritz shrugged his shoulders. "Do you blame me for what he did to you?"

"No, not in the least. There is only one man I blame for all of this. It is your cousin."

"Heinrich."

She heard Liesel's harrumph from the kitchen. Of course she would be listening to the conversation. They all shared a common disdain for Fritz's Berlin cousin. Unlike his parents and Aunt Liesel, Heinrich's family had embraced the Nazi party. His whole family became avid National Socialists with Heinrich joining the Schutzstaffel and quickly rising through their ranks.

"Do not EVER speak his name to me," she hissed.

Fritz bristled at her anger, unaccustomed to such an outburst. After a few minutes, he continued. "I tried to find you. When you disappeared from our engagement party, I looked for you. I begged him. I knew he had to know something." He hung his head in defeat. A lone tear slid down his tanned cheek. "I begged your father, your mother. No one would tell me anything."

"One day I can tell you the story, but not now. Know it is his fault. I do not blame you, I never could." She still loved the man sitting beside her, but a lifetime of experiences now separated them. The serious boy who wrote poems about rainbows and butterflies, falling madly in love with Greta when they were only six. They went to university together and worked in the same department during the war. They were forever side-by-side. He, her gallant knight, and she, his fair maiden.

"How did you end up in Bavaria, Fritz?" They were both a long way from their home in Berlin.

"After I was injured, I was discharged from the Wehrmacht and sent home. Then my parents lost their house in the air raids, so they sent me here to help out Aunt Liesel with her farm. And you, Greta, how did you end up here?"

"That is another story for another time. It was a long journey. It is most unexpected to find you here." She swept the hair away from his forehead. He leaned into her touch, savoring the softness against the hard planes of his face. "Unexpected, but entirely wonderful."

She extended both her hands, clasping his in hers. They held onto each other, silence replacing any words they could speak. He lifted their joined hands to his lips, the motion causing her sleeve to slip past her elbow. For the faintest moment, the blue numbers appeared. She held her breath, praying he hadn't seen the marks, but his eyes grew wide. With the lightest pressure, he twisted her forearm to examine it more closely.

Running his thumb over the tattoo, his face flushed with anger. He knew what the numbers meant, he had seen them before. "When I was in Poland, I heard talk of a camp." Dark shadows crossed his face as he stared down at the hideous marks. "Some despicable SS men were bragging about this place, about the people they murdered and the tattoos that marked their skin." His hand shook, as he fought memories and guilt, both raging a battle within him

"Fritz." His name was a plea. "I survived. We both did." She pointed to the kitchen, where Ezra was.

"I wondered who he was. I can't believe you were there. *He* sent you there, didn't he?"

"Yes, he did. Right from our engagement party, he sent me away."

"That's why I couldn't find you. Why you were gone." Tears of anger fell freely, but he just held her wrist, not letting go. "Did your father know?"

"I am not sure what my father's involvement was. He was there when I was taken away. Perhaps they planned it together. Or not, I really don't know." She lowered her head, trying to fight off the flood of memories, horrible memories. Heinrich's hate and betrayal was expected, but her father's was more than she could understand.

"How did you...? How did you survive?"

"I escaped with Ezra." She couldn't tell the story yet, not in its entirety. That fear still lingered so closely to the surface, preventing her from giving names to all those emotions, those memories. "What happened to your job as a translator? You were the best they had." This confused Greta. Fritz, like all men in Germany, joined the war in some capacity. He had no taste for fighting, but proved to the Wehrmacht that he could be a most useful bureaucrat and could best serve as a translator.

"Him," was the only answer he gave, revealing so much. It made her stomach lurch, forcing her to hold back the rising bile. She was not the only target; that man was determined to destroy everything for his selfish pleasure. "I wanted to find you, to save you, Greta. I worried I would never know what happened to you."

He paused and took a long, deep breath. "I was in the East, I know what happened there. What *they* did." His anger and confusion were back. "But how did you escape?"

She finally answered his question, "I was able to sneak out of a hole in the fence. The guards were distracted, and Ezra and I were able to squeeze through."

"Always thinking of others, Greta. That's the girl I love...d." His lips trembled with a shaky smile.

"I am so sorry, Fritz. I wish, oh, I wish for so many things. But this, oh, I don't know what to do with this." She pointed to both of them.

"War. It destroys more than men." He looked off in the distance, still holding onto her. A touch that begged her not to let go, because somehow, in letting go, it would signal the end. Neither of them wanted to acknowledge the gulf now separating them. How far apart they had grown.

Letting go of his hand was tantamount to letting go of the life she once knew, for an uncertain future she had yet to envision. Greta was not ready, not for admitting there was nothing remaining of the life she understood. She would become someone else entirely, but who? No, she could not let that go, not quite. They sat there for a while, holding onto the last bitter remains.

Ezra wandered back into the room towards Greta, leaning into her side. She wrapped a protective arm around him and placed a motherly kiss on top of his head. Still no words were spoken. Fritz watched with a mournful smile on his lips. Finally, Greta turned back to him. "This is Ezra. Ezra, this is Fritz."

"So very nice to meet you." Ezra waved a friendly hello and pointed to the door.

"Yes. I think it is best if we end our adventure now." The corners of Greta's lip turned up. She pulled her hands away, the warmth evaporating. Fritz wobbled as he stood, proffering his elbow to help Greta from her seat. He was forever the consummate gentleman.

He leaned down to give her a peck.

"Auf Wiedersehen, Fritz."

"Auf Wiedersehen, Greta. Until we see each other again. I am sure we will." With his words of farewell, he stroked her cheek. His eyes filled with affection and a forlorn longing. It was their chapter's end, the final goodbye to the life she once knew, to who she once was.

CHAPTER THIRTEEN

Another day, another new place to explore. This time, Greta was determined to find something far more cheerful for them to do. So off to the village they would go. Perhaps they might find something delicious to eat or a new toy for Ezra.

"Are you ready?" He nodded once. "Then off we go on another adventure!" He ran ahead of her, arms splayed wide: an airplane soaring through a field of wildflowers.

The path to the village wound around a few farms. The area was becoming more populated as displaced persons from the war struggled to find places to live. A steady stream clogged the roadways with refugees and vehicles alike.

On their way, Ezra occasionally stopped to point out clouds or gather a flower or two. They kicked stones along their path, having a contest to see whose traveled the farthest. Ezra won every single time. It was wonderful seeing him enjoy these precious childhood moments.

Rounding a corner, Ezra spied several American soldiers lounging against a jeep. Excitedly he yanked at Greta's sleeve, pointing to the group. "I see. I doubt it's Tony, but we can check."

His face lit in excitement as they approached the men. "I do apologize for interrupting, but we were wondering if Corporal Ricci might be around?"

One soldier tilted the brim of his hat in greeting. "Ma'am, I think he might be over there with Captain O'Brien." He pointed a few yards down from the group to two men standing, their heads bent, engaged in conversation.

Greta swallowed hard. She hadn't seen Jimmy since VE Day and their terrible fight. She dreaded what she might say to him, what he might say to her. Ezra jerked hard at her hand, wanting to see his friend. "I don't know, Ezra. I don't think Jimmy will be happy to see us." His tear-filled eyes melted her resolve. There was no way she could refuse him anything. "Oh, all right. You can go, but I am going to stay back."

He ran forward, throwing his arms around the legs of the unsuspecting Tony. The soldier stumbled back and looked down. Realizing who it was, he scooped the boy up and hugged him. "Hiya, li'l man! Wanting some chocolate? Some Schokolade?" Tony teased. Ezra laughed as Tony extracted a candy bar from his coat pocket and gave it a wave. He squealed in delight and took the delicious treat.

Jimmy turned, spotting Greta. He motioned for Tony to keep the boy busy. Dubiously he approached. Nervousness overtook Greta. She fumbled with her hair and attempted to smooth invisible wrinkles from her dress.

He was hesitant as he spoke. "Greta?" She arched her brow, a silent invitation to continue. "I am sorry." He raked his hands through his hair, then twisted them behind his back. Finally, he stuffed them into his pockets.

"For what?" She tipped her chin up, trying to maintain a

semblance of composure, but the hurt in his eyes weakened her determination.

He paused, searching for the exact words to say to her. "I allowed things to get out of hand. You've got me all twisted up inside and I wasn't thinking."

"You weren't."

"I was an idiot, a complete jerk to you."

"Go on, I am not going to argue." Anger flashed deep within her eyes, causing Jimmy to flinch.

Stumbling, he attempted another explanation. "I shouldn't have said what I said about you." Her eyebrow hitched up further. He raked his hands through his hair again, a few strands sticking up at an awkward angle. Greta resisted the urge to smooth them down.

"I'm making a muck of all of this." Jimmy reached for her hand, clasping it between his. He brought it to his lips, placing a soft kiss on her knuckles, then rubbed his hand over hers. "There's something different about you, Greta. You aren't them." He tilted his head towards the village behind him. "You're special." His voice turned to soft velvet.

She took a steadying breath, resisting the urge to wrap herself in his embrace. "That's nice, Jimmy. But I'm not easily swayed." She tried to wrench her hand free, but he gripped it tighter.

"I know." His eyes widened, begging her. "Please, Greta. Give me another chance?"

"And what do you mean? Another chance? Another chance to have your way with me?"

He bristled. "No, not that." He pulled her closer, giving a one-shoulder shrug. "I think it means I want to start again. I want to get to know you, Greta. To understand more about this attraction I feel for you."

Part of her wanted to leave, to turn her back on him and

forget ever meeting this man standing in front of her. The other part, the less rational part, couldn't help but notice the flame smoldering in his eyes whenever he looked at her. The burning desperation filled her with a frantic need to find the key to open him fully. And there was more behind those eyes awash with such fiery passion, a hidden pain. A secret she knew he would share with her, if only she could see him for all he was. She desperately wanted to be the one to unravel the mystery of Jimmy O'Brien.

She sighed, lured by the irrational thoughts. "One more chance, Jimmy. That's all I can give you. But no more clandestine meetings in remote office buildings."

He smiled brightly. His sultry smile made Greta's knees go weak. Using her hand, he leveraged her into a hug. "I promise, you won't regret this."

"I hope I won't," she muttered forlornly to his chest.

He kissed the top of her head. "How about I take the two of you home?"

"We were planning to go to the village. We were wanting an adventure and to hopefully find a little more food."

"I think I have a few cans and such. The village is cleaned out."

"Oh." She nudged a clump of dirt on the ground with the toe of her shoe. "I hadn't realized so many people would be coming through this area. It always felt so remote here."

"I am afraid this is only the beginning. The Sudeten Germans are being ousted by the new Czechoslovakian government. There are millions who will be needing places to live and food. But anything you need, you just let me know." He tilted her chin up. "Come on, let me take you both home."

She nodded her acquiescence as Tony approached with Ezra. "Ready to go, Captain?" Tony asked. "Li'l man, let's get y'all into the jeep." Ezra's face lit up.

Jimmy said something to the group of soldiers she had spoken to earlier. They saluted each other and he returned. He helped Greta into the vehicle, settling Ezra next to her. Tony and Jimmy climbed into the front two seats.

"Why don't you drive?" she leaned forward to ask Jimmy. She rested a hand on his shoulder, her breath ghosting past his ear.

"Officers never drive. It is the way of things, tradition, I guess," he said as Tony maneuvered the vehicle onto the roadway.

"We wouldn't want our officers to do anythin' too taxin'," Tony jeered.

Jimmy rolled his eyes. "I may have heard that jest a few too many times. You need new material, Corporal." Tony laughed and steered the vehicle through the crowded roadway.

The journey home was over quickly, a loop in the opposite direction. Ezra was in awe of the jeep. Holding onto the edge, he peered over the side watching the scenery pass by. Greta showed him how to hold out his hand, moving it up and down with the wind. His face lit up with rapt fascination, mesmerized by the gentle glide and resistance the air current created as he flicked his wrist back and forth.

Once they arrived, Ezra dragged Tony into the house, showing him everything he could imagine. He convinced Tony to climb into his hiding place under the floor. Then he demonstrated each and every one of his toys. Finally, they set up the toy soldiers, with Ezra insisting Tony be the blue soldiers. Those were Ezra's favorites.

Jimmy rested his arm along the back of the sofa, patting the seat next to him. Greta sat at the edge until he used his outstretched arm to nudge her closer. "Tell me something about yourself?"

She rested her head in the cup of his shoulder. "Hmm,

something about me?" She was quiet for a minute, then spoke in her lightly accented voice. "I never learned to ride a bicycle."

"What? Seriously?"

She snuggled closer to him, breathing in his bay rum aftershave. So divinely masculine, she wished she had a bottle of his scent to spritz around her room. "I don't know. I've ridden horses hundreds of times, but never had a bicycle. What is your secret?" He stiffened at the question. *What is he hiding?*

After a moment, he relaxed, the flat of his nails skimming up and down her spine. "I love fishing. I will spend hours sitting on the bank of a river, my line in the water. Everyone thinks I am a terrible fisherman, as I never seem to catch any. But the truth is, I say I am going fishing, only to lie down next to the river and watch the clouds drift by. I enjoy the peace and solitude."

"It sounds lovely." Greta felt all of her tension slipping away with each soft stroke of his fingers. She could hear the whump-whump of his heart, feel the slow rise and fall of his chest. If she allowed herself, she could fall asleep to this gentle lullaby. "Do you have any brothers or sisters?"

"Only a sister, Erin. She is a spitfire. Flaming red hair and a temper to match."

"Is she younger or older?"

"Younger, by eight years. And you?" He shifted against her, allowing her head to rest more solidly against his chest.

"No brothers or sisters. I wish I had a big family. I've always wanted so many children, a house full of them." She could hardly believe how comfortable she felt in his embrace, how natural it felt being so close to him. With Fritz, physical affection felt odd and a bit forced. Since they had known each other most of their lives, there were never any secrets or stories to tell. Never an all-consuming need to touch, to open herself fully.

They sat in companionable silence, listening to the soft tick of the cuckoo clock. When he spoke again, Greta felt his words vibrate in his chest. "This moment is perfect."

She hummed her agreement and wiggled closer, tilting her head to gaze at him. With a brief hesitation, as if asking permission, he lowered his mouth to hers, his lips a gentle caress. Meeting no resistance, the kiss deepened. His beautiful hand cradled her head.

It ended with a sigh. He rested his chin on the pate of her head, holding her tightly against the warm expanse of his chest.

"I am ready to tell you a bit of my past. How I came to know Ezra."

Tony walked in the room. "Poor li'l guy, he was completely tuckered out. Fell asleep halfway through my story. I'm ready to head back."

"I am going to stay here tonight. Do you think you can come back tomorrow morning and pick me up?" Jimmy kept Greta nestled into his side.

"No problem. I'll come by after formation." Tony gave a mini wave to Greta as he left the house.

"You don't have to go back with Tony?"

"No." He shifted against the sofa again, trying to elevate his aching leg. "I've been relieved of duty. No longer fit for service." He pointed to his outstretched limb. "As soon as they begin sending soldiers home, I'll be going."

"Oh, so soon?" She didn't want to feel the disappointment that this affair wasn't meant to last. She pushed those feelings down and turned to face Jimmy.

He beckoned Greta into the bedroom with his finger. "I think we should have a little privacy while we talk, if that's okay." Once inside he closed the door with a small click.

Greta stood near the bed, playing with the hem of her

sleeve. She didn't know what to do with her hands as she faced Jimmy, his pupils dilating in the soft light. He swaggered over and gripped her shoulders. Then slid his palms down to rest on her waist. He leaned in, his breath sweet and hot against her lips. With a satisfied smile, he deepened the kiss.

It began as a gentle onslaught. Jimmy tugged on her plump bottom lip with his teeth, begging for entrance. A breathy moan escaped Greta's throat, stoking the fire raging within him. On a possessive growl, he tightened his hold. Their tongues met in a tangled dance, tasting each other. Holding his hand at the nape of her neck, he angled their mouths to align perfectly. Her blood surged. She could feel his engorged length pressing against her belly, knowing that if she did not stop, she would never be able to reveal her story. Reluctantly, Greta broke the kiss.

Still holding her head in his hands, Jimmy searched her eyes. "I could do this all night, but I think you had something to tell me."

Losing her nerve, she reached up, drawing his mouth back to hers. "I think I would rather kiss you."

For a few moments, they continued, her long fingers wrapped around the back of his head, holding them together. His lips moved to the hollow below her ear, then he playfully tugged on the lobe. The bristles on his cheeks tickled and she snorted. Embarrassed, she covered her face.

"Oh, Greta, love, don't be embarrassed." He rubbed his face against the sensitive spot again, and she shivered, another snort escaped. "You are utterly adorable." He tugged her down onto the bed, throwing one heavy leg over hers, his arm along her side with his hand below her breast. Greta wriggled her backside against him, shifting to find a comfortable position. He gripped her hips tightly, urging her to stop. "Greta, love, if you keep moving like that, I won't be held responsible for what happens to you next."

She turned around to face him, her smile fading quickly after catching the desirous look in his eyes. "Oh," she uttered, withdrawing an inch to give them space. His demeanor gentled as he tucked a few strands of hair behind her ear. "I love lying here with you, holding you," she sighed against his strong chest.

"Me too." He reached down to the end of the bed, dragging up the quilt to cover them.

"Tell me about America."

"I come from a place called Reading, Pennsylvania."

"I remembered from the other night. Is it anything like New York City?"

"No, love, nothing like New York. It is much smaller. My family owns a tobacco shop on a corner, and we live upstairs. I miss it dearly."

"It must smell amazing in the shop," she sighed, remembering fondly the smell of her grandfather's tobacco and pipe. But thinking of her grandfather left her with a terrible sense of loss. She changed the subject. "Touching you feels magical." Her fingers skimmed over the soft hair on his arms, tracing over the veins and muscles under the skin.

"That it does." Greta twisted onto her other side. Jimmy rested his chin on Greta's shoulder, pulling her back against his chest. "We call this spooning."

"Spooning, what a funny name."

"It is, see I am the big spoon, and you are the little." He ran his hands over her side. She giggled. Was it the touch or his statement, maybe a bit of both? "What is *spoon* in German?"

"Löffel," she whispered.

"Loffel," he repeated.

"Almost, like this," she took his mouth in her hand and showed him how to say the umlaut. "Ö, Löffel."

"Löffel. What a funny word."

"That's what I think of spooning, but it is rather a delightful way to lie down next to someone."

"My curiosity is getting the better of me, Greta." He shifted his body a bit closer, causing the funny feeling to rise in her belly. "I know you were there, I know what the tattoo means." She stiffened at his reference. "How did you do it, how did you escape it? The concentration camp?"

"You won't let it go?" She wanted to savor the moment in each other's arms and do anything other than talk about that place.

"No, you promised you would tell me." His tone became insistent, then gentle. "Be brave, Greta."

"I did promise." A bit reluctant and yet relieved to unburden herself, she began to tell her story, talking of the night they broke through the fence. Revealing the story and the promise of Ezra's survival.

CHAPTER FOURTEEN

September 1943

"Run!" Ruth hissed into Greta's ear. *Now, it must be now.* The guards were distracted by a commotion on the other side of the camp. Greta grabbed three-year-old Ezra, hoisting him onto her hip, darting to the fence. Two inmates had already cut through the wire, using the chaos as cover. It was only a matter of time before the hole was discovered and their chance for freedom would be gone.

Without even a hasty glance over her shoulder, Greta made it to the triple fence. She took a deep breath. *Now*, she must go now. She helped Ezra thread through the opening and then followed behind, sliding along their bellies. The cut wires caught on her clothes, tearing at her skin, but she was able to wrest herself free. First fence... second fence... third fence... They were through the barrier. She felt blood oozing over her shoulder. *Run, Greta, run!*

She lifted Ezra, cradling him against her chest as they ran straight into the woods. Scrambling behind a tree, she caught a quick breath, listening intently for the sounds of them being followed. They zigzagged through the woods, using the trunks for a moment of cover before darting to the next. Quickly, they weaved through the area, moving further and further away from the camp.

There was a dry creek bed in front of her. Perhaps if they jumped, it would be harder for the dogs to follow the scent. She placed him on the ground and motioned him to stay put. She leaped forward, clearing the creek bed. Turning around, she held out her arms to him. Ezra got a running start and landed perfectly. Stumbling backward from the force of his jump, she took a moment to steady herself. Then as quickly as she could, she ran with Ezra cradled to her chest.

Now, keep going. She heard gunfire, it was closer. Behind them, dogs barked. *Run faster, faster.* Quietly, she set the boy down and they continued to run together, holding onto his hand as they wove through the trees. They were breathless and said nothing. *Come, little Ezra, fly, like a bird, fly.* Zigzagging, left, right, stop and breathe, run, left, right, left again. They serpentined through the dark forest, with only a thin strip of moonlight shining through to guide them to safety. Quickly they ran. *Were they being pursued?* There was no time to check, they must run for their lives. No stopping now.

They ran like two people possessed, their breathing coming in short, painful bursts. Long ago the sounds of gunfire and dogs had diminished. The only sounds were their panting and the dry crunch of leaves.

Further and further, they went, and the dense forest began to open up. When Ezra's young legs started to give out, she cradled him in her arms until her muscles strained under the additional weight. There was a field, with a building some 20 meters in front of them, perhaps an old barn. She quickly turned to the left, then right. However, the area around the building was bare. *Should we risk it?*

Hesitating for only a moment, she debated what to do. But they didn't have a choice. They could not stay where they were, out in the open. A cloud covered the moon, it was their one chance. "Run fast!" Ezra sprinted forward, Greta running behind him. They darted inside, as the cloud moved past the moon and the ground was lit again.

Blinking their eyes to adjust to the darkness, they huddled inside the remains of a long-neglected building. Cobwebs hung throughout the building, discarded objects strewn haphazardly around. Greta prayed it would provide adequate shelter for the night. It was their only hope. Ezra collapsed onto a mound of hay, curled up into a ball and fell fast asleep. *How long did we run?* It felt like hours. Her chest burned as she inhaled deeply. She sat with aching legs, back, every part of her throbbed.

Hopefully, something hidden within the clutter might provide comfort. She searched, lifting up the debris as silently as possible. There was no telling who or what might be near. At any moment, their hiding place could be discovered. But they had no choice, they had to rest. Ezra's breathing was labored from the quick pace she set.

She was very fearful for Ezra's mother, Ruth. They had to leave her behind, as she was too weak to follow. For as long as Ruth had been at the camp, she fed most of her portion of food to Ezra. Greta had only arrived a few weeks before. It was Ruth who woke her up. Almost everyone in their barracks continued to sleep through the noise, but Ruth, Greta, and Ezra took advantage of the commotion, watching and observing at the entrance. Then, from the corner, they noticed two women run up to the triple fence. They had smuggled some sort of shears and quickly cut through the wires, one by one. In a matter of a minute, the women were through all three fences.

Ruth knew she would hinder their ability for a quick escape. "Please," she begged, "you must save Ezra, save my son." There was no time to argue. This was to be Greta's sacred task, save Ezra from certain death.

What would happen when the guards discovered Greta missing? If she was lucky, if Ruth was lucky, no one would notice until the roll call in the morning. Ezra wouldn't be missed. The guards already assumed he had perished long ago in the gas chamber. But Greta, that would be a different story. She shuddered. The retribution would be swift and ferocious. She silently sent a prayer to everyone they left behind.

Greta refused to sleep now. She must stay awake. Ezra's breathing was ragged. He needed water. Not now, we must wait. She sat down next to him, resting her back against a box. *What could be in here?* She opened it and sifted through the contents. There were old dishes, small trinkets. Inspecting the wrapping materials, she discovered clothing and rags. There was a dress, a touch too big, but it would work. She took off her coat and uniform. Next, she put on the dress, and bundled her uniform into a rag. She must discard it, burn it hopefully. The Schutzstaffel guards must not find it. They could not be allowed to find evidence of their escape. Anything left behind would be a clue as to who they were, where they were, and where they were heading.

She put on a rag to cover her shaved head. It would draw undue attention and speculation. Luckily, Ezra still had his original clothes. Now they could pass for a Polish mother and her child, then she remembered the yellow star of David on his clothing. Her red triangle had been discarded with her uniform, but Ezra's clothes were still needed, and each piece still had a patch. She found a sharp tool and went to work, careful not to wake up the sleeping child. She snipped away the stars ever so carefully, yanking out the remaining threads. He slept soundly while she worked, the poor child was too exhausted to even know what was happening around him.

Adding these scraps to her bundle, Greta sat back and thought about the sixty-five days she spent in Auschwitz-Birkenau, all leading to this moment here. A flood of memories came to her. She remembered Ruth's kindness the first night, how she took Greta under her wing and helped her learn the rules of survival in the camp.

"Trust no one," Ruth warned. "The soldiers have spies everywhere. I have seen people betrayed for nothing more than a tiny scrap of bread. Never underestimate what people are capable of when they are starving and scared." Her dry cough caused her to wheeze terribly.

She remembered the horribly cruel guard. An incredibly sadistic woman, a veritable monster. One time, the guard found food scraps a woman in the barracks managed to smuggle. To get someone to confess to the theft, she picked Ruth, one of the weakest in the barracks. She beat her over and over. Greta saw Ezra's face peering around the stove, watching in horror as the scene unfolded before him. Something in Greta snapped, she had to act.

Greta knew there was no way Ruth would survive such an attack; she yelled to the guard, "Stop! It was me. I stole the bread."

The guard turned to her, an insidious look in her eye. "What did you say, dog?"

"I said, it was I who stole the bread." Greta lifted her chin, staring defiantly at the tormentor.

Greta's beating seemed to take an eternity, every inch of her covered in bruises and welts. The guard did not care who stole the bread, it didn't matter. She had to instill fear in every inmate, as it was the only way she would wield her power, and she was drunk on it. As for Greta, the only thing that did matter to her was the survival of the three of them. She would not stand by and watch Ruth or Ezra die. Miraculously, she healed with only a few scars as a reminder of the cruelty people were capable of perpetrating.

Then what she feared the most happened: prisoners from other barracks became aware of Ruth's secret. A few days after the bread incident, Greta overheard a conversation between an inmate and a guard. The woman was well known for being complicit. The guards used her in the past as an informant, though she received little in return for her betrayals.

"I am telling you, she is hiding something," the woman said, pointing discreetly at Ruth.

The guard suspiciously eyed the woman. He knew any information she told him came at a price. The question was what price was she willing to sell it to him and did he even want to bother with her. "And what is it that she is hiding?"

"For some more food, I will find out," offered the woman.

He scoffed at her, "Bring me the information, and then we will see about what you think might be payment." Slapping her in the face, he walked off, but not before screaming, "Get to work!"

Greta knew Ruth only had one secret, a secret that could get everyone killed. She mentioned what she heard to Ruth. "We have to find a place to put Ezra, where they cannot find him," she insisted.

Ruth clung to her son. "But where? We must escape, Greta. There is no place to hide him anymore." This desperate plea sent her into another coughing fit. She was pale and weakening every day.

So far his hiding place was behind a small stove. The inmates and Ruth had removed a few bricks, creating an opening behind it. But now the days would be growing colder, and the stove would need to be lit whenever possible. It soon would no longer be practical to hide him there. The rest of the barracks' floor was made of stone floors. Concrete served as the frame for the bunk beds and on these were immovable wooden slats, covered only by loose hay. There were no places in the wall or openings in the floor.

That night, Ruth turned to Greta. "Promise me, Greta, promise me you will always take care of Ezra?"

"I promise, Ruth." She understood her urgency. There was only so much time left.

"I know I am too weak to go on much longer, but Ezra, he must survive. For our people, he must survive."

Greta swore to her, "As long as there is a breath in my body, he will survive."

And now, two days later, Greta sat in a dilapidated building with Ezra and Ruth was alone at the camp. They must survive, there was no other way. Greta allowed one tear to fall, a tear for her dear friend and her vow.

Morning broke and it was time to move on. She picked up the bundle containing her clothes and the stars. She nudged Ezra awake. He wobbled as he wiped the sleep from his eyes. If only they could stay longer, but no, they had to continue. Peeking out of the barn door, she looked around, left and right, no one. Now it was not possible for them to run. They had to act as if they belonged.

She found the road. Judging from the position of the sun in the morning sky, if she followed the road to the right she would be heading West. That was the best direction. All she knew about their current location was they were somewhere in occupied Poland. Where exactly, she did not know. If she made it to Germany, she would be able to blend in. She had friends, people who could help her and Ezra. There was Fritz and his

Aunt Liesel, they would risk everything for her. But help was far away now, it must be hundreds of miles to Berlin.

She made a mental list of what they would need: documents, food, water, a place to burn the clothes. She would change his name. Hans perhaps, something easy to remember. But she could not, she would not let him forget who he was, Ezra Eichenbaum, son of Ruth and Daniel of Cologne, Germany. After this was over, he must be reunited with his family, Greta had made this promise. *No matter what, as long as I have breath in my body, Ezra will see his family again.*

A short distance along the road, a farmer burned leaves in a field. Walking with purpose, holding Ezra's tiny hand in hers, she marched up to the pile and threw the bundle of clothes on top. The farmer caught her eye, gave a curt nod. She stared straight at him, daring him to say something, but he didn't. He understood. He continued raking up more leaves. There would be no trouble here.

Walk with a purpose, her mother always instructed her, *if you act like you belong, no one will question you.* And on they walked, over fields and roads, past villages, barns, horses, cars. Every now and then, they would come across a stream. They would drink as much as their bellies could hold and rest. Then on they walked, neither saying anything. Greta holding onto little Ezra's hand, one foot and then the next. *Keep going west...*

"Dear God, Greta!" Jimmy raked his hand through his hair and sat up on the bed. "Your story..." His mouth agape, his eyes searched her face, words failed him.

"You don't believe me." She spoke barely above a whisper, wiping away at the tears pooling in the corner of her eyes.

Jimmy gripped her tightly. "Greta, it isn't that. I believe

you. It's just... I don't know what to say." He tenderly stroked her back. "How did you make it back to Germany?"

"With the help of a man named Gregor. He had connections to Żegota. Do you know who they are?"

Jimmy was familiar with the organization. It was a codename for the Council to Aid Jews, an underground group working with the Polish government in exile. Their members were able to disrupt the war and protect Polish Jews from the Germans.

"Yeah, their deeds are remarkable. I also met some Free Poles when I was stationed in England. I don't think I've ever met a more impressive group of fighters. Their records were unmatched."

"Gregor and a few others were able to get us here to Aunt Liesel. And you know the rest." She relaxed against his strong chest.

"You are incredible." He sighed, his chin resting on her head.

"No, I did what anyone would do. Ezra was merely a small child."

He pulled back, his eyes locking onto hers, boring through the walls of doubt she built. "Yes, but he's here because of you. You saved him."

Greta looked away, uncomfortable with accepting his praise. "I wish I could have done more, brought Ruth with me." Her lip quivered. Each night before she fell asleep, she prayed most vehemently for her revered friend's survival. "Oh, Jimmy, will I ever find her? Do you think she's even alive?"

Jimmy said nothing for a long time, instead he gripped her tightly, using his body as solace. The chance of Ruth's survival was slim at best, but the last thing Greta needed to hear were his doubts. "We will find her." His hands framed her face. "Greta, whatever we have to do, we will find Ruth."

CHAPTER FIFTEEN

The house felt so empty. A softly reminiscent sigh escaped Greta's lips as she watched Ezra playing in the yard. It was disappointing how early Corporal Ricci arrived to return Jimmy back to base. Shortly before, Greta was roused from a delicious dream, involving a rather scantily clad Jimmy and his wicked tongue.

His velvety baritone voice caressed her ear, as he nuzzled his stubbled cheek against the nape of her neck. Delightful tingles shimmered over her skin. "Good morning, Angel."

"Angel is it?" She scooted closer into his warm embrace.

"The day we met, I thought you were an angel sent to heal me." Her bottom rubbed against the hardened ridge of his olive drab boxer shorts. With a low groan, he gripped her hips, holding her steady. "I want you. I need you." His husky voice stoked her fevered longing.

She swiveled around, facing him. Her eyes captivated, pleading for him to make the next move. A hair's breadth away from what surely would have been the most passionate kiss of her life, they heard the pitter-patter of little feet coming closer. Just as quickly, the steps quietly retreated.

"It is not to be," she teased. They both felt the heavy weight of disappointment.

He lustfully groaned. "It needs to be soon. I need to be inside you. To feel your body gripping mine."

"Oh!" A flush spread over her cheeks. His pupils dilated, his eyes grew darker, heat pools of liquid brown. No man had ever looked at her with such raw hunger. It stirred an aching deep in her core. Her breasts felt full and needy. She pressed her legs together, hoping to steady the growing pulse in between.

His fingers outlined her jaw. "I can't help it, Greta. You fill me with a burning ache I have never known before."

She shuddered, those feelings remaining long after Corporal Ricci's arrival and Jimmy's subsequent departure. She replayed the next moments in her delightful daydream. The kiss started so innocently, then quickly erupted like lava flowing down a volcano, consuming everything in its path. His lips, his tongue, his hands devoured her. He tucked her underneath him, the length of his body resting against the cradle between her thighs. Together their hips rocked, the rhythm becoming urgent. Then they heard the blare of a car horn, and a deluge of ice water smothered the raging fire. He stifled a roar of frustration into the pillow, while she bit back a scream of protest. Today was not the day.

Remembering that kiss rekindled the flame. She placed her glass of water against her forehead, hoping to cool her overly heated skin. He was correct, something needed to happen, and soon. But it was more than a need to satisfy a growing itch.

After everything she revealed, after finally telling this part of her story, she wanted to fully give herself to him. To open her heart and body to this man, her Jimmy. To surrender herself to him, as she had never done before. But there was still something she was holding back. There was more to the story, was she truly ready to share *everything* with him? The reason why she was at Auschwitz?

As she flipped over the potatoes, she contemplated what would happen next. Flip. Flop. The entire time she cooked their lunch, her mind ran in a million different directions. One more flip and they were a perfect golden brown. Sliding them onto a plate for Ezra to enjoy once he was finished playing outside, she asked herself the biggest question of all - what's next?

Life could start again. They no longer had to be in constant fear of what might be lurking around the corner, what she was trying to keep hidden. She would need to start searching for Ruth.

But these feelings whirling around inside were a confusing mess. How could she go from feeling terrified every single moment of every day to having some semblance of a normal life? What was normal? To go about working, laughing, loving... living. It wasn't like turning a new page, flipping on a switch. Both she and Ezra had to learn to trust, to feel safe, to belong in a place that long ago abandoned them.

"I guess starting over is putting one foot before the other," she said to herself. "I only wish I knew where I was going."

The Kartoffelpuffer was now finished; she looked out the window at Ezra. He used a large stick to draw different shapes on the ground. Then, he took off, arms outstretched, like the wing of an airplane. He was having so much fun. Greta allowed him to simply be for a while. The potatoes could wait until he was hungry. She ate a few mouthfuls, saving most of the rest for him, and began her chores.

She made the beds and put away the extra blanket. Wiped away the dust from a few surfaces. Swept up the floor. It was monotonous, yet somehow soothing. Stopping, still holding the broom, she closed her eyes.

Caught again in a daydream, she pictured Jimmy. Could feel his arms enveloping her, his hard body against hers. She could hear his soothing baritone. Smell his masculine scent, a blend of musk, bay rum, and a hint of clove still lingering on her clothing. His embrace felt like home, so safe and protected.

A sound wrested her from her thoughts, and she reluctantly continued her chores. Tomorrow, she decided to go to the refugee camp. Perhaps then she could find a few answers, a starting point.

Suddenly, the door flew open, the bang echoing through the small room. Ezra flew into her arms. He gripped her skirt, yanking her toward their hiding place. A shadow eclipsed the daylight. There was no time to hide...

CHAPTER SIXTEEN

The doorway filled with a man in a rumpled uniform. Its distinctive gray color was immediately recognizable. *Oh, God! It's a German soldier!* Greta shielded Ezra with her body, trying to hide him from the man leering maliciously in their direction. Into her flesh gripped Ezra's tiny fingernails, begging her to not let go.

Using his booted foot, the soldier kicked the door closed behind him. He threw the lock, the slide of the bolt clicking ominously.

"I don't want to be disturbed," he uttered, his voice arctic cold. His German words were clipped, dripping with hate. "I've been watching you, seeing how you whore after the Americans." He pointed with a gnarled finger in the direction of the military encampment and spat on her clean floor. "Your betrayal cost us the war."

Menacingly, the soldier stalked around the house, keeping an eye trained on them. He lifted objects, peeked behind doors, searching for something. He spotted the Kartoffelpuffer. Taking one into his hand, he took a bite. "Not bad, you would have made someone a fine cook. Too bad you won't live."

She tightened up defensively. *Those were Ezra's!* The rage roiled within her, but she knew she must remain calm. She had to think clearly or there would be no chance of survival. "The war is over now, you will be shot for looting. The Americans won't tolerate guerilla soldiers," she stated, raising her chin in defiance.

"Looting," he laughed. "They will shoot me for something far worse than looting. I am under orders, the top orders." He tossed the food down in front of him, running greasy hands down his shirt. "We continue to fight. We have not surrendered, we are the 'Werewolves.'" A sinister smile crept over his face. "You know what werewolves are, little boy? We are creatures of the night who hide in the woods and come out to eat our prey." Each word was drawn out, enunciating every syllable.

Ezra's grip tightened more; she felt his nails digging into her skin, but she did not remove them. His grip kept her alert. She shifted around to the left, inching away from their captor, pulling Ezra along with her. She had to get him to safety. She could sacrifice herself, block the door to let him escape. He knew the way to Liesel's house. She would protect him with her life.

The soldier stared at her, his beady black eyes following every move. "Perhaps, I will bite and eat you first, you traitorous bitch." His game was over, now for the fun. He lunged at Greta, throwing her against the mantle. Her head crashed against the wood. The attack stunned her, and a loud ringing filled her ears. She tried to shake away the dizzying sickness.

Ezra ran, but only managed a few steps before the soldier picked him up. Impervious to his kicks and furious hits; he shoved the boy into the bathroom, dragging a chair against the door. Ezra was trapped. His tiny fists slammed against the wood.

Greta pushed against the wall, trying to stand. Her head spun and she could feel the blood trickling down the back. "Poor pretty girl, did you hurt yourself?" he jeered, spittle collecting on his bearded chin. His towering frame enveloped the entire room, a demonic figure in gray.

He yanked her up to her feet, gripping her wrists. She twisted and trashed against him, but she could not get free. With nothing left to leverage against him, she spat directly into his eye. A flash of anger washed over his face, he used her hand to wipe it away. "You will regret that," he hissed, a venomous snake.

Using his body, he forced her against the wall, pinning her feet, her legs, her arms. The smell of unwashed skin and cigarettes overpowered her, and she started to gag. "We come to bite and eat," he spewed the ominous words into her ear. Down her neck he ran his tongue, his putrid breath filling her nostrils. He clamped his teeth down hard on her collarbone, tearing at her skin. She let out an agonizing scream and flailed against him. He grinned, his yellowed teeth covered in her blood. The maniacal laughter reverberated off the walls of the small room.

CHAPTER SEVENTEEN

"Hey, Corporal," Jimmy called out to his driver and friend, Tony. "I have nothing to do here, so I'm thinking of heading over to Greta's to take her a couple of tins of food I found in my locker. Can you drive me?"

"Yeah, why not. I have been relieved of duty for the next couple of days." He stood up from the chair he was lounging in. "Things seem to be gettin' pretty heavy with y'all."

Jimmy nodded as they climbed into the jeep and Tony started the engine. "I'm not sure how serious we can get. But there is something about her, I can't stay away."

"She's a real dish."

"I've never met anyone like her. We haven't even, well, you know." Jimmy mimed the sign for intercourse.

Tony chuckled. "Damn, Captain. That's some restraint." Greta's house came into view. "You're a lucky guy."

"Damn right I am."

Tony stopped the vehicle in front. Warning bells clanged in Jimmy's head, he turned to Tony.

His face was tight and grim. He sensed it too. "Somethin's wrong, Captain."

Jimmy nodded. He chambered a round in his service revolver. Tony did the same. A blood-curdling scream shattered the silence around them, propelling Jimmy into motion.

Tony grabbed the radio from the jeep and requested assistance. Jimmy threw himself against the door of the house, but it did not budge. Through the door, he could hear Greta pleading in German for someone to stop, followed by sadistic male laughter. In a moment, Tony was by Jimmy's side. Together they slammed against the door over and over until it finally yielded, splintering under their assault.

The soldier and Greta both turned to face the commotion. The sight greeting Jimmy turned his blood to ice. A vein at his temple pulsed. Unable to get a clear shot, he lunged forward. The German soldier emitted a guttural growl, throwing Greta with all of his weight against a wall, causing her to fall into a small table.

Jimmy's momentum caused both men to collapse onto the floor, his forearm pressing against the German's throat. The man was able to quickly reverse their positions, leaving Jimmy to scramble back onto his feet.

Jimmy charged the man again, throwing him against the sofa. This time he managed to land a few punches into the German's jaw, a yellow tooth clattered across the floor. Their strength, however, was evenly matched. Jimmy unholstered his revolver. Before he could raise it, the soldier threw his full weight into him. Jimmy crashed through the bedroom door. Both of them fought for the gun. It slid across the wooden floor, out of reach of both men.

Tony yanked the soldier off of Jimmy and placed him in a restraining hold. It was not easy, as the German fought with animalistic intensity. He broke free, sending Tony reeling, losing his footing and crashing against a wall. Jimmy readied himself and seized the opportunity, landing a perfect right hook along the soldier's jaw. The impact violently twisted the German's neck and he fell prostrate to the ground.

Jimmy picked up the revolver from the ground and leveled it at the German's head. He felt Tony's hand squeeze his shoulder. "It ain't worth it. Put the gun down, Captain."

His hand shaking, he lowered the weapon and placed it in Tony's hand. "He twitches, you shoot him."

"Understood, sir."

Jimmy could not resist; he landed a few well-placed kicks into the unconscious man's rib cage before turning to Greta. He bent over and took several large gulps of air, trying to regain his equilibrium. Greta was pitifully bracing herself against the sofa, shifting her weight to her left ankle. Shakily, he approached her, trying to cool the adrenaline coursing through his veins.

"Ezra." She pointed to the bathroom door.

"Don't worry, Tony will see to him." Greta nodded and opened her arms to Jimmy. He gently smoothed her hair from her face, running his trembling fingers down her bruised cheek. She bit her lip, hoping to hold back the swelling sobs. Without a word, he scooped her into his arms and sat with her cradled in his lap. He pressed her against his shoulder, holding her tightly against him as they both worked to regain control.

Tony secured the unconscious German with a length of rope. "Where's Ezra?"

"He's in the bathroom, Tony. The soldier left him alone," she responded hoarsely, trying to clear her throat. Jimmy explored the bruising on her neck, his jaw twitching with each newly discovered scratch, welt, and contusion. He pressed a handkerchief to the bite on her collarbone. She winced at the sting of the cloth.

Tony acknowledged her response with a swift kick to the German's knee. The popping of cartilage brought a satisfying smile to Tony's face. He stepped over the soldier, conveniently landing on his outstretched hand. "Oops," he said, stomping down hard again, bones crunching. "Didn't see you there."

Tony released Ezra from his holding cell. He ran straight into Tony's arms, who then gathered him up. "I've gotcha, li'l man. Don't fret none, I've gotcha." The boy slumped against his neck, shaking and sobbing. Tony walked outside, still cradling him in his arms. "We got the bad man, no one will hurt ya, my li'l friend, I promise."

Greta tried to ease herself back, but Jimmy kept a tight hold around her waist. She smoothed out his torn shirt, running her fingers over his bruised knuckles. "You're hurt again," her hoarse voice squeaked.

Jimmy gently pressed their foreheads together. "I'm fine," he sighed. "You're the one who is hurt."

As they sat together in an embrace, several vehicles entered the yard. From Tony's exclamations, they knew it to be American soldiers, who then rushed into the house. They saw the fallen assailant and relaxed their stances. "What happened here?" came the commanding voice of Major Clarkson.

Jimmy snapped to attention, saluting. The major quickly returned the greeting. "That man," Jimmy waved to the German soldier on the ground, "was attacking Greta and Ezra. Corporal Ricci and I were able to intervene and that's why he's incapacitated."

The major acknowledged the response and commanded two men to retrieve the new prisoner and take him into custody. He ordered his men to search the area for more soldiers and for the medic to take care of injuries to Greta and Jimmy.

"Excuse me, Captain," a red-haired man behind him said.

"I would like to examine her, if I could?" The medic was standing at the opposite end of the sofa, gesturing to Greta. She recognized him immediately as the man who treated Jimmy before.

"Sergeant Kowalski, s-so nice to see you a-again." Her voice strained, as she attempted to speak. Both Jimmy and the sergeant grimaced at the sound.

Jimmy repositioned Greta, keeping her within his reach should she need him. She reached out, twining their fingers together. The sergeant bandaged her cuts and checked her for severe injuries. After determining that she did not need more than bandages and rest, the medic excused himself to look over Ezra. Jimmy refused help for the moment.

"Thank you," she choked out, lightly patting the man's hand.

"No problem, ma'am, happy to help you out." He stood, gathering his things. "Please take it easy, you've had quite a beating. I'm glad we could help you, what with all you did for the captain there." He smiled roguishly, tipped his hat, then walked outside. Kowalski found the boy still in Tony's care. Luckily, he was completely unharmed, but he maintained a death grip on Tony's neck.

Tony swayed left and right, allowing Ezra to gently sob into his shoulder. "There, there, li'l fella. I've gotcha now."

Greta winced as she tried to move, her whole body ached and throbbed. "I... I need..." she stuttered. Jimmy was at her side again, scooping her up and carrying her to bed, laying her down onto the feather-filled duvet.

"What do you need, my Angel?" Jimmy helped her sit up, reclining her against the headboard.

She shook her head, her thoughts clouded. "I don't know, just keep Ezra safe." She leaned back, tried to steady the dizzying nausea threatening to overtake her.

"We will, my Angel, and you, too." He stroked her cheek with the back of his hand. "I thought I was going to lose you." He paused, picked up her hand, kissing each knuckle. "The thought of losing you..." He swallowed hard, not ready to say more.

"I was so terrified for Ezra, how he might not make it. After everything we had been through, and then..." Streams of anguish flowed down her cheeks. "I thought of not being able to tell you how I feel. About not seeing you again."

Jimmy drew her to him. He held her tightly, her body sagging against him. "Don't let go," she sighed to him, "hold me like this forever."

"Captain," the major returned, "I would like to speak to her for a moment." Reluctantly, Jimmy withdrew his arms.

"I will be right on the other side of this door. I'm not leaving." He kissed her forehead, then turned and saluted the officer, leaving them to talk together in the room.

She shifted, hoping to find a more comfortable position. Pulling a chair next to the bed, the major sat down. "Miss Müller. I'm Major Clarkson. We met before when you took care of Captain O'Brien."

She nodded. "I remember, Major Clarkson. It is nice to see you again."

He inclined his head and his lips slightly turned up at the corners. "I have a few questions to ask you about what happened." She indicated he should continue. "Do you know who the man is?"

"Not really," she explained. "He kept referring to himself as a Werewolf and he was..." She paused, her throbbing head making it difficult to remember. "He was ordered to continue fighting."

"Did he say who gave the orders?"

"No, I'm sorry."

"Is there anything else you can think of?"

"No, he said he was watching us. He knew the Americans had been here."

"Did he indicate how long he has been watching this house?"

"No, he did not. Do you know what he meant by calling himself a Werewolf?"

"There have been attacks on German citizens and Allied soldiers since the war ended. We've collected evidence suggesting that a group of soldiers are using guerilla tactics and are trying to continue the fighting. We have an idea where the orders have come from, but are working out how many people are involved."

"Does this mean Ezra and I are still in danger?"

He smiled sympathetically. "We will do all we can to protect you. Our job now is to maintain the peace and begin rebuilding." The major moved the chair back to its place near the window. "I would like to leave a few soldiers here if it would be alright with you? I am afraid there may be more men hiding in the woods and if this is the case, we need time to root them out."

"Thank you." She leaned back against the bed, closing her eyes and willing the pain to stop. "Can you let the captain stay, and maybe Corporal Ricci?"

"The captain is no longer on duty; he is waiting for orders to go home. He is being discharged because of his injuries. He has my permission to stay though. And yes, Corporal Ricci can stay too, I see he is very protective of your boy and if my boys had been through that..." He shook his head and didn't continue. "We will leave a few other soldiers outside for tonight as well, to make sure no one else is out there."

"How did you know to come?" she asked.

"Corporal Ricci called it in over the radio. Because of the

recent attacks on civilians and soldiers, he had a radio with him. Luckily, we were patrolling nearby and could arrive quickly." He moved toward the door.

"Thank you, Major Clarkson. I know you didn't need to help a German."

The major shook his head. "The war is over. It is time we all start anew and rebuild. We aren't going to sit by and watch someone prey on innocent women and children."

"I'm so grateful you were here."

"As I told you before ma'am, anything we can do for you, you let us know." He tipped his hat to her. He withdrew from the room, giving orders to his men as he walked through the house.

Jimmy returned and sat next to her in bed. She sobbed painfully now. Holding her against his chest, Jimmy whispered, "It will be all right now, I am here. All the adrenaline is wearing off, let yourself relax."

"Why are you here?" She could scarcely believe her luck. Had Tony and Jimmy not returned, she and Ezra would be dead. Out of nowhere, he appeared like a knight in rumpled olive green.

"Well, Tony and I got to talking. He thought we should come by and bring you something to eat. I had found a few C-Rations I didn't need and thought you might like them." He adjusted his body and winced too. The skin was broken on his knuckles; a bruise bloomed under his right eye.

"Oh no, you are hurt," she cried, reaching out to touch his bruised face.

"I'm hurt?" he sputtered incredulously. "Darling Greta. I will heal; the medic says I strained my shoulder in the fight and have a few scrapes. Don't worry though, they got everything fixed up again."

He smoothed her hair away from her face and straightened

her dress. "Now I am not going to let you sleep tonight, not with a head wound like that. Tony is taking care of Ezra. He is telling him stories about baseball and Mickey Mouse. I'm pretty sure he has given him two or three chocolate bars to eat. So now it is all about you and your needs."

"Thank you for taking care of Ezra." Greta groaned, resting her aching head on his shoulder. "I can't think. My head is spinning."

"Rest, my Angel." He made himself comfortable, removing his boots and letting them drop with a thud to the floor. Then stretching out next to her, he ever so gently snuggled Greta into his side. "Anything you want to talk about?"

"I am not sure. You pick." The gentle rise and fall of his chest soothed her aching mind. His fingers drifted up and down her arms, leaving an eruption of goose pimples in their wake.

"As you wish, my Angel." They spent the whole night talking about their childhoods, growing up, and their families. As the dawn broke through the window, Greta allowed the exhaustion of the day's events to overtake her, the one thought running through her mind. *How am I ever going to let him go?*

CHAPTER EIGHTEEN

Warm rays of sunlight filtered through the window. Greta stretched her neck and groaned. Every muscle ached after yesterday's assault. She tried shifting her position, but a heavy weight anchored her to the bed. Her eyes fluttered open. Across her leg rested Jimmy's. His hand splayed across her belly and his head rested on the pillow near her shoulder. She was reluctant to separate herself from such a delightful male cocoon, but her muscles cried out, demanding movement.

She tried to extract her body, but instead found herself hauled against Jimmy, surrounded by even more soothing warmth. "No," came his gruff command. "You're staying put." To emphasize the command, his hand slid further down her abdomen, pressing her against his body.

"As much as I would love to lie here forever, I have a few urgent needs." She patted his hand and tried to rise again.

"Nothing doing. Medic ordered bed rest, and in bed you will stay."

"Jimmy," she groaned as his lips pressed against the hollow

below her ear, sending chills down her body. "Please, I have needs."

His tongue skated down the length of her neck and nibbled at the collar bone. "I have needs, too. Let's satisfy them together."

He nuzzled his stubbled chin against a particularly sensitive spot. She giggled. "Jimmy, please. For a moment?"

He sighed and released his hold. "Just a moment, then back to bed. That's an order."

She gave a mock salute. "Ja wohl, Captain!" His face dropped; his eyes darkened. "Oh, Jimmy. I'm sorry, I didn't..."

He shook his head. "No, Greta. It's not that." He turned her to face the mirror on the opposite wall. "Have you seen the bruises?"

Her hand flew to her mouth. "Mein Gott, Jimmy. I am all black and blue."

"You look like you went five rounds with Joe Louis." She raised her brow in a silent question. "A boxer."

"I do, but I most definitely lost." She pressed her fingers against her swollen lips, along her blackened eye.

His hands settled on her hips, and she winced. Before she could stop him, he unfastened the buttons on her dress. "Jimmy, not now."

"I know, Angel. I need to see the extent of the damage." He lifted her dress and slipped it over her head to begin his inspection. Greta could feel his agitation growing, feel the tremble of his fingers, as they smoothed over her skin. When he found the tiny crescent moons along her hips, his voice strained. "Ezra?"

"Oh, Jimmy. He was so frightened, he held onto me so tightly. Did his fingers leave marks?" He showed her the indentations. "I didn't think we were going to make it."

He held onto her, taking in deep breaths to steady his

anger. After a long moment, he finally spoke. "I want to kill him. I have never wanted the death of anyone as much as I want his." What she saw in his steady gaze, chilled her to the bone. She placed a placating hand on his chest, trying to temper the rage boiling inside.

"It's done. He was arrested. We can move on. He wasn't the first man to hurt me."

"Who was the first?" His eyes searched her face. "Was it Fritz?"

"Fritz! Ach, nein. Never Fritz. It doesn't matter. The past is the past." She smiled up at him, but his jaw tightened.

"Give me his name, Greta." His voice was deceptively soft.

"Not now, Jimmy. I can't talk about it yet. Please!" A tear ran down her cheek, his grip lessened.

He nodded once and stepped back. "Change your clothes. I am going to check on Tony and Ezra." His hand on the doorknob, he turned around and looked her over.

Her tears were flowing freely. It took three purposeful steps to reach her again. He placed one hand on the nape of her neck and another on her lower back. His eyes blazed; their lips met. Every word he could not say, every feeling he could not express poured out in that kiss. She responded with equal intensity, twisting the back of his shirt in her fist, pushing herself against him. They merged as one, their hearts beating in rhythm together.

The fire still lingered in his eyes, as he declared, "Never again, Greta. You are mine to protect. You are mine." And she felt every last syllable of those words.

After his fervent declaration, he left the room, gently shutting the door behind him. Greta sank down onto the bed, too stunned to even speak. His words echoed in her mind. *You are mine...*

Ezra sat at the table eating an apple, his legs swinging back and forth as he listened to Tony regale him with stories from high school. "Greatest game of my life was in October my senior year. I was the runnin' back for my high school football team at Woodrow Wilson. That's American football, not what you call football." Ezra nodded his head and took a big bite. Juice ran down his chin, which he wiped away with his sleeve. "With only a minute left on the clock, the quarterback threw this long pass." Tony imitated the throw. "I caught it and ran it into the end zone, winnin' the game." He threw his arms up in the touchdown sign. Ezra imitated the gesture.

"Everyone at Woodrow was cheerin'. The cheerleaders ran over and kissed me. It was the greatest!" Ezra clapped; Tony ruffled his hair.

"I didn't know you played football." Jimmy walked into the room in time to hear Tony's story. "I played too, was the quarterback my junior and senior year."

Tony grinned. "Perhaps we could teach Ezra to play. Whatcha think about that?"

Ezra nodded and jumped down from his seat. He ran to the door and picked up his ball, motioning for Tony to follow. "I'm being summoned."

Jimmy clapped his back. "We might have to find a proper football, but it sounds like a plan. I'll see you outside in a few."

"How's Greta?"

"Not great, but not terrible." Jimmy tapped his fist on his thigh. "She said this wasn't the first time." He clenched his jaw, his teeth grinding in irritation.

"Yeah? How much do you know about her past?"

"Not enough." The thought of any violence done to Greta

by one man was more than he could bear. That there was someone else, unconscionable.

"Perhaps it's time for all y'all to open up?" Tony tugged on his cap. "This ain't some li'l fling between y'all. There's somethin' more. I ain't no college boy, but I know when I see somethin' powerful workin'. Stronger than a Texas tornado. Be careful it don't pick y'all up and toss y'all in a ditch somewhere."

Jimmy hated his inability to protect Greta. How many times has she been hurt before? His anger was only growing. He wanted to rage against the injustices done to Greta, attack the men who had hurt her. It was his time to protect her now when everyone else had failed her before.

Greta came into the room wearing a light blue cotton dress, simply styled and plain. The color enriched her eyes, causing them to shine more blue than green today. Her smile glowed. Jimmy fought the urge to haul her back to bed.

"Anything to eat?" she asked, eyeing a pot on the stove.

"Tony made some sort of soup."

She crinkled her nose. "Do you think we will ever eat normally again?"

"Normally?" She took a bowl from Jimmy's hand and sat at the table. He poured them both a cup of coffee.

"Vegetables, meat..." she sighed, "desserts with sugar."

Jimmy winked at her. "I can get you dessert."

She rolled her eyes and sipped the beverage. She released a soft moan. "Real coffee? Oh my, now this is a treat." She took a longer sip and sighed wistfully.

"What do you normally eat?"

"Liesel has a few chickens. A vegetable garden with potatoes and cabbage. That's what we mostly eat. Sometimes there are surprises, like the other day, she brought over sausage! I almost forgot what it tasted like."

"Don't you normally get to eat meat?" He tore a piece of bread, dipping it into the soup.

"No, it is such a rarity. The chickens, Liesel keeps them for eggs." She took a few more bites of the soup and then put her spoon down with a clink.

"What's with the heavy sigh?"

"I am dreaming of Wiener Schnitzel with hot potato salad," she said, eyeing the offending soup.

"You know, Reading is in Pennsylvania Dutch country, you can get a lot of great German food there."

"How can you get German food in a place known as Dutch country?"

"Well, people call it Dutch, but it is from the word Deutsch. So it's actually a place with German immigrants."

"Oh, you silly Americans. Dutch when you mean Deutsch," she chided with fondness. "But I want it now, a thin cutlet of veal, breaded and fried. A big bowl of hot potato salad with bacon sprinkled on top." Her stomach grumbled in protest as she took a mouthful of the vegetable soup.

Jimmy grimaced at his bowl. "Well, now you've done it. Now I am craving it."

She laughed. "Jimmy, there is one big favor I need to ask of you." He motioned with his spoon for her to continue. "Do you remember the story I told you? About how I need to reunite Ezra with his mother?"

"What do you want to do, my Angel?"

"I need to see the displaced person's camp today."

He relented. "All right, if you promise me one thing?"

"What is that?"

"Take it easy the rest of the day. Between the two of us, we barely make one person and..." He tapped the table next to her outstretched fingers. "I need you."

As he spoke, he watched a blush creep over her cheeks and

flush her chest, her lips twitching upward. He fought the urge to haul her back to bed and keep her there for the next week. Do everything he could to keep her beautiful smile permanently.

"But, yeah, we can go today. Let me tell Tony our plans and we can get going." He lifted her chin with his hand. "Do you promise?"

"I promise." Her eyes warmed before he strode outside.

He knew she should spend the day resting, but he couldn't argue with her plea. Time was running out and trails would get cold. Now was their best chance to find a trace of Ruth. He would do anything, move Heaven and Earth, to reunite Ezra and his mother, to help Greta fulfill her promise. It was one thing he could do, when he had failed so miserably at protecting her. He shuddered, remembering her screams, watching that beast attack her. There was nothing he wouldn't do for Greta.

"Hey, Tony," he called out to his friend. "Change of plans."

CHAPTER NINETEEN

Ironically occupying a former Schutzstaffel barracks and training ground, the displaced persons camp was a chaotic network of buildings surrounded by a wire fence. Though liberated from the camps, these freed people now found themselves caged again. But this confinement was not the same, as evidenced by the euphonious sounds permeating the air. Laughter - a sound once forbidden by their captors, floated promises of tomorrow above the wired fence.

A duo of uniformed GIs sat at a long table before the makeshift entrance. They saluted Tony and Jimmy, who both returned the greeting. The shorter of the two seated men inquired curiously, "How can we help you?"

Jimmy spoke first. "We are hoping to find a woman. We think she might be here, or perhaps someone might have heard something about her."

The soldier shook his head. "Man, it is like trying to find a needle in a haystack, while blindfolded and drunk. You are more than welcome to try, but I don't want you to get your hopes up. Every day new ones come, but very few leave."

"Sir," Greta started to ask.

Jimmy gently corrected her, "Address him as Sergeant. See the patch on his arm, it shows his rank."

"You have much to teach me." Changing direction, she addressed the man correctly this time. "I am sorry, Sergeant. If we find who we are searching for, can she come home with us?"

"That all depends, ma'am. She will need to be checked out by the doctors over there." He pointed to a white tent with a red cross. "We need to make sure they are healthy enough to leave and don't unwittingly spread disease. You wouldn't believe how these poor people were treated."

Jimmy brushed the tattoo on her forearm, a gesture not lost on the soldier, whose eyes widened in a brief moment of commiseration and sympathy. "Oh, she knows. Too well in fact."

"If I were you, I would find one of the holy men. They have already managed to help reunite a few families. Wish we could do more for you, but we had no idea there would be so many."

"There should be more," Greta whispered as she took in the enormity of the camp, knowing it was merely a fraction the size of the place she left behind. The people looked the same, their clothes hanging off their bodies. Many still wore their striped prison garb. Yet, their carriage, their walk was no longer the same shuffling gait. Instead, flirtatious giggles, affection, and conversation sweetened the air.

The sergeant studied her for a moment, then drew a deep breath. "No one under the age of twelve, not one older than thirty-five. Yeah, there should be a lot more." He rose from the desk to give more direction. "Many are eating lunch right now, enjoying the warm air. I would start over there, near our kitchens. You'll probably find some of the priests or rabbis there."

A hush rolled ahead as Greta and her group slowly meandered through the camp. Blank faces stared curiously back at them, the emaciated figures wondering if perhaps they knew each other from their previous lives. At one corner they saw a man, his head bent as he shuffled through a stack of papers, muttering to himself. They all agreed he might be the person to start with.

Greta spoke in German: "Excuse me, I am hoping you might be able to help us?"

He replied in the same language, thick with an accent she tried to place. Maybe he was Dutch? "Yes, I may be able to help. At least point you in the right direction." He chuckled lightly, removing a pair of round glasses to wipe them on the hem of his shirt. Replacing the bent and cracked spectacles on the end of his slender nose, he smoothed the dark wisps of hair remaining on his head. "Now, tell me how I can help you."

"Oh thank you. I am trying to find someone, his mother." She placed a protective arm around Ezra's shoulders.

He eyed the Americans. "And them?"

"They are our friends, they want to help," she explained, smiling up at Tony and Jimmy.

"I see. Thank you, thank you," he said to them in English, clasping and shaking each soldier's hand. Then he turned back to Greta, speaking in German. "It might be a difficult task, finding his mother. Do you know where she went, what camp she was at?"

"Last I knew, in September of 1943, she was in Auschwitz-Birkenau."

He startled. "That was a long time ago, a lot of deaths between then and now. The SS - those barbarous cowards tried to kill most of the inmates before they fled in retreat." He tapped the boy's nose affectionately. "But do not fear, hold on to hope. Now, how do you know she was there?"

Greta turned up the sleeve of her dress. She had only been to the one camp, and she was unaware only inmates of Auschwitz were labeled with the distinctive blue tattoo numbers. However, this man knew. He had heard the stories and met a few of the survivors who were marched to his camp before they were all liberated. "We were together."

"You managed to escape?"

"With him too." She pointed to Ezra.

"But how? I thought they killed all of the children immediately?" he whispered, trying not to be overheard by the child.

She gave him a very brief outline of their story, about Ruth's and Ezra's luck the day they arrived, because the Red Cross was examining the camp they were not immediately sent to the gas chambers. Then she explained her promise to Ruth to one day reunite. He touched Ezra's head, saying a prayer of thanks in Hebrew. He turned to Greta and did the same.

Then he looked over the papers in his hand. "Ruth Eichenbaum, wife of Daniel Eichenbaum, both of Cologne," he kept repeating the information Greta had given him, over and over again. There were several pages, each with a long list of names. He was thorough, but said to her, "Please, double check. My eyes are old, and I do not want to miss a name."

She handed the papers to Jimmy and Tony. They helped with the search, reading over the pages with desperate hope: Eichenbaum, Sara; Eichenbaum, Israel; Eichenbaum, Miriam. Each time she saw the last name her heart skipped, and she uttered a prayer, *please, oh please let it be her*. But it was never her name. He scanned through the last page, shook his head, no luck. She grabbed it, maybe he missed the name. But then again, the chances of them finding her so easily would be nearly impossible. Ruth had been in the General Government, the area of German-occupied Poland. Now Greta and Ezra were in Germany, hundreds of miles away. She couldn't help it, the tears came. She realized now how this was an impossible task. Jimmy reached out and held onto her.

"There, there, it is too soon to lose hope." Their guide's avuncular face crinkled kindly. "Let's go find someone of authority. They might have a better list, and they can write down your information. This way, she can also find you. Do not underestimate a mother's love."

Trying to stifle the tears, Greta nodded, his wisdom poetic. They followed him through crowds, zigzagging left and right. She was beyond grateful for this help. How could she have possibly navigated this on her own? They stopped in front of a group of scholarly looking men. A short conversation ensued in Hebrew. She assumed her guide wanted some assistance. Ezra squirmed as a boy of five does.

Then she felt a frantic tug on her hand. "Ezra, what is it?" Frantically, she looked around, trying to see what he saw. She was terrified. Was it a guard from the camp? Was it something horrific? She followed his line of sight and saw in the distance a woman standing in a dress much too large for her slight frame. Her close-cropped hair curling at the ends, her boots worn and tattered. The cup she held tilted, its contents spilling to the ground. Ezra and the woman were locked in a stare.

Finally, Ezra cried out, "Mama!" He broke free of Greta's grasp and ran.

Recognition dawned. It was her stance, her general shape. She had lost even more weight, if it was possible. Her face was sallow, with an unhealthy pallor. But there was no mistaking her. It was Ruth! They had found her!

"What is Ezra doing?" Jimmy turned to Greta as she squeezed his hand in jubilation. "My God! Is that really her? Is that Ruth?"

A crowd formed, watching a mother and son reunite. Ruth

spun around and around, holding Ezra to her chest, kissing him all over his head. Tears streamed down onto the boy she clutched in her shaky arms. Exclamations and cheers of jubilation filled the air, as the gathered crowd cheered and clapped.

A hot, salty tear fell from Greta's eye. She turned to Jimmy, noting how the emotion affected him equally. She mouthed: "We found her!"

Wrapping his arms around her, he spoke affectionately against her ear. "I knew we would, somehow I knew we would."

Tony finally declared, "Well, I'll be damned!" He grinned at them, wiping the back of his hand over his wet cheeks, before heading over to Ruth and Ezra, standing to the side of the ebullient reunion.

"See, if one has a bit of hope," their helpful guide said to them, listing their names on his paper. "Found: Eichenbaum, Ruth, Cologne, Germany, mother of Ezra, wife of Daniel, former inmate of Auschwitz." Then he made a second note, "Found: Eichenbaum, Ezra, Cologne, Germany, son of Ruth and Daniel, former inmate of Auschwitz. And you, my dear?" He held up his pen, motioning to the paper and Greta. "I need to make my list, people need to know."

"Müller, Greta, Berlin, daughter of Helga Müller," she recited to him, her eyes never leaving Ruth and Ezra. He jotted down the notes.

"And your father?"

"I have no father."

He lightly patted her shoulder. "You have fulfilled a great deed. Now it is time to find who is looking for you."

"There is no one left for me," she whispered.

"Ah, but there is someone, perhaps someone who is hoping to be found." He winked at Jimmy before disappearing through the sea of tents.

Ruth motioned to Greta. "Come, come, please come here." When she made her way over, Ruth embraced Greta. "I knew you could do it. I feared for you when you left. I heard the dogs, the shots, but I prayed and prayed. I knew God would bring you to safety." She held Ezra to her tightly, kissing his face over and over again.

Then, it happened, as if the dam holding all of the water burst forth and the river flowed free. Ezra began to talk, to say everything he hadn't for a year and a half. He spoke in rapid German. "Mama, Greta has been so kind. She met an American, well, several Americans. She actually saved his life. Then, his friend Tony, well, Tony's my friend too, he gave me chocolate." He pointed at Tony, "That's him, Mama, that's him. He is my best friend, my very best friend. And I ate so much chocolate, I had a huge stomachache, but I didn't care. I love chocolate, Mama, I love it. And then Tony, he showed me a magic trick. Do you want to see it, do you?" He ran to find a ball.

The laughter burst forth from Greta, completely unrestrained. The mirth was infectious, all of them joined, even Ruth, who wasn't exactly sure why it was funny. Finally, Greta explained. "Ruth, he has said exactly three words since we left you. Chocolate, Tony, and Mama." Greta wiped the tears from her eyes.

"My poor son, my poor, poor baby."

Greta placed her hand on Ruth's shoulder. "He has been saving every word for you, Ruth. He knew he would see you again." They embraced like long-lost sisters.

Greta spoke in English. "Ruth, this is Jimmy and Tony. They have been our absolute saviors since the end of the war. They are why Ezra and I are still here."

Ruth smiled at them. She spoke in English, with the faintest hint of an accent. "I am so grateful to you. Thank you."

"You speak English as well?" Tony asked, confused.

"Yes, I was an English teacher before the war, but then I lost my job. Jews were no longer allowed to teach."

"Well, you speak it beautifully."

"Thank you." She turned away shyly away from him, a faint blush staining her cheeks.

Ezra came back with a rock and started speaking immediately in German, "This will work. Now watch. Are you watching Mama? Keep your eye on the ball, I mean, rock." Ruth stood there, watching him, wrapped in the moment. He showed her a few other magic tricks Tony had taught him. Then he started asking questions, "What is your favorite color, Mama? Mine's blue."

"Pink..." he interrupted her to ask the next question.

"What is your favorite food?"

"Any..."

"Mine's chocolate. I taught Tony how to say it in German, Schokolade. Remember Tony?"

"Schokolade," Tony repeated, not entirely sure what the boy was saying in rapid German, but from Ezra's expectant pause, he knew he was supposed to say something.

And on and on Ezra went, until finally, Ruth said, touching his face tenderly, "Ezra, my darling boy. Rest for only a moment." And like magic, he was quiet. He beheld his mother with pure adoration, the very woman who had risked it all and was finally here with him. He never wanted to leave her side again.

"Ruth, you must stay with me," Greta said. "I have a small house, it is where we have been living for the past year and a half. It is safe and comfortable."

Ruth nodded. She was weak and tired. The reunion had sapped what little strength she had. "I need to discuss this with the Americans first." She pointed toward the front gate. Together, they wandered through the maze of tents until they reached their destination. They joined a line at the registration desk Ruth tugged Ezra's hand lovingly, and he gazed adoringly up at her. Finally, they were called forward. "I have found my family. May I leave with them?"

The sergeant they had spoken with before checked for her name on his list. He said she must first be examined by a doctor. "If the doctor releases you, then you are free to go. Just let us know."

The examination was quick but thorough. They returned to the sergeant, who made a note of her information, again in case someone else was seeking information about her and Ezra.

"Now we will go to my home and there you will find comfort and a hot bath." Greta chewed her bottom lip, resisting the urge to unload every last detail of the past year and a half. Ruth needed time to adjust.

"Bath," Ruth uttered, "I can think of no better word right now." Then she stopped, realizing that the struggle for survival was truly over. "I don't know what to do now that I no longer have to keep fighting and surviving. What do I do with myself?"

Greta understood completely. "I have been feeling the same way. How do we go back to being us?"

"Who are we?" Ruth uttered the exact question that had been running through Greta's head as well.

Ruth and Greta walked hand-in-hand, two sisters, a bond deeper than blood. What they endured, what they experienced, would forever tie them together.

"Tony," Ezra called to him. Tony caught him in a hug. "Did you see who we found? Can you believe it? I knew it, I just knew it. She would know where to find me. Isn't she pretty? She is the best mother." His English was startlingly good.

"He speaks English?" Ruth stumbled over her feet, shocked.

"At the suggestion of a most wonderful woman, Liesel, I have been teaching him for the past year and a half. We had so much time together, we had to do something." They all stared at him, blinking. "I didn't realize he actually learned it!"

Tony roared with laughter, aware he knew something no one else did. "They didn't know, did they?" He tousled his hair. "You finally let them in on your li'l secret, huh? Ez."

"Yes, I did Tony. Don't they look funny?" He made a face in imitation. "Like fishes who fell from the sky."

"How did you... but how?" Jimmy stuttered.

"I didn't know until this mornin', when he came to wake me up. He ran into the room and whispered in my ear. 'Do you want to know a secret?' I was so shocked, I think I nearly screamed. Then he says, 'I can speak, English.' And with that, he was off, zoomin' around the room. Kids, man." He shook his head.

They walked toward the jeep, everyone taking their time. Tony offered his elbow to Ruth, helping her to walk the short distance to the vehicle. No one seemed to have a care in the world right now. "Do they know I am Jewish?" she whispered to Greta in German.

"Yes, and they will adore you. You belong to us." Ruth visibly relaxed.

They climbed into the jeep. Ruth, Greta, and Ezra all sat in the back, the men were up in front. The ride back home was joyful and quick. Ezra talked almost the whole way, nonstop, and in nearly perfect English. Greta could not believe he kept this secret from everyone for so long. She couldn't help but wonder about Tony and the reasons Ezra chose to embrace him like a father. What made Tony so special in Ezra's eyes?

They arrived at the house. Ezra grabbed his mother's hand and started showing her around the yard, pointing out his favorite places. Ruth spun around in awe, muttering "home" over and over to herself.

Jimmy held onto Greta, keeping her near him. They stayed back, waiting for Ruth to continue her exploration. Ezra peered over his shoulder at them, stopping everyone else from entering the house.

"Hey, Jimmy? Are you going to kiss Greta again?"

Greta nearly swooned. She stumbled a bit on her feet, but Ruth pushed her back upright. She felt the burn across her cheeks, down her chest. Everyone stared at Greta. *Oh please Lord, open a hole for me right now to jump into.*

Jimmy's eyes twinkled with a devilish gleam. "Would you like for me to kiss her?"

Ezra contemplated this, his brow furrowed in concentration. "Hmm, no, well, maybe. But no, I think you should marry her. Yes, that's what you should do. Marry her and then we can all go to America. Would you like that Mama, would you like to move to America?"

"Yes, anywhere but here." She spat on the ground.

Tony kicked dirt over where she spat. "Technically, this is America now. We liberated this place, Germany has to earn it back."

"Oh, then I must beg for your apology." Ruth was mortified that he caught her making such a rude gesture. But her anger had been building every day, it had grown animated and fierce. She felt impotent rage.

"No apologies necessary." His hazel eyes sparkled mischievously at Ruth. She couldn't help but hold her breath. He spat on the ground too and whispered into Ruth's ear, so she was the only one who heard. "Fuck Germany."

It felt so liberating, she had to say it too. "Fuck Germany," she mouthed to him.

"Attagirl, Ruthie. Attagirl." Tony patted her shoulder.

Jimmy rubbed his thumb along Greta's jaw. "He thinks we should get married. What do you think?"

Marriage? She couldn't even imagine the word. To get married sounded like a far-off dream, and to Jimmy. Could it be possible? Her eyes widened, thrilling at the idea. It was enough of an answer for him, for now.

"See, Mama, he is going to kiss her," Ezra's voice broke through the moment.

Jimmy chuckled. "Well, not now anyway."

Ezra was clearly disappointed and said to Tony, "I was hoping they would. It always makes Greta happy after they do. She starts singing and stuff."

Tony choked on his laugh and said, "Well, I won't kiss Greta, but how about your mom?"

Ezra's eyes opened wide. "You think she would start singing?"

"I dunno, let's see." He took hold of Ruth, who was completely oblivious of the conversation. Sweeping her into his arms, he leaned her back slightly and kissed her fully on the mouth. At first she was surprised, but then stopped resisting. She melted into his arms and began to kiss him back. "Welcome home," he said to her, ending the moment. She stumbled, trying to regain her equilibrium, completely bemused.

"Huh, no singing," Ezra said. "And she looks all funny."

They all laughed loudly, except Ruth. She touched her fingers to her lips and mouthed "wow" to Greta.

CHAPTER TWENTY

After celebrating Ruth's return well into the dark hours of the night, Greta and Jimmy retired to her bedroom. The pale-yellow walls gave the room a soft glow, an invitation to peaceful serenity. The homemade quilt spread across the small bed provided loving warmth. It was paradise.

"Jimmy." Greta cupped her hand around the face she adored so much. "Can you teach me to defend myself?"

"Why?" he questioned, his brow drawn together in consternation. "I can take care of you."

She loved his confidence and knew he would protect her. But it was only a matter of time before she was alone, yet again. "I know, but perhaps one day you might not be with me."

His jaw flexed and his body stiffened as he looked over her bruised face - a painful reminder that he would not always be by her side and the dangers he could not protect her from. He cleared his throat and nodded. Placing her delicate hand in his, he began his lesson.

"Take your fist like this," he said, untucking the thumb. "Lower it to your side, and swing from the hip. Make your arm a dead weight." He showed her how to swing it across her body. "Make a connection with the attacker, somewhere on his face would cause him to let go of you." He had her practice.

"What if he holds onto my arms, standing behind me?"

"There are a couple of options for you." Moving behind her, he held her arms at her side. "One, you take your foot here," he nudged her instep with his foot, "and then rub it down his shin." She imitated the maneuver without using her full strength, but Jimmy still flinched.

"I am so sorry," she cried.

"No, no, Beautiful, don't cry. That's how effective it is, it doesn't need to be hard." He continued the lesson. "This next one uses your head. Lean it all the way forward and use your head to smash it into someone's face. If you break his nose, he can't keep a hold on you." Hesitantly, she rehearsed the move. "It also works well facing someone, you have to lean backwards and smash it with your front. But this will hurt you too. It may even stun you."

Straightening her stance, she reviewed what she learned. He smiled at her, his eyes sparkling with pride as he cupped her chin in his hand. "One more thing," he added. "If you try to kick him, kick him in his bladder. It will cause him to urinate on himself and makes him easier to identify."

"Um, how will I know it is his bladder?" she asked shyly.

"Here." Laying her hand in his, he placed it above the junction at his thighs. "Now this," he said, sliding his hand down onto the hardening ridge of his pants, "is too low."

"Jimmy!" she chided, shaking her head, and laughing.

"Only a little anatomy lesson." His lips curled into his lovable grin. He kissed the bridge of her nose.

"Thank you." She felt relieved. "I remember when I first

saw you, I was terrified of who you were and helpless to defend myself."

"You were an angel." He drew her into his arms, his breath ghosting her ear. "I would not be here without you."

"And I would not be here without you." She threw her arms around him, sobbing.

"My precious Angel, it is over now." He held her, letting her emotions run free, no longer bottling the hurt and fear inside. "I think it is time for bed."

She yawned, it had been an exceedingly long and tiring day. Yet, she wanted to savor all of the moments she had remaining with the hero standing before her. With a heated gleam in his eyes, he captured her attention by flicking the buttons of his clothing open, revealing inch by glorious inch of his chiseled physique. Greta's mouth watered in anticipation.

His voice deepened as he advanced towards Greta, her feet rooted in place, her eyes devouring this man she adored so completely. "See this, this is where you removed the bullet." He took her hand and traced his scar with it. He slid her hand to his thigh, moving from his knee to just under his boxer shorts. "And here, this is where you sewed my leg together."

She took his hand and placed it on her chest, her heart accelerating under the warmth of his palm. "Here, this is what you stole the day we met."

"I may have your heart Greta, but you possess my very soul."

"Oh, Jimmy." The back of her legs hit the bed frame as his lips trailed from her mouth to her throat. As much as she wanted this moment, she resisted, pushing against his chest to break the contact. "I'm afraid."

His eyes danced back and forth, his forehead creasing. "Of me?"

"Of this." She pointed in the air between them.

"Are you a virgin, Greta? I will be gentle, so gentle with you, sweetheart." The pads of his fingers drew soothing circles over her shoulder.

She bit her lip, too afraid to speak. Could she truly be honest with him? What would he say if he knew the whole truth? The reason she was in Auschwitz? "No," she squeaked. "But I'm not ready, Jimmy."

He cradled her against his chest, his hands working carefully over her back. "I understand, but, Greta, we don't have forever. I would never force myself on you." She started to shake her head. She knew he was not that type of man, but he stopped her from speaking. "Let me make love to you." He captured her earlobe between his teeth, giving it a playful tug.

She squealed, burying her face against his chest. "Jimmy," she protested, "not tonight."

His weary sigh filled the room, followed by the one question she could not answer. "Why?"

She shook her head, biting her trembling lip. Why couldn't she open herself to him? Why was she such a coward?

"There is one thing I cannot abide, and that is someone keeping a secret. I sense how afraid you are, but you must trust me."

She was tempted, but could she trust him? She nodded, as he tucked a strand of hair behind her ear.

"One more day, Greta. Take one more day to find the courage to tell me what it is you are so afraid of. I need you to trust me." He gripped her hand in his, pressing it against his heart. "You have me, body and soul. There is nothing you need to fear. Trust me." He pressed his forehead against hers. "I need you to trust me, please."

Shortly after, he drifted off to sleep, his arms wrapping her in a cocoon. His soft snoring was a siren's song, a false lullaby luring her to peaceful slumber. She fought against sleep, her mind racing. Could she trust him with such a terrible truth? Ruth showed Greta long ago how to bury the pain in order to survive. And she had, Greta survived, but at what cost? Would her past be something Jimmy could ignore? She shuddered and he hugged her tighter into his chest, wrapping her in his protective embrace.

"One more night," she whispered. If she told him the truth, he would leave; if she could not tell him the truth, he would leave. "Either way, he will be gone." She squeezed her eyes shut, praying for an answer that never came.

CHAPTER TWENTY-ONE

Jimmy leaned against the door frame, gazing hungrily at the woman mending his shirt. Between her teeth, she gripped the needle as she snipped the thread from the spool. Then she stuck out her tongue to wet the end, threading it through the eye. After knotting the ends together, she began sewing up the hole in the sleeve. Watching her hands flutter in a hypnotic dance of domesticity caused a tightening in his loins. How could simple housework be so alluring?

He cleared his throat, and she lifted her head. Her sparkling smile: every time, it stole his breath away. "I have something for you." He held up a small brown basket.

"What is it?" She set down the shirt, jumping up in excitement.

"A picnic. Tony's friends with the cook. He arranged for us to have a basket and Liesel gave me a special treat."

"When did you meet Liesel?"

He motioned to her to follow.

"Funny thing, she came by the house the other day when

you were sleeping. Ezra and I thought you needed your rest. Then she handed me a little surprise, gave me a sly wink, and said: 'Save it for a special occasion.' Come on, I've scouted the perfect place for the two of us."

Greta folded the extra blanket at the end of the bed. "I haven't been on a picnic since I was a young girl. This will be heavenly."

From the front door, they headed towards the trees lining the property. In one hand he held the basket, keeping the other wrapped around her waist. The path through the woods opened to a small clearing filled with grass and tiny white flowers.

He spread the blanket across the verdant grass and patted the spot next to him. Reaching into the basket, he set out a few sandwiches wrapped in wax paper, a tin, and two glasses. "I have a few more surprises." With a flourish, he rested a bottle against his forearm. "For you, madam. The best vintage this soldier could find."

She giggled. "Where in the world did you find it?"

He waggled his brow. "A man never reveals his sources." He uncorked the bottle and filled the two glasses. "Cheers!" he exclaimed while clinking his glass against hers.

"Prost!" she returned. "To us." They linked their arms together and sipped the thick, dark wine. "Oh my, this is delicious. It must have cost a fortune!"

His laugh rumbled through his chest. "Not so much, this is what Liesel gave to me. Insisted we partake."

Greta grabbed the bottle and examined it more closely. "Oh, Jimmy. This was the wine she saved for when her husband returned from the war."

The dusty label was difficult to read, but he could faintly make out the year. 1914. He swirled the liquid around, watching the wine form legs. "I'm really without words."

"She is terribly romantic. She probably laced it with a love potion."

"Then we should change the toast. To Liesel and her romantic machinations."

"May they work in our favor." They sipped the velvety liquid, enjoying the hints of vanilla mixed with the smoky tang of oak.

"I've another surprise." He handed her his glass of wine and dug around the basket. He pulled out a silver and black camera. "I thought I would take our picture. It has a timer, so we could be in one together."

"You've thought of everything!"

He sat the camera on a rock a few feet away and had Greta pose for him. "Perfect! Leave the spot to the right of you open." He set the timer and dove onto the blanket. Throwing his arm around her shoulder, he grinned at the lens, while she gazed adoringly up at him. It clicked. "Fantastic! Let's do another one."

"That way we can both have one."

He paused at the implication. They both needed a photograph because all too soon they would be apart again. He shook his head to clear his thoughts. *No, not today.* Today was perfect, no need to fill it with nagging doubts about their uncertain future. He kissed the tip of her nose. "Great idea."

After the second picture, he picked up the camera. "Say cheese, Greta." She tipped her wine glass towards him, her smile glowing. "You are truly the most stunning woman."

"No, it is you who is stunning." She gestured to the camera. "Can you show me how to work it? I would like another picture of you."

He wrapped his arms around her, showing her how to focus the lens. "Over there." She pointed to near the treeline. "A Kaninchen, um, bunny." The camera clicked quietly, capturing the moment before the rabbit hopped away. She turned to Jimmy. "Now, you pose for me."

He sprawled across the blanket, his head resting against his hand. One leg bent at the knee, the other straight. "Is this what you are wanting?"

"My handsome prince, yes." She focused the lens and took his picture.

"Maybe one with more skin?" He unbuttoned the top portion of his shirt.

"Jimmy," she laughed, sitting on her knees next to him. "I can't take a picture of you barely dressed."

A wicked smile tugged at his mouth. "Would you let me take a picture of you like that?" Cheeks flushed, she slowly shook her head from side to side. "I didn't think so." He tugged her down onto the quilt.

Languidly, he kissed her. The pressure light at first, reverent. Her hair fell around her face like a glowing halo. Everything about this woman made his heart pound, his body ache with need. He ran his thumb over her brow, down the bridge of her nose. "I love you, Greta."

Her eyes fluttered open. She took his hand and pressed her lips to each of his knuckles. "And I love you."

It all fell into place, this perfect moment. He loved her. There was no holding back anymore, no hiding behind feelings he didn't want to name or explore. This was it, love. For the first time in his life, he truly felt the dizzying splendor of love. And she was his, she belonged to him and no one else. He lowered his mouth, his lips working over hers, his hands exploring every curve of her body.

Two fat raindrops fell from the sky. "Ever made love in the rain?"

She released a lusty groan and shook her head. A peal of thunder drowned out her response. He gathered everything into the basket. She draped the quilt over both their heads as they set a steady pace home. His limp slowed them down, but nothing could dampen the warmth spreading through his chest, as he hurried home with the love of his life right next to him.

CHAPTER TWENTY-TWO

The deadline had passed. Yet he demanded nothing, no great reveal of the secret she kept. With each passing day her confidence waned, she was certain she would lose everything. The minute she said those words, told the whole story, he would no longer look at her like he did at this very moment. And she would lose him forever.

Jimmy appeared at the door holding up a wooden fishing rod and small basket. "I've decided to take you fishing."

She jumped up from the sofa, where she and Ruth were discussing plans for the future. "I thought you only like to fish alone?"

"Normally. But for you, I'll make an exception."

Ruth nudged her forward. "Go with him or else I will take your place."

They meandered through the meadow to the creek that edged its northern border. The water trickled lazily over smooth rocks. "I asked the guys in my unit, and they said this is the place if you like to catch pike."

He stood at the shore and motioned to Greta to join him.

"This is how you drop the line for the fish. Swing it back over your shoulder. Then cast it back into the water."

The line gently sailed through the air. Jimmy wrapped his hands around her waist, settling his lips against the pulse in her neck. "What exactly are you fishing for?" She angled her head, giving him better access.

"You." He reached for the pole, but as Greta let go, her foot slipped on a rock. Plop! Down she went into the cool water. Jimmy doubled over with laughter. He stretched his hand out to her.

"No." She smiled wickedly. Wrapping her hand around his ankle, she yanked his foot forward. Splash! Into the water he fell.

She giggled triumphantly. Without a word, he scooped her into his arms, holding her just above the water. The grin on his face was worrisome. "No, Jimmy. Don't!" He pretended to drop her, and she squealed.

He pressed his lips against her hair. "I would never drop you." He started towards the shore. At the rocky ledge, he set her down to climb out.

"Come swim with me." She sunk into the water, letting the current carry her downstream where the creek widened. She crooked her finger at him.

He contemplated the shore, then shrugged his shoulders. He floated toward her, before sinking beneath the water. She waited, but he didn't resurface. She stood, frantically searching around until she felt his strong arms wrap around her waist. "Miss me?" he asked after emerging behind her.

"You always tease me." She could feel his grin against her cheek.

"Hmm, but you are always so much fun to tease." His voice hummed low in his chest.

Gingerly, he lifted the hem of her dress up, the cool water

drifting against her legs. His fingers skated along her thighs, then skimmed across the waistband of her panties. "Jimmy! Was machst du denn?"

"What's that?" His fingers dipped lower, brushing against the soft curls. His index finger parted her folds.

"What are you doing?" Her skin tingled. Never before had she felt such a sensation as he cupped her most intimate area.

"Exploring," was his breathy reply. One finger dipped inside, stroking in and out in a slow and intoxicating rhythm. Her body filled with a tantalizing sensation, building deep within her belly. Her legs weakened, his grip at her waist the only thing keeping her head above water. Then his thumb pressed against the nub at the apex of her femininity, and she lost all sense of her surroundings, enveloped by the quickening sensations.

Pressure built from within as he added a second finger, curling them inside and discovering the most heavenly spot. Her hips worked rhythmically against him as his fingers thrust urgently inside. Her head swam, her pulse raced, every nerve lit on fire.

"Don't fight it. Come for me, Beautiful."

She didn't understand his words, but the timbre of his voice spoke of forbidden pleasure. The sensation overtook her, as she pushed against him mimicking his adroitly clever hands. In an instant, she flew apart. His name became a declaration of pleasure.

His fingers stilled inside her but stayed cupping her sex. The water flowed gently around them, the air filled with the sweet scent of spring. "Ach du Lieber!"

He cradled her in his arms. "We may have scared the fish away."

She released an inelegant laugh. "Perhaps, but wow..." How could she explain how she felt?

"Was that a first for you?"

"Oh my, yes." The current swirled around them, their clothes lifting and floating on their bodies. "Delightful," she sighed breathily.

"Glad you enjoyed it." His lips worked along her temple, jaw, and neck. "We should probably head back home." The sun dipped low in the sky, casting long shadows on the ground.

"But do we have to?"

"I'm thinking a bed might be more comfortable for what I have planned next."

His words caused her to stiffen. What would he expect to happen next? Could she freely give herself to him before he knew the whole truth? No, how could she take advantage of him? She muttered in agreement as he helped her from the creek. Gathering their things, they began a slow walk home. The air against their wet skin and clothes was freezing. By the time they made it home, she was a shivering, trembling mess. Was it the state of her clothing or nerves?

Her dress was indecently damp, hugging all of her curves. He stood before her in the pale-yellow bedroom, his nostrils flaring as he released a low groan. "It's time to get you out of these things before you catch your death." Without a word, he loosened the buttons and lifted it over her head. Then wrapping the quilt around her shoulders, he said. "Get warm, sweetheart."

She sat on the bed and watched as he stripped out of his clothing, showing her only his backside. He wiggled his bottom at her. "Like what you see?"

"Oh, yes."

He wrapped a towel around his waist. His chest was bare and covered with a light sprinkling of hair. Below his navel was a trail of dark hair setting her mind ablaze, wondering what could be hidden below.

He moved on to the bed, laying her down. He aligned their bodies, pressing his burgeoning arousal against her. However, she held a hand to his chest as she said, "Not yet."

"Why, Greta, why not now? After what happened at the creek?"

"I have to tell you something." Her voice cracked. Did she want to say these things now? Wouldn't it be better to let the moment continue and then later reveal the truth? But no, she couldn't do that to him. He deserved her honesty before the physical intimacy started. The time had come, and she could no longer delay. It was not fair to him. She could not give herself to him without first revealing the whole horrific story.

"Then what?" His caresses were tender.

"I have to tell you something. I fear you will not feel the same afterwards. I cannot give myself to you, not until you know." He was about to speak, but she stopped him. "All of it."

"What is it, Greta? This is why I told you how I felt the other day. I need you to know you can trust me. I love you and nothing you say will change how I feel." Jimmy raked his hand through his dark brown hair, the locks scattering in disarray.

Greta trembled. "Oh, Jimmy. For so long I have kept this inside me, I am not sure how to form the words. I'm terrified."

Cradling her within the circle of his muscled arms, his thumb drifted along the edge of her jaw. "It is time to trust me, Greta."

"I am still afraid. What I have kept from you will change everything about how you feel about me." She shivered as Jimmy pulled her closer.

"Greta, I assure you, there is nothing that would change how I feel about you now." Resting his chin on her head, he began to rub large circles over her back.

But she was still terrified. She could not bear the thought of him looking at her differently, doubting his affection. How could he still feel the same about her once he knew what had been done, how she had been used? No man would want a woman who was already soiled. Her mother had been blunt with her from an early age. A woman's virginity was sacred and only to be shared with one man, her future husband. It didn't matter if it was given willingly or taken, all men would view her the same. Damaged, forever damaged. She couldn't tell him the truth, not after he was so open with her.

There was more to fear. Would he be as brutal, as demanding as *him*? She gripped the bedsheets, trying to taper down the butterflies fluttering around like mad. No, not Jimmy. He wasn't like *him*. Already, he showed Greta how gentle and tender he really was, he would never hurt her intentionally.

"Oh, Jimmy, I can't." She buried her head into his shoulder, as his hands dropped. Heat crept up her spine, nausea overwhelmed her.

"Greta, not telling me is the same as lying. Do you understand that I can't be with someone who cannot trust me?" His sigh was heavy and long, but there was still the same tenderness filling his eyes. He was begging her to tell him about her past, but the words stuck like molasses in her throat.

"And if I tell you the truth, and you find me distasteful, what then? What would be served by telling you?" She wanted to beg him to stay with her, to not leave, but she couldn't trust herself to tell him. Not yet, not when she couldn't even say the words to herself. How could she explain all of her fears?

"Then I guess you have made your decision and I have to make mine." He turned away from her, his back rigid and taut. He threw on his clothes and without a backward glance, he left her in the bed.

"Jimmy!" she cried, her voice rising. "Please, don't go."

"Greta, I can't do this right now. I need time. Let me think."

He walked into the living room. Greta hastily threw on her dress, desperate to stop him from leaving.

Tony rose from the sofa, with Ruth peering around his shoulder. "What's goin' on here?"

Greta stretched out her hands to Ruth, pleading. The hurt in Jimmy's eyes caused Greta to flinch. He spoke to Tony. "I need air, care to drive me?"

Ruth patted Tony's back. "Take him out for a while, let me talk with Greta."

"Is this goodbye?" Greta bit her lip to keep from crying.

Ruth answered in German, "No, I think you two need a different perspective. Tony will take Jimmy for a short drive, and you and I can have some girl talk."

Tony gave her a sympathetic look. "Time, Greta. Just give him some time to sort things out. We'll be back tomorrow morning."

"Jimmy, I love you," she pleaded, hoping to keep him from leaving.

"I know you do." He hesitated at the door, gripping the wood tightly. She could almost hear his thoughts warring inside his skull. He tapped the door twice and left.

She ran to her room, throwing herself across the bed. She heard the front door slam behind him. A few minutes later the jeep started. Greta collapsed in a fit of sobs. She lost him, the only man she ever wanted to trust and to let love her. And because of *him*, because of that monster, she lost the only man she truly loved.

She felt a pair of bony arms wrap around her. A soft voice asked, "What happened, Greta?"

"Oh, Ruth, it was dreadful. He was ready for us to finally be intimate, and I rejected him."

Ruth studied her face. "Because of Heinrich?"

Tears streamed down Greta's face. Ruth stroked her hair

and cradled Greta in her arms. "I am so afraid. Surely Jimmy will think I'm undeserving of his love and unworthy of his affection."

"Do you really think after all the two of you have been through, he would think any differently about who you are? For something you had no control over?"

Greta closed her eyes. She could still picture her father's face when she begged for help. With utter disgust, he turned away from her. She felt so soiled and used. Surely Jimmy would feel the same way. How could he not? If her own father rejected her, why would Jimmy not do the same?

"Ruth, how could he not see me as anything but damaged?" She felt Ruth's grip tighten. "How could he treat me the same when my own father turned his back on me?"

"You, my dear friend, are wrong." Ruth lightened her grip and continued to stroke her hair. "You will see. You will tell this man who you are so obviously in love with the whole story, and you will find out he has more character in his pinky than any man you ever knew."

"And how do you know this?" The tears had long since stopped. There were none left to fall. Instead, she felt the heavy weight of sleep tugging at her eyelids.

"For one, my son. He spoke of this great affection between you and Jimmy. For another, it is obvious by the way the two of you look at each other. Like the world ceases to exist when you are together. It is honestly rather nauseating for anyone who is around you."

Greta laughed and relaxed slightly onto the pillow. Could Ruth be right? "I can't believe he left. Do you think he will ever come back?"

"Yes, and I suspect it will be early tomorrow. Tony and I talked when we heard you arguing. We think you both need to sort through your thoughts separately."

Greta puzzled over what Ruth said. "Where was Tony?"

"Sitting on the sofa, talking with me."

"Oh."

"Don't say 'Oh' in that tone. I know what you are thinking. I could not sleep, I can never sleep. So, I went to the kitchen to drink some water and Tony started talking with me. He is a nice man and that is all."

Greta tried to smother a knowing smile. "Nice?"

"Hush, this is about you. Now, rest." Ruth tapped her shoulder twice. "I will stay here and keep you company."

Greta lay in bed counting the passing minutes on the ticking cuckoo clock. She ran through the words she would say when she hopefully saw him again. Debated each way to finally tell the story, but every time she recited the story in her mind, it ended the same disastrous way. Of all the horrible experiences she had lived through, this terrified her the most. Losing Jimmy was not an option. But how could she keep him if she did not reveal the one event which changed her life forever?

CHAPTER TWENTY-THREE

Jimmy watched the landscape fly by as Tony navigated the darkened roads. They sat in silence, the whoosh of the wind cooling his skin as he tried to clear his mind of Greta. But all he could do was think of her, her tender smile, and beguiling blue-green eyes. She stirred feelings within, deep feelings he could hardly name, let alone explain. And he screwed it all up. She admitted she was afraid, and instead of trying to soothe her fears, to help her open up, he walked out on her. He regretted leaving the moment he got into the jeep with Tony.

And now what did he have to show for all of it? A raging erection and no end to the amount of self-pity he felt. He demanded full disclosure in all of his relationships, but was that entirely fair? He wasn't being fully honest with Greta either. There was so much more to his story, but he didn't trust her. To be honest, he didn't trust anyone with the whole truth. The only one who knew what had happened on the night so long ago was Hugh. So why couldn't he allow Greta her secrets? Jimmy growled in frustration.

"You alright over there?" Tony peered across the front seat.

"Peachy." Jimmy kicked the floorboard.

"Listen, I think it's time we talked." Tony drove the jeep onto the shoulder, then turned it off. He slouched and propped a lean wrist on the steering wheel. "Ruth is houndin' me to talk with you. And since I have every intention of keepin' on her good side, I am reluctantly talkin' to you."

Jimmy looked up at his friend, arching a brow. "What's going on with you and Ruth?"

"A lot actually. Seems we have hit it off and I am not about to let her get away." Tony smoothed out a few wrinkles in his pant leg. "You know me, can't resist a woman in need."

"Yeah, seems to be your M.O." Jimmy removed a cigarette from a pack, then offered one to Tony. "What does she want you to nag me about?"

"Greta." Tony took a long drag on the cigarette. "Apparently, somethin' truly awful happened to her, and she is terrified you will think less of her."

"So she has decided I will condemn her for it, instead of trusting me?"

Tony eyed his friend skeptically. "Man, I know you are not being honest with her either. I've known you for far too long and we've been through too much shit together. I know there are things in your past you are not being honest about. Know you haven't told her everythin' about you. So why are you sittin' here, actin' like a total jerk, when you could be with her?"

Jimmy was too shocked to be angry, Tony had never taken such a heated tone before. "She's a German. It's not like anything could happen with us."

"Ah, don't give me that baloney! You know the ban on marryin' Germans won't last forever and we ain't talkin' about marriage yet. The truth is, you're different with her. Better. I've seen it. Hell, half the guys in this outfit see how you've changed. No longer strait-laced, can't-crack-a-joke Captain O'Brien. Go back to her." Tony crushed out the cigarette. "This morning."

Jimmy laid his head against the seat. Was Tony right? Had he really changed? Should he trust Greta, allow her to open up to him on her own time? Her terror was a punch in the gut. He wanted to erase the fears, the doubt. How could she possibly think, after everything they had been through, he would ever think less of her?

He resisted putting a name to what he had been feeling. Each day, it grew stronger, like a thread being pulled, drawing them closer. Yet, he was deeply afraid their delicate bond could be so easily broken. One thing was for certain, he was not ready to let her go. It was time they both faced that uncertainty together.

The two men sat in the jeep, each lost to their own thoughts. Only the occasional strike of a match intruded on the silence. Long after the sun crept over the horizon, the sky shifted like a kaleidoscope from navy to magenta to periwinkle. "Hey, Tony?"

Tony crushed out his cigarette. "Yeah?"

"Turn the car around."

CHAPTER TWENTY-FOUR

"Tony's favorite sport is baseball? Did you know, Mama?" Ezra hopped from one foot to the other as Ruth tried to wipe off the crumbs from his face. "It's my favorite sport too. I am going to be a baseball player just like Babe Ruth!" He tried to squirm away from his mother. "Or maybe I can play football, like Tony. He played in high school and was really good, Mama."

"Ezra Eichenbaum, stop moving. You've got crumbs from ear to ear." Ezra broke through his mother's hold, grasping his baseball as he ran out the door.

"Later, Mama, off to play ball!"

She sighed, shaking her head. "I can't believe that is my son."

Greta sat at the table with Ruth, pouring them each a weak cup of substitute coffee, Sanka. "It is remarkable how much he has changed in the past few weeks. Honestly, it gives me such hope for the future for all of us."

Ruth reached her frail arm across the table, clasping Greta's hand. "It does for me too. I see so much of Tony's influence on him. Not to mention the chocolate all over his face."

Greta chuckled. Every time Tony came by the house, he brought a new treat for the boy. "I think half the weight he has gained is thanks to Tony."

"What do you think of him?" Ruth skimmed her finger across a wet ring on the table, trying not to look up at her friend.

"Why, I think you might be a tad smitten."

Ruth answered with a blush.

"I think Tony is a good man, but I think he's married."

"Oh, well, there's more to his story." Ruth leaned forward, whispering conspiratorially, but stopped at the sound of a vehicle braking outside.

The door slammed open to Ezra exclaiming, "Tony's back!" He ran outside, then returned in a blur. "Oh, and so is Jimmy." Turning on his heel, he rushed to greet the men.

Greta stumbled to her feet, the chair overturning behind her. Frantically, she smoothed over her hair and dress. "Relax, Greta. You are as lovely as ever." Ruth stood, wrapping her arms around her friend. "Stay strong, I'm here for you."

Greta swallowed hard. "Would you mind taking Tony and Ezra out for a while? I would like to speak to Jimmy alone."

"Only for you will I endure the endless discussion about sports and Ezra singing Tony's undying praise. Oh, how I suffer for you, dear friend." Ruth mockingly laid a hand across her forehead.

Tony listened to Ezra chattering away about the game he had been playing outside. Ruth walked over to them, leaned in to whisper something in Tony's ear, and shooed them outside. Jimmy remained at the door, squeezing his hat in his hands.

Greta tried to move forward, but her feet felt mired to the floor. She gave Jimmy a wobbly smile, feeling utterly exposed.

"Hi." Her voice cracked and she winced. "I'm glad you are here." There was nothing she could do to squash the torrent of nervous energy. Her body sent conflicting signals, demanding she throw herself into his arms and stay rooted exactly where she stood. Her fingers turned white from gripping the chair so tightly, and she had smoothed over the same spot on her skirt five times.

"Hi, Greta. You are lovely as ever." He approached the table; her inner voice screamed, *hold him!*

"Coffee?" She gestured to her cup in front of her, her trembling hand giving away her nervousness.

"No, thank you." His mouth opened and closed repeatedly, as if searching for the right words to say.

They continued staring at each other in silence. Each waited for the other to speak, to say something to break the tension around them. She longed to throw herself into his arms, wrap herself in the strong expanse of his chest, run her fingers through his sable locks.

Finally, Jimmy was the first to break. "I'm sorry. I should never have left, not while we were talking." He rushed the words so quickly, it sounded like one long word instead of a sentence.

She nodded, trying desperately to hold back the flood of tears his apology caused. "It is so hard to trust people, after everything I've been through. I find it hard to open up, especially to reveal such horrible things."

He reached out to her, grasping her elbow in his hand. "I understand more than you would believe. But you can rely on me. I am here for you, all of me."

She took an unsteady step towards him. Reaching out, she played with the edges of his collar. "I think I'm ready to tell you." Chewing on her bottom lip, she dared to look up into those deliciously chocolate brown eyes.

He rested his hand on hers. "Let's sit on the sofa, so we can talk."

"No, the bedroom."

He swallowed deeply, his eyes darting between Greta and the doorway.

"So we can ensure privacy should Ruth or Ezra come home. I don't want anyone else to hear what I have to say."

He nodded and steered her to the room. They both sat on the bed, their shoulders touching, their backs stiff. "I have nothing but time for you, Greta." He held her hand in his, giving her the strength to tell her story.

She took a steadying breath and began.

July 1943

It was absolutely thrilling! Greta twirled around. Today was the day she and Fritz were to announce their engagement! Greta and her mother worked for days, altering the gown she had worn for her eighteenth birthday party. The dress was a stunning royal blue silk slipping elegantly over her hourglass figure. The gown draped delicately around her shoulders, ending with a slight plunge at the back. Her long butter-blonde curls were pinned away from her face and adorned with small white flowers from their garden.

She giggled with delight, if only Fritz could see her. *When Fritz sees me*, she thought, blushing as she remembered the proposal last Saturday. He was so gallantly dressed in his uniform, and she was sitting on a bench in her father's garden, wearing her favorite scarlet and cream sundress. He bowed, holding her hand in his. "My dearest Greta, may I have the honor of your hand in marriage?" She jumped up, delighted.

"Yes, Fritz, yes!" And then he kissed her, so gently, his lips pressing lightly against hers. Their first kiss! Her lips still tingled a little from the tender sign of affection.

Once the war was over, they would live in a terrific house and fill it with beautiful children. The perfect blend of the two of them, so happy together. After telling her family about the proposal, her mother insisted they host a party the very next weekend. During times like this, there was no sense in waiting for a proper lengthy engagement and wedding. They were to be married in two weeks' time, and then the wedding night. The thought of that made her blush from within. *The wedding night.* She erupted in giggles again.

The room was beautifully lit with candles everywhere. Her house was an old but gorgeous home from the time of Frederick the Great. It had been in her family for generations and was right in the heart of Berlin. The windows were large, and, during the day, the sun bathed the room in a soft glow. But with the war, the windows had to be covered at night to keep the light in. She was twirling and twirling around the dance floor. She felt intoxicated.

During the party, she danced with everyone, her best friend Katja, her fiancée Fritz – even her overly stern father danced once with her. This was a night she would never forget. Twirling, twirling, twirling, she had to catch her breath.

Greta headed to the punch bowl and heard a distinctive "Ahem" behind her. The voice! Her skin crawled; it could only be one person. Fritz's cousin – Heinrich Braunfeld. The night before, she had begged Fritz not to invite him.

"But why does he have to come?" Greta whined.

"He is family, darling Greta, we must invite him," Fritz said firmly but with an understanding smile.

"Oh." She stomped her foot in childish frustration. "He is

really creepy. There is something about him that makes me feel dirty just standing next to him."

"I will be there with you the whole night. You don't even have to dance with him. I promise," he said, sweetly giving her hand a chaste kiss.

But now, Fritz was off playing billiards with his Wehrmacht buddies, and she was left alone at the punch bowl. She could feel Heinrich's leer before she even turned around. The way his eyes raked over her, it was like he knew what she looked like under her dress. She shuddered. "Hello, Heinrich." She glanced over her shoulder seeking help.

"Is that any way to greet your cousin?"

She sighed. She knew she must be the consummate hostess to everyone, even Heinrich. Reluctantly she turned around and gave a quick curtsey.

"Ah, much better," and he returned a bow. "May I have this dance, I believe it will be a waltz?"

"No, thank you," she said curtly. She did not know what it was about him exactly that made her feel so unsettled, but every time she saw him, she wanted to run as far from him as possible. Maybe it was because she realized as a member of the Totenkopfverbande, there was no way he could be a good man, he had probably killed dozens of people without any sign of remorse. Or maybe it was all of his not-so-subtle innuendos. Or maybe it was when she once saw him kick a puppy. He actually kicked a real puppy. She couldn't put her finger on it. She always hated Heinrich and she was not going to ruin this most beautiful of nights by dancing with *him*.

"How very rude of you to refuse my pleasant invitation," he sneered. He towered over her, making her feel weak and helpless.

"I am sorry, Heinrich, but I have a bit of a headache. I think I shall lie down for a bit. Then I will probably feel like dancing again." This lie was all she could think of on the spot. "And when I return, you will be the very first person I will dance with." She smiled with forced sweetness up at him and turned as quickly as she could with a hand covering her forehead. She hoped the gesture would strengthen the subterfuge.

She headed out of the ballroom and quietly down the hall into her father's study. Closing the door behind her, she switched on the small electric lamp on his desk. Now, she could be alone to enjoy this amazing mood.

She hummed a few notes of a waltz and continued to dance, pretending she stood in front of a prince. She executed a perfect curtsey. "Why yes, Prince Ludwig, I would be honored to have this dance." She then swayed left and right, back and forth, her skirt rustling.

Greta suddenly stopped. She heard the click of the door shutting and the sound of boots on hardwood. Turning around she hoped to see Fritz – perhaps they could enjoy a clandestine meeting with a few kisses. To her shock and horror, it was Heinrich. His muted brown hair slicked back, his black uniform neatly arranged, almost too neat. He had a thick scar running down his cheek. Fritz told her a story about the scar which turned her blood cold. When Heinrich was at university, he got a girl in trouble. He refused to marry her, and the girl's brother challenged him to a duel. The outcome was unknown, but it was the supposed origin of the scar. *Dueling, in this age, what a total barbarian.*

"Perhaps you feel better?" he asked, his eyes leaving a scorching trail, finally settling his leer upon her chest. His tongue darted out and he licked his chapped lips. Instinctively, she folded her arms to shield herself.

"Yes," she stammered, "I do. Now I really must rejoin the party."

"Not so fast." He grabbed her arm tightly, squeezing it in

his hand with bruising intensity. "You must not cover yourself." He moved her arms, purposefully rubbing his hand over her breast.

"Stop. You are hurting me, and you will leave a bruise." She tried to break away, but he tightened his hold. Her skin molded like putty in his aching grip.

A sickly smile crept across his face. "I like to leave bruises, it always reminds me of my conquests later, how much we have enjoyed our time together." He thrust his erection against her pelvis. "How much she begs for it, wanting me."

"Stop this at once," she demanded. "I am to be your cousin. I am a proper lady and not some trollop."

His laughter echoed ominously off the wooden paneling. "Is there a difference? Aren't all women whores?"

She narrowed her eyes. "Was your mother a whore then?"

He slapped her with the back of his hand, the crack resounding loudly in her ear. She tripped over an ottoman and landed on the floor. Stunned, she lay there, trying to recapture her senses.

"Don't ever speak to me like that!" He loomed over her, blocking her only escape.

Her muscles straining, she shoved herself up from the floor. "I will speak with you any way I want to." She felt like she was at the absolute mercy of this sadistic puppeteer, but she would not back down.

"Come to me." He crooked his finger at her.

"Never, not even if you are the last man to ever live. Not if the devil himself was behind me. I will never do what you tell me." She knew it was futile. There were far too many steps between her and the door. The study was at the back of the house, no one could hear, no one would hear. *You are such a stupid girl, why would you leave the party?* She defiantly lifted her chin.

In two steps he was on her, his mouth devouring her lips. His body pressing against her, she felt him growing harder, as he plunged his tongue in over and over, molded her body against his. She gagged, hoping to throw up. She tried to gag again, tried sticking her finger down her throat, but he forcefully trapped her arms against her side, long fingers squeezed her flesh. She spat in his face, directly into his eye. "You will most definitely pay for that."

His hands were at her throat, then she heard the ripping of her gown, her beautiful gown. Hot tears flowed from her eyes as she thrashed, kicked, and scratched at him. It was no use, he was too strong. He tore at the remnants of her gown, tore open her undergarments. She heard his pants open. He threw her onto the desk, forcing her legs apart. She felt him invade her. She hit and hit him, grabbing for something to stop him, anything. She knocked everything off the desk, she was reaching and grabbing, slapping, and flailing. His grip on her neck tightened, pops sounded in her ears, and then there was nothing, blackness.

She woke up on the floor of her father's study, her dress torn, hanging in shreds at her shoulders. Her legs were sticky and wet. Her head swam as she listened to the commotion around her. Peering up, she saw the one man she was certain would help her. "Father," she rasped, "help me."

He merely glared at her. *Why doesn't anyone help me?* "Please, someone, help," but no one came. She crumbled back to the floor, weakened, desperate. "Father, please," she begged him.

Finally, someone helped her to her feet, peeling off the torn dress and replacing it with something plain. She begged her father. "Please help me, I am your daughter."

"I have no daughter," he declared, turning out of the room, leaving her there. Someone grabbed her arm and yanked her out of the study, down the hall, out the front, and into a waiting taxicab. She saw her mother run through the door toward her, screaming, but was stopped by her father. He yanked her inside, slamming the door shut.

Inside the taxi was a man wearing an SS uniform and shaking a sympathetic head. "You made a powerful man very angry." Giving her his handkerchief, he indicated to her to wipe the blood from her face. "I wish I could do something for you, but I am afraid I have no power here." He tsked. "A girl as pretty as you would have made a perfect mistress for some fat general. I would take you myself, but we know Hauptbannführer Braunfeld would find out. You poor girl, being a mistress to me would be a lot better than the place you are going." He took his handkerchief from her and stuffed it in his pocket.

They arrived at a distant train station, far removed from the view of Berlin and its residents. "Here we are. I wish you luck, it's your only chance of survival now."

She was yanked out of the car and thrown into a crowd of people. They were being jostled forward, loaded onto trains. But these were not ordinary trains, these were cattle trains. She lost her footing; a soldier screamed at her. *What is happening?* Panic set in. She was shoved into the back corner of the car. There was but a small window above her, covered in barbed wire. There was nowhere to stand, and the smell was abominable, worse than she had ever smelled before. *Did they even clean the cars?*

No one looked at each other, no one said a word to anyone. They rode like this for days, their legs aching, backs tired and sore. There was no place to sit or lie down, no food to eat or water the drink. The sanitary buckets overflowed, so many people. *Going where?*

The train finally stopped. Suddenly the doors flung open, the sunlight blinding everyone. More screaming, out, out, everyone must get out. Women and children to the right, men to the left. From the mass of women and children, they started to rip away the young and healthy. The mothers and children, the old, were sent to the right. Dark clouds of smoke swirled in the sky, the stench of death intense.

It was a massive camp with wired fences, towers, guards, dogs everywhere. She marched along with the other women. They were led into a room where other inmates waited for them. Greta called them inmates because they were all wearing the same prison uniform. Most had the yellow star of David emblazoned on their chest and shoulder. Their heads shaved. Someone tattooed numbers on their left forearms, a swab of dirty alcohol, and then the numbers. Finally, they gave her a uniform. She fingered the red triangle, *but I'm not a Communist?* She was confused and terrified.

They all marched along to different barracks. She was thrown inside one, with a blanket and white enamel cup. Only one woman greeted her. She was taller and slightly older than Greta, with hauntingly beautiful blue eyes. She appeared to be frail, her hands were without calluses. She was not used to hard work, not like the others she had seen. The woman pointed to a bottom bunk filled with straw. "This is where we will sleep," she said. "Hold onto your belongings, everyone steals here."

Greta fingered the red triangle again. "You'll get used to it," the woman said to comfort her.

"I am not a communist," Greta muttered.

The woman regarded her strangely. "If you are not a Communist, then why are you here? Are you married to a Jew? Or married to a Communist?"

"No." She burst out crying.

"Oh, do not let them see you cry. They love to torture those who do," she said sympathetically, pointing out the window towards the guards.

"I was at my engagement party. It was beautiful and then my fiancée's cousin was there and he..." She could not say the words, she could not describe what happened to her.

She gently gripped Greta's shoulder, rubbing small, soothing circles. "I am Ruth," the woman said. "This place is filled with terrible people who do terrible things. I am not sure why you are here, but there is no escape for any of us now."

Greta still did not understand everything she was being told, but she was afraid she would learn soon. "I am Greta."

Ruth looked over her new friend, noticing the bruises covering every inch of exposed skin. "Did he do that?" She circled a finger, waving it over Greta's face.

Greta gave a nod, wiping away a lone tear. "Yes," she choked out. Ruth nodded in understanding.

She tugged on the hand of a toddler hidden behind her, who appeared to be no more than three. "This is Ezra, my son. Welcome to Auschwitz."

CHAPTER TWENTY-FIVE

Jimmy blanched and stood up, pacing the small room. He said nothing for what seemed like an eternity, running his hands through his thick hair and over his face. His actions concerned her, was it what she feared most? *Is he disgusted with me? Will he leave me knowing I am not pure? Knowing how a man violated me?*

Then Jimmy finally spoke, his jaw flexing. "If he isn't dead already, I will kill him. I swear to you." He spat out the words like venom, his fists balled at his sides.

"You can't, it would be murder," she pleaded with him.

"You think anyone would care? Care about a man like that? I told you before, Greta, men do not hurt women. They do not hit them, they do not *rape* them." He enunciated each word, the syllables punctuating the stillness.

The word stabbed at her heart, she never once uttered the word, never truly admitted to herself what he actually did to her. She shook her head. She hoped Heinrich was dead, she hoped someone murdered him, or he was run over by a tank, or stuck on a pike a-la Vlad the Impaler. Somehow, all of those deaths still seemed too good for him. But Jimmy felt differently now. This was what she feared the most. Her head fell, a small sob escaped.

Long moments of silence passed, then finally he spoke. "Greta." She raised her head, feeling the weight of emotions surge through her. He knelt in front of her, his large hands resting on her knees. "Please understand, Greta. I think I respect you now more than ever. You survived the way he tortured you, then so much more – Auschwitz, hiding, Ezra, the German soldier, rescuing a lost American soldier – and look at you. Here you are. You survived; you helped Ezra survive. You helped him find Ruth. You healed me. You healed me in ways I didn't know I needed." She rested her head against his shoulder, feeling his breath against her cheek. "Oh, Greta, Greta," he sighed to her. "I was a broken man when you met me. Defeated by the war, defeated by loneliness. You saved me." He repeated himself, "You saved me and now I must do the same for you."

"You already have," she exclaimed. "For the first time in too long, I feel like there is a possibility of a future. The word 'will' means something more than a dream that could never be." She smiled at him. "Last night, for the first time in as long as I can remember, I had a dream. An actual dream. I stopped dreaming the night I was sent to Auschwitz and now, because of you, I can dream again. I have hope for the future."

They lay on the bed, holding onto each other. They desperately needed to keep each other close, to feel each other's warmth, each other's heartbeat. He rested his forehead against hers. "Are you going to tell me about the dream?"

She kissed him lightly on the lips. "Yes, I was in Reading." She could feel his heartbeat quicken. "Your parents answered the door, and you were there, as was your sister, Erin. They all reached out to me and said, 'Welcome to our family.' I had a family again." She sighed deeply.

She felt a warm tear trickle down her cheek. Jimmy was crying. He said quietly, "I am not sure that is a dream."

"Oh no?"

"I think you saw into the future." He kissed her hard and long, letting his lips express the feelings within his heart. "I too have a secret."

"Will you tell me?" she asked. She had already opened so much to him, it was time he revealed a little to her.

"Not yet, Greta, but soon. I promise."

She understood the need to hold back all too well. For now, there was nothing left to say, their lips hungrily working over their bodies, desperate for more. They gripped tightly, not wanting to let go of each other, let go of the bond they formed. They fell asleep from exhaustion, holding onto one another, never moving from their embrace.

CHAPTER TWENTY-SIX

The next morning, Greta found Tony sitting alone in the kitchen at the table. Cheerfully she greeted him, searching the cabinets for ingredients for breakfast. There was not much to find. As normal, they contained only a few odds and ends.

"Mornin'," he muttered. He looked up and saw her examining the almost bare cabinets. "I went over to the camp this morning. I had to mail something. I brought back a few things." He waved his hand over to a table by the door.

Greta stared in utter shock. She couldn't remember the last time she had seen so much food. "How did you…" was all she could manage.

Tony laughed. "Oh, that?" His smile was pleasing, warming his entire face. "Helps to have friends in the right places. So, I got you bacon, eggs, a little flour, milk, and a few tins of somethin'. The coffee Jimmy had in the jeep. Can't live without a good ol' cup o' Joe." He walked over to the coffee can, handing it to her. "Think you can make some? I am dyin' for a cup."

"Gladly. It is a luxury we have only had since we met you

and Jimmy. Before then it had been years since I had the real stuff."

"I am a pretty amazin' cook, I have to say. I was fixin' to make a heapin' stack of pancakes." He waved a hand over the ingredients.

"Pancakes? I wonder if they are like our pancakes. In Berlin we call them Eierkuchen, but here in Bavaria, Liesel calls them Pfannkuchen."

"Pfannkuchen?"

"Literally translated as pancakes."

"And the other word, um, what was that: *eye cookin*?"

She stifled a giggle. "Eierkuchen."

He tried to say it again, his face tingeing red. "You Germans have a funny way of talkin'. Rollin' y'all's r's and such." Then his lips spread into a glowing smile. "But I bet y'all ain't tried nothin' like these pancakes. So ya go on and make the coffee. Then sit back and watch the magic unfold." He clasped his fingers together and stretched them in front of him. From a bag he had brought with him, he pulled out glass containers with sugar and butter. Then he set down a glass bottle on the table. Greta opened and smelled it, the sweet liquid thick and sticky. "Syrup," he said, getting to work.

Greta brewed the coffee. "And the sugar and butter?" Unheard of luxuries, even sodas were sweetened by fruit now.

"I have my ways," he whispered conspiratorially. "And it helps to be best friends with the cook."

She could only imagine. Tony was more than likely best friends with almost anyone he happened to meet. His delightful and gregarious personality was one of the many reasons why Ruth was growing so fond of him. How could anyone not find his charm infectious? He radiated positive energy.

Tony worked quickly, measuring out ingredients and

heating a pan with oil. Greta watched him flipping pancakes and turning over crisp bacon. The way he worked over a stove reminded her of the artistry of a conductor with his symphony. It was pure artistry.

"So what does the other word mean? The Eierkuchen." His pronunciation improved, but still contained his distinctive American twang.

"Egg cakes. Our word for pancakes actually describes a pastry filled with jam and dusted with sugar. What Liesel would call Krapfen, but we haven't had in years. I'm very excited to try these and this syrup you have." She set two mugs down on the table.

"Well, here you are." Tony set down plates, a large pile of bacon, and a huge stack of pancakes. "I left you the eggs. Ezra can eat them later. He is a growin' boy."

Neither of them ate. They both picked up their beverages and sipped quietly. "Tony, I'm a tad curious. Ezra seems to be completely taken with you, so where does that leave you and Ruth?"

Tony sighed genuinely. "Well, truth is, Greta, Ezra is one of the reasons I am fallin' in love with Ruth."

Greta leaned forward, anxious to hear more of Tony's feelings for her friend. She sensed a spark between them when they met. The kiss they shared hinted there was something more than mere infatuation. She was so happy her two friends found such affection for each other, but wondered how it was possible to form a bond so quickly.

"I know it's crazy, but the moment I first saw her, I knew I loved her. Like Cupid's arrow, pfitt, straight to the heart." He thumped a fist to his chest. "It was her strength, the way she carried herself. I couldn't believe this tiny, frail woman survived such a place. And she did it for Ezra, for no one but Ezra."

Greta encouraged him to continue. "And then, I found out there is nothing frail at all about her. She is all piss and vinegar; she would spit fire if she could." His boisterous laughter filled the small kitchen. "And God, I love her for it. I don't care if she gets angry with me or is sweet and lovin'. Every one of her moods is intoxicating. I can't get enough of her."

"She is an amazing woman. Truly one of a kind." Ruth was someone many would underestimate, but not Greta. She had seen the unbelievable strength her friend possessed the moment she set foot in Auschwitz. Ruth's ability to continue fighting gave Greta her chance for survival. She understood everything Tony tried to explain.

He picked up a plate and piled it high with pancakes. He handed a stack to her and then served himself. "Thank you, these look tasty."

"Best way to eat them is with butter and syrup. We don't have no more butter left, but syrup we do have." He drizzled it on her stack and then on his.

"You seem to want to be needed, Tony. I truly hope you can find someone who can be that person for you."

He munched on a piece of bacon. "I think you are right. Ezra needs a father, and I am here for him. At least until his pa comes home."

"His dad isn't coming home. Didn't Ruth tell you?"

He reached for another piece of bacon, holding it to his mouth. "Really? How does she know?"

"Ruth told me the story when we were at Auschwitz. Shortly before she and Ezra were deported, she received a telegram. It was cruelly blunt: Spouse died Dachau Concentration Camp, signed the commandant. He was sent there before Ezra was born." She set her cup down. "She was having such a hard time coming to terms with what happened. I think sometimes she kept him alive for Ezra's sake."

Tony's eyes glittered with unshed tears. "I admire her more and more. What she's gone through." He shook his head and ate a few bites of pancakes. "A widowed mother of a young boy, and then left to die in a camp."

They ate in silence for a while, there was nothing else to say. "These are so delicious." Greta decided they needed to change the conversation. Ezra ran into the room, his hair sticking up, sleep lines across his face.

"Hiya, Ezra!" Tony greeted him, the boy ran into Tony's outstretched arms. "Want breakfast?" Tony held him for a bit longer than normal, and Ezra just let him. He sensed how Tony needed him.

As Ezra gaped in awe over the heap of food. "All of this for us? I want bacon and those, and what is this?" He held up the bottle of syrup.

"It is pure sugar, you are gonna love it."

"Pour it on, Tony." He took a bite, his eyes rounded. "This is the greatest breakfast ever. I love it. We need to eat it all of the time, with mounds of eggs, and bacon, and these things." He held up the pancake on his fork.

"Pancakes," Greta explained.

"Mama needs to eat with us." He jumped up from his chair, scooted it across the floor, and ran out of the room.

Tony smiled and laughed. "He's the greatest!"

Ezra returned, dragging a grumbling Ruth behind him. She was obviously still sleepy. "Ezra is insisting I eat." She sniffed the air. "Is that... is that real coffee?" Her voice was filled with hope. "With actual caffeine?" Since the Nazis had taken power, decaffeinated coffee had been lauded as the healthier option. Then came the wartime rationing and trade embargo, making the acquisition of any coffee near impossible.

Tony poured her a cup and placed it in her hand. "Real coffee for a lovely lady."

Ruth shyly accepted the hot mug. "Tony, you are too much."

They sat down, everyone with a plate. "Wait," Ezra exclaimed, "Jimmy!" and ran out of the room.

"Jimmy ain't gonna know what hit him." Tony winked at Ruth, causing her cheeks to pinken.

Ezra ran back into the room, dragging a very sleepy Jimmy behind him. "I was summoned," Jimmy mumbled, his voice rough. He then leaned down and pecked Greta on the head. "Good morning, my Angel. Now, what's this I hear about pancakes?" Greta retrieved a chair from the living room and brought it to the table so he could join them. "Who made these?"

"Tony," Ezra said. "They are a-maz-ing!" He drew out every single syllable of the word. "Best thing I have eaten my whole life."

"I think he exaggerates," said Tony, beaming with pride.

Ruth sighed. "Probably not, Tony. Poor boy has never really eaten so well."

Tony looked lovingly at Ruth. "Well, I guess it is time he did."

Their eyes met across the table, a flicker of passion drawing them together for the briefest of moments. She sighed like a lovesick schoolgirl and started eating. "Oh my, he is right. This is a little plate of heaven right here. And the bacon, oh, how I have missed meat." She took minuscule bites, savoring each flavor, and being careful not to eat too much. She had been starved for so long that her stomach had shrunk in size. For now, she could only eat small meals, until her body adjusted to the correct portion of food. Yet, in the short time she was at Greta's, her color improved and her hollow cheeks a bit less prominent.

"Come to America with me. I will make sure you both get

whatever you want to eat. You would never be hungry." Tony's bold suggestion surprised everyone.

"But your fiancée," Jimmy stuttered, regretting the words as Greta shoved her elbow into his side.

"She called it off. Actually, got a letter from her yesterday. She married an old flame." Tony stared at Ruth, waiting for her to respond. Ruth's mind was a jumble of thoughts running through her head.

"I can't be your mistress," she blurted out.

Ezra pushed away from the table. "I am going to play outside. Things are awfully goofy here." Off he ran, the door shutting behind him.

"Never asked you to be," Tony responded huskily.

"Oh." Ruth took her time eating bites and savoring each tasty morsel. The air was thick with awkward tension.

Jimmy took another piece of bacon from the pile and nudged Greta to eat more. She told him no and patted her stomach. "No matter how much I want to, I cannot possibly eat another bite. I swear I ate two plates full of food."

"She did, man, she ate more than I did. I was impressed," Tony teased her.

Jimmy leaned back, satisfied. A pretty woman at his side, a belly full of food, and not a care in the world.

"Ruth?" Greta inquired. "What are you going to do?"

She sighed and held up her cup to Tony. "Can I have more, please?" He refilled the cup and set it down. Then he picked up her hand, rubbing his thumbs over her knuckles. "I hardly knew Daniel before we were married. It was arranged by our parents. The marriage was short, too short. We were married and a few months later I was pregnant. Then the Gestapo arrested him and sent him away to that awful camp and the Nazis killed him. He never met Ezra. I'm not certain I'm ready to jump into anything just yet, but I've applied to immigrate to the United States. I am currently awaiting my approval."

"Do you know where you will settle? America's an awfully big place."

She shook her head. "Hadn't thought yet, where do you suggest?"

"My house." She shoved his arm. "How about Dallas? It's where my family lives. We can take care of you and Ezra."

"I'll think about it."

Greta stood up and began to clear the table. Everyone sat around, not sure what to say or do now. Tony held Ruth's hand, caressing it with his thumb. "Can I kiss you?" he finally asked.

Ruth startled. "Why?"

"I dunno, I just feel like I need to." He shrugged.

"One proper and dignified kiss would be fine." She rose to her feet, about to say something else, when Tony made his move. He cupped her chin and tilted her head over his arm. The kiss grew in intensity. Ruth melted into Tony's arms. As he broke apart from the kiss, he steadied her against the chair, her fingers tracing over her tingling lips. A satisfied smirk crept across his face, and he winked at Jimmy and Greta. Then he spotted Ezra by the door.

Ezra laughed. "Oh boy." Then ran back outside. Tony's laughter filled the room as he followed Ezra out the door. Ruth was still frozen. Jimmy and Greta stared at her, waiting for her to say something.

Greta finally spoke. "Are you all right?"

"What was that?" she asked, fingers still touching her lips.

Jimmy chuckled and headed outside, leaving the women to talk to one another.

"It's what you asked for, Ruth."

"A kiss? Do men really kiss you like that?" Her eyes

widened. "Daniel never kissed me with such, um, enthusiasm, and twice now, wow. Can other things make you feel all tingly?"

"Other things?"

"You know, in there?" Ruth pointed to the bedroom.

"I honestly don't know yet, I am still waiting to find out."

Ruth shook Greta's shoulders. "You have to find out for me, and then tell me everything."

Greta stuttered. "But-t, Ruth, you were married, didn't you and Daniel, um... didn't you do such things already? I mean, you do have Ezra"

"No, nothing close to that." She shook her head. "Our marriage was an arrangement. We were fond of each other, but we didn't know you could do things like *that*. I mean, he would lay on top of me and, you know, move a little, and then it was over. I didn't even fully undress." They worked around the kitchen, cleaning up.

"I think you were missing out," Greta teased.

A sly smile crept across Ruth's face. "I think you are right."

CHAPTER TWENTY-SEVEN

For Greta, there was one question remaining unanswered: what happened to Greta's beloved mother? That moment, from seemingly a lifetime ago, remained burned in the forefront of her memory. The anguished cry of her mother as she pleaded and begged Greta's father to intercede. A slam of a door. The final goodbye.

There was one person who might know something. With the help of Liesel, Greta had sent a few letters covertly to her mother, letting her know she was still alive. They received no response to them, but she hoped somehow those letters, like messages in a bottle, found their way home. It was for this reason alone Greta found herself walking along the lonely path between her home and Liesel's farm. Perhaps Fritz might have answers, after all, he had been in Berlin for the latter half of 1944.

As she clutched and unclutched her dress, hoping to temper the butterflies in her stomach, she found herself smiling over her morning conversation with Jimmy. After she told him of her intention, he volunteered to accompany her.

"No, I think it will upset Fritz." Jimmy looked away from her, the disappointment in his face weakening her resolve. "It isn't that I still love Fritz. All this happened to him in a way as well. You are a reminder of what he has lost."

He reluctantly agreed she should go, but he didn't want to let her go yet. "Please promise me to be careful." He leaned over her, caressing her cheek. "You are too precious for anything to happen to."

"And Jimmy, you are..." She stopped, searching for the right words. Precious felt silly, but it is what he was to her. Something tangible and dear.

"Kind? Fabulous? Irresistible? Perfect?" he joked with her, filling in the phrase.

"You are too much," she sighed, placing her hand against his chest.

"Eh, I was hoping for magnificent." He gave her his wickedly charming smile, causing her heart to flutter. "I mean it, Greta, be careful. You are my everything."

My everything. The words caused heated tendrils to run over her spine and a giddy laugh to escape. Oh, how she loved this man.

Summer was finally here. The earth was awash in a rainbow of color with honeybees flitting from stem to stem. The bees' song drew Greta further into the field, where she gathered the happy blooms in a bouquet. She found herself sighing heavily, dreaming of Jimmy's touch, the feel of his arms around her. *Her Jimmy.* How fortunate it was her door he stumbled upon.

She heard a voice cheerfully call out, rousing her from her sweet musings. "Greta! What are you doing here?"

"Fritz!" She waved to him. He limped along the dirt path, returning after a hard day's work maintaining Liesel's modest farm. "I was wanting to talk with you and Liesel, I had a few questions and brought Liesel these flowers."

His face broke into an easy smile. "As always, it is wonderful to see you. Unfortunately, Liesel stepped out a while ago. But please, come inside." He looped his arm through hers and together they entered the house.

They sat in the comfortably appointed living room facing each other. "I can make us tea." He started to stand.

"Oh, you're so kind, but I don't need any." She smiled sweetly at him. He was always so generous, thinking of the comforts of others.

He lowered himself back down onto the sofa. Using a ray of sun peeking through the window, he studied her, before his jaw noticeably began to twitch. "Why is your face bruised? Did your American hit you?"

"What?" Her hand flew to her cheek. "Oh no, never. Jimmy is not like that." She didn't want to tell the story of the brutal soldier, but had no choice, catching a glimpse of anger she never even imagined the gentle Fritz could possess. "An awful soldier, a German, broke into the house and attacked Ezra and me."

Fritz jumped to his feet and hauled Greta towards the light to inspect her face and arms. "Was Ezra hurt?"

"No, thank goodness. Luckily, Jimmy and his friend, Tony, arrived and stopped him. He was arrested by the Americans."

"I'm so sorry, Greta, I've failed to protect you yet again." Devastation flashed in his cornflower eyes, his arms dropping from the agony of not being able to prevent such violence.

"You have never once failed me, Fritz." *Oh, poor Fritz, he has never deserved any of this.* "If you had been there, you would have done something to stop him. I know you." She searched his face for some sort of recognition. "You are a good man, my darling Fritz. You have always been all that is pure and decent in this world. And you have never failed me." She pleaded with him to understand.

He shook his head but did not make eye contact. "Fritz, please listen to me." His pale blue eyes met hers. "I am fine. Ezra's fine."

Finally, he nodded. But he did not let go of her. "What do you want to ask?"

"I was hoping you might be able to answer a few questions."

"I assume you are wanting answers about our engagement party." He looked away from her and off to the distance. "I tried to find you. I knew Heinrich did something to you. Your father wouldn't talk to me or your mother. She tried, but your father was acting strange. Like he couldn't trust me." He shook his head, trying desperately to hold back the tears, the pain Heinrich caused. "I stopped working. I was on a mission to find you. My actions did not go unnoticed, though I strongly suspected Heinrich was the one who informed on me. I was stripped of my duties, demoted, and sent East to fight."

"Heinrich always let power go to his head. Ever since we were young, he would do anything he could to make us miserable. Remember what he did with my pet rabbit?" Greta shivered over the memory. Her poor French lop never allowed anyone to hold it after the incident with Heinrich.

"Threatening to feed her to his dog and holding her for ransom? Yeah, hard to forget. Most of my memories are of him torturing us, even your friend Katja from time to time. I remember him cruelly taunting the girl just a few years ago, calling her a piglet." Fritz shifted, trying to relax his stiff muscles.

"I don't understand why he seemed obsessed with me."

"You don't? When he found out you and I were engaged, he tried everything to convince me that you were less than honorable." Greta gasped at the revelation. "But, of course, I didn't believe him. He was jealous. I had a beautiful woman, a woman he couldn't have. You turned him down many times, which he was never going to forgive. You were the one woman he couldn't convince of his superiority."

"So, he wanted me to pay?" She had long guessed at Heinrich's motivation but discussing it with Fritz reopened old wounds she wanted to forget.

"Yes, because you chose me over him. It's all my fault."

She gripped his hand tightly. "It was never your fault." It was all so unfair, for him to blame himself for the actions of his cousin. To see her once carefree Fritz so worn down by life caused an aching sorrow far worse than she had imagined.

"Are you managing alright?" she finally asked.

"Better than I probably deserve," he stated. "Greta, I know I can never make any of this up to you, but I want you to know I will do anything for you, anything at all." He grasped her hand in his. She wanted to pull away from such a declaration.

She shook away the thoughts. "I know you would. For now, I am hoping you might have information about my family. What happened to my mother?"

His sigh was heavy and drawn out. "Unfortunately, I do not know. Things were so chaotic when I left Berlin to come here, I haven't even heard from my family since I left. Naturally, I am hoping they are well, but there is no certainty. Especially once the Soviets advanced through the city at the end of the war."

"If you hear something, will you let me know?"

"Absolutely. I will also be here for you, whatever you need."

"Always my knight. Please take care of yourself. Find a little piece of happiness." She gently stroked his cheek, but he flinched at the touch.

"I will, Greta, and I hope you will as well. Goodbye." Tears gathered in the corner of his eyes.

"Goodbye, Fritz." She tenderly kissed him for the last time and walked away. One fat, heavy tear trailed down her face, but she did not wipe it away. She turned around, hoping to see him watching her. Instead, he limped back into the house, with no final wave over his shoulder.

The walk home was longer than she remembered. The emotions of the day washed over her as she processed everything. In the distance, she saw Jimmy and Tony engaged in conversation near her door, where they waited for her. The joy in seeing him there, her Jimmy, filled the aching void left in her heart. She fought the urge to run the rest of the way home and fling herself into his arms. Instead, she kept her head held high and gifted him a brilliant smile.

He met her halfway, his confident swagger filling her with desire, a need for him to hold her, to consume her. She was ready to fully become his. As Jimmy approached, his brown eyes darkened with lust. "I missed you."

She kissed his cheek. "I am so glad you are home."

"Me too." He captured her plump bottom lip with his own. Too quickly, he broke away. "You can try to distract me all you want, Greta. I still want to know. What happened? How did things go with Fritz?" She sensed a tinge of bitterness wrapped around the name.

"He knew nothing of my family. I still do not know if they are alive or dead." Her voice trembled.

"I'm sorry. I know you were hoping to find some answers," he said, decidedly softer, the tension in his jaw easing as he rubbed light circles across her back.

"I'm afraid it will be a long time before I know. Things are chaotic with the division of Berlin. The mail is sporadic at best and there is no way of knowing if they are still in their home. I am afraid I am a bit without hope." The tears flowed. She cried for her home, her memories, for her love of Fritz, for her innocence lost. Finally, she was free to mourn all that once was. Jimmy remained, lending his strength until the sobs faded into hiccups and the last tear for her past fell. Jimmy was her future now.

As the tears subsided, Jimmy nudged Greta towards the house. "Tony and I have a surprise for you and Ruth. The major told us it was too damaged to spend time repairing, but if Tony and I could fix it, we could have it." Removing a handkerchief from his pocket, he tied it loosely around her head as a blindfold. He guided her through the threshold.

At the doorway, she felt him loosen the knot. "Open your eyes," he whispered into her ear.

A chorus of voices yelled, "Surprise!"

Against the wall was a blue Steinway piano, very similar to the one she saw in the American camp. Tony sat before it in a kitchen chair, his hands hovering above the keys. With a flourish and wide grin, he played a melody familiar to them all.

"*Für Elise*! Oh, I love this song." Ruth clapped with glee. "I've missed music so much."

"A Victory Vertical! I can hardly believe it." Greta threw her arms around Jimmy. He picked her up, spinning her around in a circle. "What a wonderful surprise, and it's blue!"

"Don't look too closely at the left side, we had to make some patchwork repairs, but didn't have the right color paint." Jimmy took her hand, leading her into the center of the living room. "Play something catchy, Tony."

Without pause, Tony switched to a lively tune. "Don't sit under the apple tree with anyone else but me," he belted out in his richly accented voice.

"Can you jitterbug?" Jimmy asked Greta. Answering, she kept hold of his hand, twisting her feet in rhythm to the music.

Ruth and Ezra joined as she demonstrated easy steps for her son to follow along. Gales of laughter filled the home, as

Jimmy twirled Greta around the room. He showed Ezra how to slide across the floor and jump back to his feet. Jimmy even attempted to lift Greta over his back, but his shoulder gave out at the last minute. They ended in a heap on the floor with Ezra tsk-tsking over them.

In a voice far too old for his age, he scolded them. "That's not dancing."

Ruth giggled, then called out to Tony. "Play something else we can dance to."

Tony seamlessly changed to another familiar but slower-paced melody. Greta helped Jimmy to his feet. Then he settled his arms around her waist, keeping her close while they swayed to the music as in a dream.

Ruth stood by Tony, singing along to the song. "I'll be seeing you. In all the old familiar places. That this heart of mine embraces. All day through."

After the first stanza, Tony continued playing but stopped singing. "How do you know this song?"

"Before the war, my girlfriends and I would play smuggled records in the basement of one of their houses. This song was my absolute favorite." Ruth sang the next stanza, while Tony watched her with glowing adoration.

The music swelled and the world around Greta and Jimmy faded into the background. She stared into Jimmy's rich, dark brown eyes. Their hands rested against his chest, where she felt the steady *whump-whump* of his heartbeat. It declared *love you, love you* over and over as they drifted along to the melodic harmonies of Ruth and Tony. The clarity in Jimmy's gaze. The surety of Greta's heart. This was the moment. Love - all around, embracing and welcoming them home.

CHAPTER TWENTY-EIGHT

After an evening filled with dancing and singing, Greta and Jimmy retired to her room. It was bathed in moonlight, the lace curtains framing the window, creating delicate shadows on the walls and floor. Greta went to draw the shade at the window, but Jimmy stopped her. "Leave it, I want to see you in the light." He wrapped his arms around her. "Are you really all right?"

"Yes, mein Schatz. I feel better than ever." She stood on her tiptoes and pressed her mouth to his. Jimmy held her possessively. His mouth claimed hers, their lips parting, tasting, and savoring each other. His hands trailed up and down her arms, moving his wicked fingers to the front of her dress, unbuttoning the top button, then the second and third. Their lips never left each other. She placed her hand on his and whispered, "Stop."

He sighed, his shoulders slumped in resignation. She continued, "I am sorry, it's, um, I really have never done this before." Then she confessed breathlessly, "I am so nervous."

"Oh," he uttered, completely surprised. A wash of doubt clouded his face for a moment. "Not even with Fritz?"

"No, I was taught to only give myself to my husband on our wedding night." She pushed the top button in and out of his shirt. "I know nothing about what to do and how to do *it*."

He smiled wickedly, sending ripples of desire coursing through her veins. He leaned in, his breath ghosting across her cheek. "I can teach you." He nibbled the spot below her ear, that deliciously sensitive spot she only recently discovered. "Show you how to please me." His tongue thrummed against the pulse point of her throat. "Bring you to the height of ecstasy." He blew cool air, causing an eruption of gooseflesh. "And show you again." Nibble. "And again." Kiss. "And again." Lick.

She fisted his shirt in her hands, using it to steady her wobbly legs. Her breath whooshed from her lungs, anticipating his dark promises. But he was not finished, without saying a word he flicked open a few more buttons and slipped her dress down her slender shoulders to pool at her feet. His fingers, light and nimble, undid the rest of her clothing. *Breathe, Greta.*

Her nerves alit with desire. She was completely bare, bathed in the light of the moon. Those chocolatey brown eyes she always loved, now shone with the hunger of a predator. She had never felt so utterly aroused. Her nipples grew into taut buds under his scrutiny. He licked his lips, watching her every breath, every shiver.

She wanted to cover herself, hide under layers of clothing. His eyes trailed fire up and down, as he took in the lush curves of her body, lingered over the tiny mole on her hip, and stopped at the perusal of her full breasts and pale blush nipples.

His rumbling, sensuous voice filled her with an aching need to be consumed by him. "Do you remember, as a child, being so hungry, but you couldn't eat yet? You are sitting at the table, while your mother brings in dish after dish. And you stare at all the food, waiting to devour it." As he was talking, he slid his finger around her collarbone and around the nape of her neck. He lifted her hair, blowing against the skin. Then faintly scratched the tip of his fingernails down her side, causing her body to quiver from the ticklish sensation.

"You can taste it simply by looking at it, but you still can't touch it. Then they say prayers, everyone passes the plates, but still you do not eat." His gravelly voice caused heat to burn between her legs. She pressed them together, hoping to subdue the ache building with each drawn-out syllable. He trailed his fingers over her bare stomach, circling her navel.

"Not until everyone has their food. Then, after an eternity, you can finally put the first morsel to your mouth." His hands slipped between her thighs; he combed his fingers through her golden fleece, feeling her moist center. He groaned as he felt the dampness. His pants grew tighter around his arousal. He outlined the soft folds of her femininity, then dipped inside, pressing in and out. She inhaled deeply. "You bring it up to your lips, the first tasty bite. Your mouth is watering before you even open it to eat. And then, finally, you do..." He raised his fingers to his lips, his tongue darted out and licked the wetness. She stopped breathing, watching in shock and fascination as he savored the very taste of her. "And it tastes like heaven."

He prowled around her, his fingers memorizing every inch of her skin. "That is what we are doing tonight. Looking, waiting, wanting. Waiting as our mouths watered, wanting to savor every last morsel, every last taste." Standing behind her, he lifted her hair again, his tongue gliding a path along her exposed flesh, fingers racing down her spine until he gripped her hips, thrusting his body against hers. His heat warmed her cool skin instantly, nearly burning at the merest contact with such sinewy muscles and contours of his body against her own. She could withstand the torture no longer.

Turning around, she pressed against him, drinking in her fill of such a glorious specimen of male form. "It is my turn," she purred, as she tore at the buttons of his uniform shirt. Then she unhooked his belt, finally free to push his pants down his long, firm legs. She raised a finger and commanded, "Boots. Underclothes. Off. Now."

He gave the sexiest of salutes and followed her command, seductively removing the rest of his clothing. His eyes never left hers. "Yes, ma'am."

His body was finally bared to her, and she studied it thoroughly. He was an Adonis of magnificent proportions. His well-defined muscles were sprinkled with a dusting of sable. His flat stomach flexed as she followed the line of hair down from his navel to the perfect V of his torso. The trail led her eyes lower, to his very essence standing at attention. Her heart quickened as she took in the sheer size of him, thick and pulsing with need. She dragged her gaze back to his face. Around his neck, he wore a chain. Gingerly, she picked it up. "What is this?" He flinched as if her touch seared his skin.

"My dog tags. My identification." His voice was husky with unspent desire and want.

"Oh," she breathed, draping the chain around her neck. She ran her fingertips over the raised lettering and kissed it, allowing it to drop and nestle perfectly between her plump, full breasts. He groaned, his fingers twitched, reluctantly holding back the urge to haul her against him.

She stalked around him, running her fingers around his body. Hard and muscular, his sinewy body flexed under each touch. She stopped at his scar on his shoulder and kissed it. He let out a low moan. Then she cupped his firm buttocks, squeezing lightly. She rubbed her finger along the scar on his thigh, watching as his member bobbed its approval.

It fascinated her, how it jutted so forcefully from his body and responded to her touch. Her hand twitched, wanting to feel it against her palm. She fingered the tip, swirling the bead of moisture gathered there. Then slid her hand down further towards the base, feeling the silky skin gliding over the hardness underneath. He placed his hand on top of hers, stopping her.

"No more, my Angel." He swept her into his arms and laid her gently down on the bed. Tenderly, he kissed her lips, then trailed the tip of his tongue along her throat. He lightly pressed his lips to the hollow of her neck, then to her shoulder. Her breathing quickened. He ran his tongue down to the center of her chest, his fingers moving up her arms.

The kisses and touches sent waves of pleasure throughout her body. Ecstasy as he cupped her breasts, rubbing his thumb over her tautly budded nipples. She groaned with pleasure as he asked, "Which one first, left or right?" He blew circles of cool air around the tip of her breast. She arched her back to him, gripping his hair in her hand, begging to feel his mouth around it. A sly smile crept across his face as he flicked his tongue against the bud and then took the whole tip into his mouth, suckling and nipping at it. The act soothed the ache only temporarily, as now she was consumed by the desire for more. "More!" she moaned loudly as he repeated every thrilling second of the delicious torture. Her nerves were on fire, begging for fulfillment, begging for more.

A strange sensation built below as his hands traveled lower, tickling and yet not tickling the skin. She could only incoherently beg for more, shouting his name. "Bitte, bitte! Mehr, mehr!" she cried, English failing her. She begged for more as she gripped his shoulders, desperate for him to do something to prolong the fantastic sensation growing within her. "Mehr," she demanded.

"As you wish." He grinned devilishly. He continued trailing kisses across the flat of her stomach to the junction at her legs. Running his hands along her legs he applied careful pressure, so they would drop to the sides. His hands were rough with callouses but deceptively gentle as he caressed her. With exquisite ease, his fingers slide in between the soft folds of her skin, feeling the heat and moisture build. He issued a low groan, before taking his finger and rubbing the swollen pearl at her center. With the pad of his finger, he stroked little circles over and over again.

Pressure built deep within her, her mind clouded as the feeling continued to intensify, and she thrashed with each touch. Greta lifted up and cried, "Ach, mein Gott!" Pleasure rippled through her, she raked her nails over her legs. He grinned at her reaction, then lowered his mouth to the spot, licking it at first, then gently sucking it in. His fingers slid inside, pulsing in rhythm with his tongue. The pressure deep within soared to an intensity she had never felt before. Her inner walls gripped his fingers as he worked them back and forth, using his thumb to keep pressure on her bundle of nerves. Erotic pleasure exploded within with blinding intensity. "Jimmy!" she roared and then sunk into a pool of resplendent satisfaction, shuddering to completion.

He leaned down over her, resting his forehead against hers. "Look at me." She dreamily complied, both sets of glassy eyes meeting and holding onto each other. "Stay with me, my Angel." He then took his cock and began to rub it around where his fingers and mouth just played. She felt his blunt tip at her entrance, but his eyes stayed with hers. He pushed inside, but only the tip.

"Deeper," she begged, wanting desperately to fill the aching emptiness inside.

"Not yet," his voice constricted. "I will go easy for your first time, Greta. Trust me, love." He skated his palms over her nipples, building the pressure she felt deep within. He pushed his hardened length in further, then slid back out. In a few more inches, then back out, in a little further, and then back out. The rhythm was smooth and controlled. Their breathing grew heavier, sweat glistened on his brow.

Finally, he ceased his torment. He plunged in deeply, embedding himself fully inside of her. She thrust her hips against his, the fullness satisfying the ache within. The thrusts became longer, more forceful, but entirely pleasurable. The plunges propelled the pressure further, building with the pulsating desire to feel the release again. His pace quickened, they rocked together as one. She could feel her inner muscles tightening around him, holding him inside. Then every nerve lit on fire with a flash of white lightning. She ground her hips against him, taking him to impossible depths. His moans thickened as her inner muscles spasmed around him. With a final thrust, she felt him spilling his warm release inside her. He groaned his pleasure and collapsed onto her. Then he wrapped his arms underneath, cradling her to his chest.

She held him to her, their breathing fast, sweat glistening over their skin. He chuckled but didn't stir. She could not stop smiling, it was all unbelievable. All her nerves felt alive and yet, she was completely sated. She could still feel the utter ecstasy of what they'd just done.

"You're trembling," he sighed into her ear as he lifted up and rolled to his back, tucking her into his side. Gently, he kissed the pate of her head, trailing his fingers down her side, tickling her.

"You were incredible," she sighed. He shuddered with each rake of her nails across his back.

He allowed her words to fill him. Then he countered, "I was thinking the same about you."

She blushed. "Is it always like that?"

"And so much more. There are other ways to make love, different positions, and techniques."

Her eyes widened at the thought, the memories of their experience flooding back to her. "Oh, can we try them all?" she asked, teasingly.

"Well, it depends." He clasped her hip, his lips twisting into a devious smile.

"On what, mein Schatz?" She smiled at him, as she wrapped her legs around him. His burgeoning arousal pressed against her belly.

"On how sore you are." His voice grew concerned, as he gently traced his fingertips over her spine. "Did I hurt you?"

A pink blush spread across her cheeks. "No," she whispered so quietly, Jimmy had to move forward to hear her. "Did I please you?"

He smiled into her hair, attempting to temper his enthusiasm. "Yes, Greta. Very much." They lay together in a tangle of limbs for a few moments. "Greta?" he asked hopefully.

"Mmm," she sighed, completely sated.

"About wanting to try them all?" He smiled, the corners of his mouth curling with devilish delight. "How about we try this," he said, swinging her up on top of his hips and with the same swift motion, plunging inside to the hilt.

And so it went for most of the night, lying in each other's arms and making passionate love. Greta felt her heart soaring. Would it always be like this? Would she always feel so completely loved and worshiped by him? What would the future bring?

CHAPTER TWENTY-NINE

Jimmy awoke with the startling realization he was in danger of losing himself completely to this petite woman snuggling so peacefully against him. He was already in love with her, but this was something more. So much more. She mewled in her sleep, stretched, and rolled to her other side, wiggling her bottom against his groin. He sucked in a breath, counted to five, before she ceased her torturous movements and resumed lightly snoring. She had to be exhausted. He woke her up no less than three times during the night to make passionate love to her. And passionate it was, and that was worrisome.

With other women, it had been so different, less fulfilling. The sex was good, enjoyable, a few orgasms and two satisfied people. But with Greta, it was something more, something tangible, important, special. He felt completely twisted up inside, to the point he didn't recognize himself. She unwittingly filled this gaping chasm that revealed itself the moment he first met her, and nothing, absolutely nothing could fill the void except for her.

Staring up at the ceiling, he counted all the ways she had opened herself to him, revealing things that would taint her in the eyes of others. He was the hypocrite, demanding such honesty from her, yet refusing to return the same. Now was the time; there could be no more waiting. He had to risk it all if they were to build a life together. He owed it to Greta, to lay himself bare. He hoped he would come out the other side reborn and free.

"Greta?"

She was exquisite in the morning light. A radiant goddess with mussed hair and pink cheeks. He could scarcely believe his luck, a woman as beautiful as she was with someone like him. He wasn't unattractive, a bit worn with a large scar doing little to attract the attention of women. He was more ordinary than handsome, but she stole his breath away. A painful knot grew in his chest; he longed to hold this perfection for a while longer.

Gingerly, she stroked his firm jaw. Moving closer against him, she rested her head against the taut expanse of his broad chest. The curly mat of hair tickled her nose, as she nuzzled against him. "Yes, Jimmy?"

He took a calming breath, bracing himself for what he knew he had to reveal to her. "My Angel, I need to talk to you about something." He paused, sighing deeply. "But I am afraid, Greta. I am afraid it will change everything there is between us, change how you feel for me."

"Can it really be so bad?"

"I am afraid it is." Pulling away from her, he leaned against the headboard and rubbed his eyes.

"I revealed things about myself to you. You were completely understanding, even outraged on my behalf. Do you think I wouldn't be the same?"

Looking down at her blue-green eyes, which blinked

rapidly trying to stave off the flood of tears, he knew he had to hold her. He needed her there beside him to give him the courage to reveal the truth. "I'm afraid, Greta."

She enveloped him with her arms. "Don't be afraid, mein Schatz. I am here and I won't leave."

With a weary sigh, Jimmy told his story.

May 1938

LIFE HAD ALWAYS BEEN easy for James Patrick O'Brien. He never had to study hard in school, earning the best grades with almost no effort. He always had a girl on his arm. He wasn't always the most attractive man around, but his crooked half-smile and self-assured swagger drew women to him like bees to sugar. He liked people and they gravitated toward him.

After finishing high school, Jimmy enrolled at Pennsylvania State College. While relishing the camaraderie and freedom of college life, he earned his degree and was accepted into law school. The gregarious son of a tobacconist had a golden path at his feet, he only needed to put one foot in front of the other to follow it. One more year of law school, then the bar exam. Then he would return to his hometown and open his own firm, with a wife and family to follow.

It was the perfect American dream fulfilled. In fact, he already picked out his ideal wife, Catherine Walsh. An Irish Catholic girl, his mother would be so proud of his choice for a bride. She was very pretty, with long curling auburn hair. Her skin was flawless, except for a tiny spray of enchanting freckles across her nose. And emerald-green eyes. But what he liked best was her fiery temper. He had many good verbal sparring with her over the past year. Her witty retorts helped keep him in line, something he needed most of all. Someone who wouldn't be blinded by his charm. Someone who could see through his facade to the man inside.

Tonight would be the perfect night to ask for her hand in marriage. It was the end of the school year and there was a big celebration at the country club on the outskirts of town everyone would be attending. Jimmy headed to the jeweler to pick out the perfect ring. A thin gold band with an ostentatious diamond. He wanted anyone who looked at Catherine to know he staked his claim on her, she was his property. He only had to decide how to purpose. Down on one knee perhaps? Too on-the-nose though. Something romantic, with music?

Jimmy arrived at the party with his best friend from childhood, the always witty and clever Hugh Bates. In the parking lot, they sipped whiskey from a silver flask Hugh had brought along. Liquid courage, he called it. They sauntered inside, checking the crowd for Catherine and their other friends.

Hugh scanned the room, hoping to find a dance partner. Unlike Jimmy, he had not settled down yet, preferring to find company in the arms of any willing and mostly pretty girl. "Aha, check out the pegs on the dish over there!" He motioned with his shoulder to a petite brunette, who sipped punch at the edge of the dance floor. "Time for me to go fishing." Hugh rubbed his hands together in anticipation.

"Poor girl doesn't stand a chance." Jimmy chucked Hugh on the shoulder. "See you later, I am off to find Catherine."

"So you're really going through with it? You're really going to ask her tonight?"

"That's the plan. I don't want to risk her getting snatched up by anyone else."

"Weren't you just with Mary Stalworth last night?" The two of them were well versed with each other's exploits.

"Yeah, she was great too. But she knows it is only a fling

and my heart is set on Catherine." Jimmy surveyed the crowd to find her. In the corner, he saw Mary talking with Catherine's brother. Sean looked directly at Jimmy, sipping at his beer, and never breaking his stare. He hadn't said a word back to Mary but nodded along with what she said.

Hugh followed Jimmy's gaze and observed ominously: "That doesn't bode well."

"Ah, Sean is always scowling, and I know Mary's got a thing for him." Jimmy shrugged his shoulders, trying to find Catherine. "Ah, there she is." She emerged from the bathroom with a group of giggling girls. The men parted company and headed in opposite directions.

Jimmy grabbed two beer bottles from a table and reached Catherine in three quick strides. He tapped a shoulder and pinched her bottom.

Catherine spun around, swatting at his hand. "Christopher Columbus! Watch your manners."

"Ladies." Jimmy inclined his head to the group. Several of them twittered as he reached out for Catherine and kissed her on the cheek.

She smiled coyly at him. "Oh, hello, Jimmy."

"Catherine, would you like a drink?" He offered her a beer.

"You know I don't drink beer, Jimmy. I would like punch please." She flicked her hair over her shoulder.

"Well, I will be back then." He downed both beers. He found the punch bowl, poured her a cup, and snatched a beer on the way back. "Here you are, Sweets."

She took the punch from him and began to twist around. "Let's dance."

He downed his beer in a few quick gulps and spun her onto the dance floor. The beers he drank, plus the whiskey he had chugged in the parking lot, helped relax his inhibitions. His dancing was decent, doing the jitterbug steps he had learned from his sister. It was exhausting and after a few songs, Catherine requested they adjourn outside. Jimmy grabbed another beer, and they exited into the cool night air.

They walked away from the building, making their way to the putting green nearby. Her auburn hair caught the light, casting a reddish glow. Jimmy was mesmerized by her and her perfect green eyes. "Jimmy," she sighed, "kiss me."

Without hesitation, he leaned in, his lips loose and wet. She turned away, after he opened his mouth, trying to place his tongue in hers. "What?" he asked.

"You taste like beer." She scrunched up her nose. "I don't like beer."

"But you like when I kiss you?" He beckoned her closer to him.

"But not like that," she chided him. "I like soft, tender kisses on the lips. You are much too drunk, Jimmy O'Brien."

"I categorically deny it." He attempted to sound like a lawyer, but knew the effect was lost after it sounded more like "cathegoriathy".

Behind them, they heard Sean calling for his sister. "Catherine, come here."

Still staring up at Jimmy, she asked, "Why?"

Sean stalked over to them. "He is no good for you, Catherine, come here." He separated her from Jimmy, placing himself between the couple.

"What do you mean, Sean? How is he no good for me?" She poked her brother in the back.

Jimmy attempted to rise to his full height, but he stumbled. "Take a powder. Catherine's with me." He leered at Sean, challenging him to throw the first punch.

"You don't want me to say it in front of everybody, do you?" Sean asked, anger building inside of him.

"I think I do, I think I want you to say it." Jimmy stabbed a finger into his shoulder.

Sean looked down at the place Jimmy had just touched, his ire radiating with palpable energy. "Mary," was all he managed to say at first.

"What about Mary?" Catherine asked. "What happened, Jimmy? What happened with Mary?" The fear in her voice tore at his heart.

"They had sex, Catherine," Sean said to her. "Last night, when he told you he was busy, they were having sex."

"No," she managed to whisper in horror before bursting into sobs of anguish. She ran away from the two of them, straight into the arms of her friends. They had followed Sean to the door, having watched the whole scene unfold.

"Catherine!" Jimmy called after her, but she moved inside. Sean blocked his chance to run after her.

Her brother squared his shoulders and shoved hard against Jimmy, too hard. He started to lose his balance and fall backwards. He managed to catch himself before completely falling down. "Hey, man, what gives?" His words slurred, his vision blurred. "You've been with Mary, too," he muttered as a lame defense.

Sean's jaw clenched. "The difference is I loved Mary. And then I found out about you!" His fist slammed against Jimmy's chest. He was prepared this time and didn't stumble. He shoved his shoulder into Sean.

"So this is about Mary?" he stupidly asked.

Sean landed a firm right cross against Jimmy's nose, blood spurting out instantly. "This is about my sister, you stupid asshole!" he screamed, landing punch after punch into Jimmy's face. "You betrayed her, for what? One night with an easy woman? She was prepared to be your wife!"

Jimmy was able to block a few of the punches, even

managing to return a few. He blackened Sean's eye, bloodied his lip. The two of them locked onto each other, each trying to bring the other down. Finally, they were wrenched apart.

"Break it up!" screamed Hugh.

"You need to leave now," said the man holding Sean. "You can't fight like this here. This is no place for this kind of behavior. Move on."

Hugh urged Jimmy to walk away. "Let's go, man, there's no reason to stay." Jimmy reluctantly followed his friend. He used his sleeve to staunch the blood flowing from his nose. As they passed by the door to the dance hall, he caught Catherine's eye. He stopped and turned to her.

"Catherine." He held his arms open, pleading with her.

"What?" she hissed at him.

"Catherine, I am sorry. I didn't mean for you to find out." It was the wrong thing to say to her. Her beautiful green eyes filled with tears. "I didn't mean that. I didn't want to hurt you. I love you!" With the last words, he reached out to her, but she yanked away from him.

"Well, I hate you!" Her hands were balled in fists of rage. "I hate you and hope you die!" she screamed and ran back into the building.

For a moment, Jimmy stood there, dumbly staring after her. Around her the rest of the partygoers shook their heads and walked away, disgusted. Jimmy's plans crumbled around him. There was nothing left to do but leave.

Hugh led them to the car. Reaching into the back, he fished out a handkerchief and gave it to Jimmy to wipe away the blood. Hugh threw him the keys. "Man, I can't drive. I don't have my glasses; I can't see a thing. And I am entirely too drunk."

Jimmy took the keys and hopped in behind the wheel. "Where next?" he asked, not sure what to do or say.

"I don't know, just drive somewhere far away from here." Hugh waved off to the distance.

The road was dark, with no streetlights to break the darkness of the night sky. Jimmy popped the clutch and pressed the gas pedal down. The car lurched forward, moving faster and faster. The air whipped around their faces through the open windows. Neither of them said a word, there was nothing to say right now.

Jimmy's face ached. He could feel his lip swelling, but the bleeding from his nose had stopped. He counted his teeth, pressing his tongue against them. Nothing was loose. Faster and faster they drove, the blackness surrounding them creating a tunnel with their headlights throwing the only light. And then in a moment, he saw it. A deer suddenly darted in front of them.

There was no time. Slamming on the brakes, he prepared for impact. There was a horrific boom. He felt himself being thrown from the car, felt his body slam into the pavement, skidding across it, his skin burning. He felt flayed alive. Then there was silence, only the light from the headlights to illuminate the scene. The deer lay dead in front of him, the car flipped over, broken. But where was Hugh? He screamed his name, "Hugh! Hugh!"

There was no answer. *No, no, don't be dead. Don't be dead!* He searched, desperate to find him. He scoured the ditch, behind the car, the darkened roadway. "Hugh! Answer me, Hugh!" With all the strength he could muster, he wrenched a car door open, and there he was, crumbled in a most unnatural angle. Bone protruded from skin, blood everywhere. "No!" His agony ripped the air. "Hugh, answer me!" He felt around Hugh's neck, on his wrist. He could not get a pulse, could not find a heartbeat. Tears, blood streamed down his face. "Not like this, Hugh, not like this!" And then finally he saw it, the faintest shudder of breath, shallow but unmistakable. Hugh was alive.

Careful of his friend's precarious position, Jimmy dragged him free. They were in the middle of nowhere and he had to get him help. Jimmy lifted Hugh up, gently, placing him into a fireman's carry. He was still unconscious but released a weak groan. Jimmy could feel his breathing, shallow and shaky against his neck. "I don't know how far we have to go, but I've got you." Jimmy took each step with care. His right leg throbbed with each step. He limped along the road.

In the distance, he saw the headlights of an approaching car. Determined, Jimmy continued to carry Hugh, trying not to jostle his friend more than necessary. "I see a car," he told him. "Help is coming."

The car came to a quick stop. The lights illuminated both Jimmy and Hugh. An older man in pajamas jumped out, running to them. "My farm is nearby. I heard the crash and came to see if I could help." He motioned to the back seat. "Let me take you to the hospital." He helped Jimmy settle Hugh in the back of the car. "Here, lay him on this blanket."

"Thank you." Jimmy patted the man's shoulder.

"The hospital is not too far from here. Get in and I'll take you both."

Jimmy sat down and now noticed the gravity of his injuries. His shirt was ripped open, blood seeping out from where he slid across the pavement. In the rearview mirror, he saw a gash from his eyebrow through his cheek, it was deep and needed stitches. As he stretched out his leg, he groaned. His ankle was almost certainly sprained and carrying Hugh had injured it further. Then, there were the injuries from the fight, his blackened eye, bloody nose, busted lip. "My car," he muttered.

"When we get to the hospital, we can call someone to get

it." The man spoke with concern. "What happened? You didn't hit anyone else? Do we need to go back?"

"No, it was only us. We hit a deer." Jimmy tilted his head back against the headrest, taking deep gulps of air, trying to calm his nerves.

"Deer are deadly, I lost a cousin that way. Rest now, we will be there soon." The man was affable, reminding Jimmy of his own father. "I am Bob, by the way." The car accelerated quickly as he navigated the dark streets with caution.

"Bob, thank you. I'm Jimmy and the man you are saving is Hugh." Jimmy swallowed hard; all he could think about was his best friend since the first grade. They did everything together, including going to university. Pictures of their childhood flashed through his head: baseball games, playing pranks on their younger siblings, chasing girls in high school. The image of Hugh's wide, lazy grin flooded his thoughts. The world without Hugh by his side was too much to bear. He hung his head, he wanted to weep but no tears came, only a deep, earth-shattering sadness drowned him.

Bob nodded. "We've got to help each other. It's the reason God put us all on this Earth. We have to take care of one another, no matter who they are or who you are."

His words struck Jimmy's heart, *take care of one another, help each other.* His whole life he was only concerned with himself, what he needed and wanted. Now, look at him. His relationship with his girlfriend destroyed, his friendship with Sean gone, and Hugh lying broken in the back of this car. At that moment he knew his path needed to fundamentally change, he needed redirection. He knew he had to be better, to become someone good and honorable, challenge himself to become the best man he could.

They arrived at the hospital fifteen minutes later. The orderlies rushed Hugh to an operating room. Bob turned to

Jimmy. "Do you want me to stay? I would be happy to sit here with you, pray with you."

"Thank you, Bob, but I think I just need to be here alone." He stopped for a moment and gazed at the tile. "I thank you from the bottom of my heart, I don't know how we could ever repay you." Jimmy reached out a bloodied hand to Bob. He took it and gave it a careful shake.

"You're welcome, son. Take care of yourself." He turned to leave, but Jimmy stopped him.

"Pray for him, Bob. Pray for Hugh," he pleaded.

"I already am, and for you too, Jimmy." Bob left through the glass door and headed home.

Jimmy took a seat in the hallway and waited. A nurse called him back to an examining room. There, they stitched up his cheek and wrapped the sprain. His wounds would heal, the scars would serve as a reminder of how he could never be so careless again. He asked about Hugh, but nothing was known yet, so he returned to the hall to wait. He stopped a nurse, who directed him to a phone at the end of the hall.

Shaking, he held the receiver and made a collect call to Hugh's parents. They needed to know. A sleepy voice answered the phone, it was Hugh's mother. "Mrs. Bates?"

"Jimmy? Is that you?" He heard the concern in her voice.

"Yes, there's, um…" He searched desperately for the right words. Resting his head against the wall, he swallowed hard and continued. "There's been an accident. Hugh's hurt."

A sharp intake of breath, then a sob crackled through the line. He knew she was trying to maintain her composure. "How bad, Jimmy?"

"I don't know." He honestly didn't. They had wheeled Hugh straight into the operating room and he had no word on his condition.

"We will be on the road in a few minutes. Is there anything

you need, Jimmy? Do you want us to call your parents?" Mrs. Bates's voice wavered. He heard Hugh's father asking what was going on.

"No, don't worry about me." He was afraid of how much time they would have, if Hugh was not going to make it. The drive was at least three hours.

"We will be there soon." Jimmy heard the receiver drop with a click. There was no need for questions now, the Bateses were only thinking of their son and how dire his condition was.

Alone with his thoughts, Jimmy relived the accident over and over again. Through the night, every agonizing second of the day's events plagued him. Finally, an hour later, he was called into Hugh's room. The doctor explained the gravity of his injuries: a broken arm, broken hip, internal bruising. They sewed up lacerations to his chest and legs and set his bones. Then the gravity of the doctor's voice deepened. "He may never walk again. He broke his back."

Jimmy choked back the tears. "How paralyzed is he?"

The doctor shook his head. "I am not entirely sure, there is no way to know for certain right now. He reacted to stimuli in his upper torso, so there is a chance the injuries only affected the lower extremities."

Jimmy's sigh shook his body. "So, there might be hope Hugh can walk again?"

The doctor flipped through Hugh's chart. "Son, I don't want to get your hopes up, we are a long way from knowing for certain what the damage may be. We have to wait until his body has a chance of healing before we can offer definite answers. At this point, everything is a matter of time."

"Thank you, Doctor. His parents should be here in an hour."

The doctor nodded. "Go home and rest, son. That's what

you both need now." He inspected Hugh, adjusting a few bandages, then left the two of them alone.

Jimmy stared at his friend, watching his breathing, even now, rhythmic. Finally, he slumped into a chair on Hugh's right side and began to weep. He reached out for his friend, clasping his hand. "I am sorry. I am so very sorry!" Hugh managed a slight flex of his hand, one small squeeze.

"Jimmy," Mrs. Bates's voice meekly called from the door. Hugh's mother and father stood at the entrance to the room, gazing down at their boy. Mr. Bates had both hands on her shoulders, trying to keep her steady.

"What happened, son?" Mr. Bates's voice was heavy and strained.

"There was a deer, the car flipped." Jimmy could not tell them more, not all of the story. Not about the drinking, the fighting, his irresponsible actions which might have caused his friend, his best friend, to lose his ability to walk, to maybe even father children. The guilt was eating him alive.

Mr. Bates gave a single nod. "And what does the doctor say?"

"Hugh should make it."

Mrs. Bates fell into the chair opposite Jimmy and took Hugh's hand in hers. She wiped a handkerchief around his face, caressing his cheek in her hand. "My darling boy, my darling, darling boy." The sobs overtook her. Mr. Bates moved to comfort her.

"Now, Darla. The boy doesn't need your tears." Even as Mr. Bates spoke, Jimmy noticed the man's own red, watery eyes.

Jimmy continued, "They think…" He studied the ceiling, begging for the strength to continue. "He might be paralyzed."

The anguish in Mrs. Bates's wail tore through Jimmy's heart and soul. No more words were said between them. The room was silent except for Hugh's mother's hiccups.

Morning dawned, and Hugh continued to sleep. After hours of sitting vigil, Jimmy limped away from his friend, hobbling out through the hospital doors. He didn't know where he was going, but he replayed Bob's words over and over again in his head. *We are here to help each other.*

He passed by shops, and curious onlookers stared at him. He knew he must appear frightening, but he did not care. On and on he limped, broken and lost. Searching for an answer, searching for a reason for why he was here, why he had survived. Hoping for a way to make amends to Hugh. On his right, a sign drew him toward it. It was an Army recruiting station, advertising for men to serve. Without knowing why, this place called to him, and he went inside. As the door opened, a man in uniform looked up, his eyes widening at the sight of Jimmy. "My name is James O'Brien and I want to help, I want to serve my country."

CHAPTER THIRTY

"So that's how I ended up here. Unlike many others, I actually volunteered and have been serving since '38, before the war even started here." He rubbed his eyes with his fingers and stretched.

Greta sat up straight. She chewed on her lower lip again, lost in thought. *I knew this would happen, I knew she would change, she wouldn't love me anymore.* A cold sense of dread swept over him as he watched Greta stiffen. This was what he feared the most - rejection. Ever since that night, Jimmy felt less than worthy of love, of relationships, because of the damage he was capable of inflicting. Of hurting those he cared about most. Sean. Catherine. Hugh. The casualties of his carelessness. Now, he risked it all to open his heart again to Greta. What he knew would happen, did, she knew he was nothing more than a shallow, damaged man, incapable of selflessness. The hollow emptiness came back rapidly. The void opened, threatening to swallow him again.

Finally, she asked, "Do you know what happened to Hugh?"

"Before I left for the Army, I saw him again. He was in the hospital still recovering." Jimmy shifted against the headboard. "His legs were still unresponsive, and he was getting ready to start therapy. There was hope he might learn to walk again, but it was a very, very slim chance. Everything else had healed well. Thank goodness."

"Oh good, I was so worried about him," Greta said, still chewing on her bottom lip.

He needed her to hold onto him, to love him. He needed her acceptance, he craved it. But she sat there, in quiet contemplation. "Greta?" he asked, his voice raw.

"Hm?" She was still lost in thought.

"Say what you are thinking. You can tell me how you really feel now, I can handle it." With those words, he knew he could not, in fact, handle it. Her leaving, no longer loving him. It was the one thing he could not manage to survive.

"Oh, Jimmy." She threw herself around him, her thin arms drawing them together. "How horrible, how dreadful!" She started to sob on his shoulder. "And you are all right, you have healed, yes?"

"Physically," he said, "except for this." He took her finger, using it to draw along the scar from his eye through his chin. "To me, it is a reminder to think of others and how my actions have consequences. It keeps me steady, instead of completely foolish."

"On the day we met, I wondered about your scar." She trailed her finger down the length of it. "I am so sorry you went through such a terrible time, how Hugh nearly died."

"I am most sorry for Hugh. For his injuries." He stiffened, all the memories flooding his senses. "Because of me, his life is over."

"No, there's no reason to think like that. You don't know what he may have become, where his path has taken him." She shook her head. "I refuse to believe Hugh would accuse you of causing the accident. Could he blame you for the deer?"

"I don't know. There are many times I wish I could see him again. If only I could write to him and let him know how sorry I am. But when it comes to Hugh, I am still afraid. Even after all of this time, with fighting and the war, facing Hugh is the only thing that actually scares me."

"I think I understand. It is hard to face the consequences of our actions, when we have hurt those, we love the most," she said, her eyes filling with tears.

Such blue-green eyes. "Can you forgive me for what I have done?"

"It is not for me to forgive you, mein Schatz. I am so sorry you lost her, Catherine. She was the love of your life." Greta turned away from him.

"What? No, Greta no." He reached for her, resting his chin on her head. "I am not sure I even understood what love was back then. She would have been a good wife, and she probably is a good wife to some man now. But I was a fool then. I didn't know what love was." He began stroking her arms tenderly. "I didn't understand love until I met you." He lifted her face to him. "I love you, Greta."

"Jimmy." The way she said his name was like a loving caress, like storm clouds parting for the sun after a storm. "As much pain as your actions caused you, it was your destiny to be here. Ezra and I would not be here today without you. You may feel like you took Hugh's life away, but you didn't. And hopefully he has found his purpose, because, Jimmy, your purpose was to be here. Because of you, we are here."

"I feel like I am here because of you, Greta. You saved my life." His grip tightened. "More than that, you gave my life meaning. All this time I have felt lost, like I was searching for something, but I didn't know what it was. I was a broken man, drifting through life. And now, I know why I am here."

"And why is it, Jimmy?" She held onto him.

"You," he said. "You are my reason for being here, my heart. You mean everything to me." He held onto her tightly, wanting her to feel through his touch, all the emotions flowing through him.

"Jimmy, I love you." The tension in his body melted as she repeated her declaration.

For a few brief moments, they stared at each other, admiring their nakedness. His hands kneaded along the curves of her body: her full breasts, the flair of her hips, her soft thighs. He rained hot, wet kisses along her shoulders. She writhed underneath him, trying to mold her body to his.

He drew her to him, pressing his hardness against her. "Greta," he whispered, "I want you, now."

"Jimmy, I love you."

Her declaration sent waves of heat through him. He needed her love, needed the reassurance she felt the same way he did. "And I love you." His voice was husky with need as he lifted her into his arms, cradling her against his chest. He leaned back, watching how the sunlight shimmered in her hair, the faint blush creeping over her body under his scorching perusal. "My God, you are the most beautiful woman."

"I was thinking something similar about you. You are truly a picture for the gods." She sighed, running her fingers down his chest. He sucked in his breath and let out a low, guttural moan as her hand reached down, touching him. Arching her back, she leaned into him, grabbing him by the waist. "I don't want to wait another second. I want you inside of me, now."

"How can I refuse such a request!" He positioned himself on top of her and plunged inward. They both let out moans of pleasure as he continued his rhythmic thrusts. Pleasure, wanton lust filled their very cores as they came together as one. As he reached his climax, he called out her name. He would never be alone again, Greta's love filled the aching void. Jimmy was whole again.

CHAPTER THIRTY-ONE

Their love grew exponentially, becoming this unyielding, all-encompassing bond holding them together. The revelation of his story finally explained the sadness she had seen lurking in the depths of his eyes and with it an understanding of how the events of his past tormented him. His openness broke down the barriers he had erected, and his heart was finally free to accept the love Greta gave so freely. She was his world.

Next to her, Jimmy snored softly. Uninhibited by his slumber, Greta could explore his gloriously naked form. She wound a sable lock around her finger; his hair had grown long enough to curl around his ears. Lightly, so as not to disturb him, her fingers explored the length of his torso, following the well-defined lines of his abdomen. Lifting the sheet, she shyly peeked underneath, watching in awe as his turgid member rose in salute.

"Like what you see?" She dropped the sheet, her face glowing a guilty red. His voice was a throaty whisper in her ear.

"Don't be embarrassed, love. I do the same when you're sleeping."

She released an inelegant snort. "I'm not sure we are supposed to admit that."

"You're beautiful and I'm not ashamed of admiring you like some sort of sculpture on display at a very naughty museum." His pupils dilated; she felt engulfed by his gaze. "Since you've got his attention," he looked pointedly down at the sheet tenting between his legs, "why don't you continue whatever you were planning?"

He lifted Greta by the hips and placed her on top of his thighs. Taking the pad of her index finger, she circled the blunt tip of his member. Sliding her fingers down to the root, she gave him a gentle squeeze and placed him inside her mouth.

"God, Greta! You are going to be the death of me."

She hummed as she suckled him, running her tongue up and around his length. He growled, flipped her onto her back, parted her legs, and slammed fully inside.

"Sorry, love, this won't be gentle." He withdrew himself, leaving only the tip inside, then thrust again fully. He wedged his hips against hers, pressing her further against the mattress as he set a fierce pace.

The hunger in his eyes inflamed her desire. She wrapped her legs around his hips and rocked with an equally bruising rhythm. The bed creaked in unison. His groans of pleasure, her moans of desire propelled their arousal, crescendoing higher and higher until it reached an apex of euphoria. The ecstasy spiraled out of control until they exploded together, coming completely apart. They collapsed into each other, panting for air.

"I can't move." She felt like a pool of melted butter.

"Sorry, love." He tried to roll off of her, but she held him tight.

"I wasn't complaining."

He rested his head on her shoulder and squeezed her tightly. "Good, because I really don't want to leave this spot."

They lay as one, glowing in the aftermath of their joining. The house was quiet, too early for anyone else to be awake. Birds outside the window sang their songs. Twined together, they drifted back to sleep.

Greta was roused from her peaceful slumber by the raised voices of Tony and Ruth. After quickly getting dressed and lingering a moment to admire the sleeping form of her love, she ventured into the kitchen. Tony and Ruth were on opposite sides of the table, arguing with each other. As soon as they saw her, they stopped suddenly, staring sheepishly at the floor. "What is going on?" she asked.

"He is the most impossible man!" Ruth threw her hands up in frustration.

Simply shrugging his shoulders, Tony went back to an old radio he was attempting to fix. "See!" Ruth said, pointing at him. "He doesn't even say anything, just..." She imitated his shrug.

"But why are you arguing?" asked Greta as she poured herself a cup of coffee and sat down at the table.

"We are arguing about how our paths have crossed, whether it is fate or coincidence. I say it is all mere coincidence, he stubbornly declares it is fate." She pointed an accusatory finger in his direction. "He won't listen to reason!"

"I think I need more clarification, if I am to give an opinion," stated Greta as she sipped her coffee in mock contemplation. She held the cup carefully to her mouth, hiding her smile. Clearly, things were developing further between Tony and Ruth. *No one can get that under your skin if you don't have feelings for them.*

"What's going on?" asked Jimmy as he entered the room

yawning and scratching his side. "I woke up with the horrible feeling I was back in the middle of a battlefield." He wore his t-shirt and uniform pants, a week's worth of salt and pepper whiskers covered his face. He enjoyed being relieved of duty and not having to shave daily. Having only just woken up, his hair was still disheveled. Leaning over to Greta, he kissed the top of her head and greeted her. "Morning, Beautiful." Then he poured himself coffee. Moving a chair next to Greta, he sat down, resting an ankle on his knee.

"You explain," demanded Ruth, throwing herself into a chair and glowering at Tony.

Tony set down the screwdriver he was using on the radio and filled in the details. "I was explainin' to Ruthie here, that everything in her life is fate. She is helpless to fight her feelin's. Her destiny brought her to this particular point in time."

"It is not fate, it is coincidence," she demanded. "And stop calling me Ruthie!"

"OK, Ruthie." Only a corner of his mouth turned up into a smile. He clearly enjoyed riling her. "Then explain your feelin's for me?"

"My feelings!" she exclaimed, glaring at him. "I feel you annoy me."

"Good," he continued. "You enthrall me." He stopped working and stared straight at her, challenging her to argue. She gasped, unable to respond.

"Explain what you mean, Tony." Jimmy gestured to him to continue. "Explain why you are calling it fate and not coincidence."

"To begin with, fate brought Greta to Auschwitz. She coulda been sent to some place in Germany, but no, the devil sent her as far away from him as he could." Tony knew most of Greta's story, as Ruth had filled him in after gaining Greta's permission to share the details.

"Coincidence," hissed Ruth.

"Then, you were brought to this refugee camp," Tony pointed in its general direction, "the very one Greta comes to with Ezra, looking for you. Fate," he said.

Ruth started to argue, but he continued, "And then, Greta happens to walk past all the other people, tent after tent, and who does Ezra see..." Again he pointed, this time to Ruth. "You!" he exclaimed.

"No." She shook her head again.

"Where does Greta end up? She could have gone anywhere after escapin', but she ends up here at this apparent nexus of the universe. Here, where you are." Standing up, his voice grew louder. "And who is it who meets your son, gets him to talk again, to open up?" He was almost yelling, pointing at his chest, "Me!"

He then went over to Ruth, helping her up onto her feet. His voice changed its inflection, growing tender and loving. "Then who is it you fall madly in love with, who happens to have won your son's heart as well? Who you open your heart to night after night. Who happens to be here, too."

"Coincidence." Her voice was less sure.

"Fate." His voice was hardly above a whisper.

"Coincidence," she insisted one last time.

"Fate," and he pressed his lips against hers. She encircled him with her arms, drawing him closer. The two of them fervently embraced each other. Finally, he broke the kiss, as she slumped into him.

"You win, it's fate," she sighed. Tony rubbed his chin across the top of her head, then transferred her into Greta's waiting arms to help support her and started to leave.

He leaned down to Jimmy, whispering, "I love doin' that to her. Kissin' the sense right out of her."

Jimmy agreed. "You've fused her brain." Everyone but Ruth laughed. She leaned against Greta, sighing.

"I had better get ready," said Jimmy. "Tony and I have some things we need to take care of." He headed to the bedroom. A few moments later, he had his rucksack in hand. He leaned down to Greta, saying, "I love you."

"I love you too. Don't be too long." Greta hated seeing Jimmy leave. Their time together was drawing to an end far too quickly. Where would she be without Jimmy? What would happen to her? The insecurity of what their future held, the possibility of a permanent separation, was more than she wanted to think about, it filled her with an overwhelming sense of dread.

Tony waved his goodbye. "Ladies, we will see you later."

Ezra, hearing the door shut, ran into the room. "Did I miss them?" He sounded so disappointed.

"Yes, dear," Greta explained. "But they will be back later."

"What's the matter with Mama?" a confused Ezra asked.

"I am not exactly sure," Greta said. "Perhaps you had better play in your room for a while."

"Nah, I am going outside to do man things," and off he went.

Ruth came out of her bemused state asking, "Man things?"

Greta shrugged her shoulders and fixed a light breakfast. Ruth washed the dishes and folded Tony's blankets, then put away his tools. "Do you remember how I asked you about the other things?" Greta muttered a small yes. "Can you tell me a little about them?"

She blushed, but it deepened to a bright crimson as Ruth continued. "The walls here are very thin and, well, I could hear you all the past few nights. I couldn't imagine what could cause you to make such sounds."

"Could Ezra hear?" Greta was absolutely horrified,

knowing that Ruth currently shared a bed with Ezra. If she could hear, then surely he could as well.

"Oh no, he was fast asleep in dreamland. You know me, I can never sleep right." She looked ruefully over the blankets she held. "Not since we were there. I wonder if I will ever sleep properly again?"

After all of this time, neither of them could quite say the name Auschwitz-Birkenau. To them, the name was a reminder of the atrocities they left behind and would rather forget than to relive them. However, at night the memories came flooding back and they both struggled to find restful sleep. They were both ready to heal, and by healing, bury the memories and build a future, a new life. Perhaps others would question both of them falling so fast in love, but both Jimmy and Tony represented the life both women longed for, a life filled with happiness, security, and most importantly promise.

"What do you want to know?" Greta asked, not wanting to reveal everything. Some things should remain a secret between lovers. And how could she describe all of her feelings, the explosion of pleasure and release? Do all lovers experience such sensations, or was it another sign showing how she and Jimmy were truly made for one another?

"What does he do, um, to get you to feel such things? To make those noises?" Ruth walked closer to Greta; she was afraid Ezra might come inside at any moment.

"Well, you know how Tony kisses you now and how you feel afterwards?" Ruth's eyes lifted. "Well, Jimmy kisses me the same way, *everywhere*." She enunciated the last word and lifted her eyebrows.

"What do you mean, *everywhere*? You mean..." She paused; Greta was nodding her head. "*There?*"

"Yes, *there*," she said. "He does things with his mouth and fingers that aren't fit to say!"

Ruth started laughing. Greta could not contain the mirth and joined in. They gripped at their sides, each one doubling over every time one of them whispered "there."

Ezra peeked in the door. "What is wrong with you two?"

This comment caused another fit of laughter. He shook his head and ran back outside. There was something distinctively Tony about the way he shook his head. Tony was becoming more and more a father to Ezra, picking up not only phrases Tony would say, but also his mannerism. Finally, the laughter died down, and they regained their senses. "Oh, how good it is to laugh!" Ruth said, clutching her ribs.

"On a serious note, what is happening between you and Tony?" Greta lowered her voice, making sure Ezra would not overhear.

"I am not sure. There is something about him. It makes me want to find out more and more. I want to be near him, all of the time." Looking out the window, she held back the curtain. Ezra played a game in the garden, happily running in circles. "I feel so guilty at times. I never felt that way about Daniel."

Greta wrapped her arms around her friend, resting their heads together. "If the war hadn't come, you would have been happy with your life with Daniel and things would have been the same. You didn't want this life."

Ruth shook her head slightly. "But I did, Greta. Not all of it, but this I did." Hanging her head down, tears streamed down her face. "He wasn't cruel or unkind, he just was there, and I didn't love him." She tugged at her sleeves, trying to find a way to explain what she felt, to help assuage the guilt eating her alive since she first met Tony. "Once the Gestapo came for Daniel, I was so angry at him. Angry for not getting us out of Germany when I begged. And in the end, I forgave him, but I knew I never loved him. If both of us had survived, there was no way the marriage would have. He's the type who would hold on to the pain, wear it like a badge. Me, I want to forget. I want to move on."

Greta held her friend tighter – the guilt. It had to be all-consuming. "It is all right Ruth. There is nothing to feel guilty about."

"But I have fallen in love so quickly." Taking her hand, Ruth roughly wiped her face, trying to hide her tears. "It makes me a terrible person."

"Again, no. I will not let you feel that way. You and Daniel were apart longer than you were together. In the beginning of a marriage, you need to build it together. How could you when you lived hundreds of miles apart, going through what you both did? He died over two years ago." Spinning her around, she forced Ruth to look at her. "You were a good wife to Daniel. You lived out your promise to him, to God. Now, you have a choice. You can choose to make yourself and Ezra incredibly happy or stay miserable." A sly smile formed on Greta's face. "Besides, it's fate."

Ruth laughed through the tears. "Not you too!"

"Can't argue with fate, can you? It is time you see this all as a gift. You and Ezra have a chance at something new, take it."

For a moment, Ruth was silent. She lifted her head, a strength within her grew. "I walked through hell and came out the other side." Her back was straight, pride radiating from within. Turning towards Greta, Ruth saw defeat wash over Greta's face. "You escaped from hell," Ruth added with ferocity, attempting to console her friend.

"I have always felt guilty for leaving you behind."

"What? Because of you, Ezra lives. Because of you, I survived. The day you left, I altered my very outlook on life and survival. I was weak and losing faith. I felt like I was going to die there." She gripped Greta's shoulders hard, begging for her to understand. "The day you left, I vowed I was going to make it and I was going to hug my son again. Now here we are, my vow is complete. Your vow is complete. When you left, you gave me strength. The strength I needed to stay alive, it gave me purpose and a will to live."

The emotions were raw, overpowering. "And now look at us," Ruth quietly whispered. "Both of us, in love with American men and maybe, just maybe, we have a chance to start fresh there."

"Don't you think other Americans will hate us? Two German women?"

"Yes, but we are not two German women. We are two women without a country." She took her left forearm and pressed it against Greta's. "No amount of hate they throw at us will matter. Nothing they say or do will ever compete with what we have gone through. None of that matters. Who we are matters. And we are survivors."

CHAPTER THIRTY-TWO

The heat of the afternoon faded to a cool evening breeze, the din of insects buzzing their mating calls filled the air. The sun sank lower in the sky beyond the trees casting long shadows across the wooden floor. Ezra had exhausted himself playing in his world of fantasy and now sat on the sofa reading from a book Liesel brought with her. Earlier, she stopped in for a brief visit, happy to finally make Ruth's acquaintance.

Liesel excitedly sipped a freshly brewed cup of coffee with Ruth and Greta. "My stars, I am jealous of you lovely ladies and this delicious coffee. It's been so long since I've had such a luxury, I almost forgot what it tasted like." She hummed with delight. "So, tell me all about your Jimmy."

Greta blushed. "He's really something special."

"Special, hmm. So much meaning behind such a little word." Liesel set down her cup as she asked the next question. "Are you in love?"

"Yes, very much so."

"Be careful he doesn't break your heart or leave you with a baby."

Greta spit out her coffee, choking on the implication, while Ruth exclaimed "Liesel!"

"What?" She waved away their shocked expressions. "Johann came after only seven months of marriage. I'm no fool, but a lady in love can be." Her tone altered from light-hearted teasing to something more weighty. "My darling girl, you have been through so much. I like Jimmy. He's not my darling nephew, Fritz, but he's still a good man. Please know I want to see you happy."

Greta nodded her head. Liesel's concern was justifiable, as she expressed the very thoughts plaguing Greta's mind. What did the future hold? Would there be marriage, could there be marriage?

Ruth asked a question about a topic that worried her. "You know all about your other nephew, Heinrich, what he did to Greta. How do you feel about him?"

Liesel waved her hand dismissively. "Heinrich? Bah! He was my nephew by marriage and nothing like his cousin Fritz. My husband's brother's son. The father was a coward, and his son was a monster. I only hope he has been punished, as I am sure his misdeeds were numerous and exceedingly cruel."

Greta nodded her agreement. Ruth wanted more clarification. "I'm confused about your family tree, Liesel. How is everyone related: Fritz, you, and Heinrich?"

Her eyes glittered, any chance to talk about her beloved husband was met with eager enthusiasm. "My husband, Wilhelm, had two brothers and a slew of sisters. His parents owned a farm with this house and the one I live in. His brothers were Gerhard and Stefan." She paused for a moment on a wistful sigh, then continued to explain. "Gerhard, who is Heinrich's father, found a doctor to lie about a supposed heart condition and escaped service during the war – the Great War mind you. He managed to find a government position and stayed in Berlin." She harrumphed in disgust.

"Wilhelm never did like his older brother. Told me not to trust him, but his younger brother, he was always kind and generous. Stefan was much younger than the other two brothers, only a boy when Wilhelm and I married."

"Stefan really is a delightful man, so much like Fritz." Greta remembered Fritz's convivial father fondly. The three women sat in companionable silence, each lost to their own reminisces.

"Mama, do you think Tony will be here soon?" Ezra leaned his head against Ruth's shoulder.

She patted his head lovingly. "I'm not sure. He's been gone a long time. Hopefully, he'll be here soon."

Ezra nodded solemnly and sat back down on the sofa.

"Such a change in that boy! I despaired we would ever hear him speak and now, such a chatterbox! Such a delightful child!"

Ruth beamed. "He's my heart."

"Now," Liesel leaned across the table, "who is this Tony? Another American? I know Greta is absolutely smitten with Jimmy." She winked and Greta blushed.

Over the next hour, the two women expounded on their favorite subjects: Tony and Jimmy. Never one to be left out of a good story, Liesel prodded them to provide the juiciest bits of gossip. Ruth told her about the plan to immigrate to America. Liesel nodded approvingly. She commiserated with Greta and the fear of her eventual separation from Jimmy. Before it grew dark, Liesel pushed away from the table and said her farewell, making sure to give Ezra a grandmotherly kiss on the head.

Shortly after Liesel's departure, the blare of the Jeep's horn signaled the arrival of the two soldiers. Ezra ran to the door, threw it open, and leapt into Tony's outstretched arms. "You're back!" he cried.

"Ya missed me, li'l man?" Tony tousled his hair. He handed Ruth and Greta two envelopes. "The major wanted us to give these to y'all."

Before Ruth could open hers, Tony dipped her backward. He swooped down and pressed his lips to hers. "Antonio Alberto Ricci Junior, what in the world are you doing?!" Ruth exclaimed furiously, but a betraying smile tugged at the corner of her mouth.

"Oh, my full name! It must've been some kiss." With a roguish grin, he pinched her bottom. "Ya know ya like it."

She answered by smacking him with the tea towel. Then she mouthed behind him to Greta, *God help me, I do!*

Greta chuckled. Jimmy turned down to her, a grin widening across his weary face. "What's so funny?"

"Nothing," she said, unsuccessfully trying to stifle her giggles, not wanting to betray what Ruth said.

Ruth opened her envelope, scanning the letter quickly. She threw her arms around Tony's neck and squealed, "We're approved! Our immigration papers have been accepted."

He lifted her and they twirled around and around in circles. "Ruthie, I'm so happy!" He rained kisses over her face.

Jimmy nudged Greta's hand. "Open yours."

With shaking hands, she gently tore open the flap and unfolded a neatly typed letter. *Dear Greta Mueller, we regret to inform you that your application for immigration to the United States of America has been denied. At this time you do not meet the requirements for refugee status. Further inquiries...*

A sob escaped, she couldn't continue reading. Her head swirled, darkness gathering at the corners of her eyes. Collapsing, she felt Jimmy's strong arms cradling her against his chest.

He pressed his lips against her temple. Lovingly, he

smoothed her hair back from her face and whispered soothing words over and over in her ear until she began to stir. When she opened her eyes again, she met his chocolate gaze. His beautiful eyes, how will she survive him leaving?

"I was denied," she choked out, tears streaming heated rivulets down her cheeks.

His face fell. He gave a solemn nod and picked her up into her arms. One arm lifted her knees, the other banded around her back.

Ruth ran to Greta's side, opening her mouth to speak. Tony placed a hand on her shoulder, keeping her next to him. "Give her time, sweetheart." Ruth began to protest, but Tony tightened his grip around her waist. "Let Jimmy take care of her."

In her bedroom, Greta gave the letter to Jimmy and collapsed onto the bed. After reading, he crumbled it into a ball and threw it across the room. When it landed with a pathetic flop, he picked it up and ripped it into tiny pieces. But the rage still burned. "We can't give in. There are other ways." He paced the room, running his hands over and over his face.

"How, Jimmy? There is a ban on marriages. Unless I was pregnant, there is no way they would let you marry me. If I cannot immigrate, I have to stay here, and you have to leave." Bile churned in her stomach. The room began to spin again.

"Well, I guess it's our last option."

She turned her head and quirked her brow. "What are you going on about?"

"Well, you can't immigrate, and we can't marry unless you're pregnant, soooo," he wiggled his brows. She laughed entirely too hard. "A man must make sacrifices." He gave a mocking sigh and lay down next to her.

"So, that's your plan?"

His broad smile could not hide the actual pain she saw

shadowed in his eyes. "When duty calls, I must answer the charge."

She smiled, the edges wavering as she fought the sadness in her heart. "This is not the way to start a life together."

"Greta, I will do anything I can to keep you with me. Cut your hair, give you a beard, dress you in uniform, and call you Bill – done. Find a loophole in immigration laws – done. Build a box and stow you away on my ship – done. Beggar myself by bribing officials to let us marry – done." He released a sound somewhere between a sigh of despair and a laugh. "Getting you pregnant so my government allows us to marry – done. With far more enthusiasm than all the other options, I might add."

They lay in silence, he stroked her face, she wrapped around his waist, begging for him to never let her go.

"The ban on marriages will not last forever, Greta. I will come back to you."

Greta resisted begging him to do that. "And what of you staying here? Didn't you ask to be a part of the peacekeeping force?" She knew it was their last option for the time being.

"I was rejected." He drew her closer. "With my injuries, I am not suited for service. They are sending me home. My Army career is over." Greta thought she would cry, but the tears did not come. It seemed she had no more left to spill. "I promise you, this is not the end." With this statement, he lifted her face, his eyes pleading.

"But, Jimmy, we can't make such promises. Not now, we can try, but we can't know for certain we can make this situation work." She was utterly defeated.

His eyes sparkled with unshed tears. "We have to, I can't live without you. We have to make this work, somehow." He paused, brushing a stray hair away from her face. "You complete me in a way I never knew was missing. You fill up the void in my heart and make me whole again."

"Jimmy?"

"Yes, my Angel?" His voice was rough with emotion.

"Make love to me?"

He answered without words, pulling her dress off and all but tossing her onto the bed. After removing his clothes in a matter of seconds, she felt the mattress shift under his weight and then his arms wrapping around her waist.

Their lips searched, hungrily devouring each other. They made love with fiery desperation, as they both sought to savor each taste, each sensation, as it may be their last chance to feel this way for another human being, to love as they have loved.

CHAPTER THIRTY-THREE

A few nights later, Greta awoke freezing, the duvet and quilt no longer sufficient enough to keep her warm. She reached across the bed, searching for Jimmy, but there was nothing left but an indention in the pillow. Where could he be?

Throwing on a threadbare robe, Greta crept through the house searching for her wayward lover. Tony was snoring softly on the sofa, his large frame comically sprawled over the cushions with a leg resting on the floor. She retrieved a fallen blanket off the floor to lay across her friend. He mumbled, rolled to his side, his snoring growing quieter.

The front door was open only a crack. She pushed it gingerly. Standing in the center of the yard, gazing up at the night sky was the object of her search. Her footsteps crunched across the gravel, but he did not react to the sounds. As she approached, he reached out a long arm and wrapped her into his embrace. Her head rested against his firm chest, as she let him encase her in his warmth, the steady whump-whump of his heart a soothing beat. His arms rested across her shoulders as they listened to the night music.

With a spiritless sigh, Jimmy's baritone rumbled through his chest as he said the words Greta feared the most, "I received orders today."

She could feel the tears forming. Her mind screamed *No* over and over again. "And what did they say?"

His grip tightened as if he was trying to draw her inside of him. "I leave in three days."

It was all she could do to not wail and collapse onto the ground. But she knew she had to remain strong for Jimmy. To show she was not weak. It was another challenge, another test she would not fail, could not fail. "That soon." She was proud her voice did not waver, it was deceptively light.

"They are moving fast. The Europe first plan was successful and now it is time to end things in the Pacific."

"They won't let you stay longer, send the soldiers who are able to fight first?" It was the only thing she could hope for. It would mean Tony would leave before Jimmy, but things were already settled with Ruth and Ezra. They would leave in a month and had arranged to stay with Tony's family to take Ruth and Ezra in until Tony returned home, hopefully before the year was over.

"No." He shook his head in denial. She was glad for the darkness, glad she could not see his beautiful face more clearly, or else she would be unable to maintain this crumbling wall of strength. "Most of us are heading back. Especially those of us who have been here the longest. Major Clarkson tried to help us, Honey. He is fond of you and understands we want to marry. But there is nothing he can do." He reached into his breast pocket and pulled out a cigarette. Cupping his hands, he lit it and took a long drag. Ever since they realized their time together was nearing an end, he had taken up smoking more and more.

"How many cigarettes have you had tonight, Jimmy?" She could tell how he was feeling by the number he would consume.

"Honestly? Lost count."

"That bad?" He didn't answer, instead gripping lightly at the nape of her neck, his thumb working at the knots of tension.

He offered her a cigarette. She took a few drags. She never liked to smoke, but the intimacy of the moment cried out for it. She knew she could never again smell acrid tobacco without thinking of him. All his scents. Bay rum and cloves.

"And us? What will happen to us?" A sob escaped.

"I don't know. I wish I could see down the road and know everything will work out. But that's not possible." He rested his chin on her head. "What do you think we should do?"

Stow her away in a trunk. Fly her to America. Anything to be together. Reluctantly she answered with the only sane choice she could. "Perhaps we wait a year and then decide. Can you? Can you wait for me, Jimmy?"

"I would wait a lifetime for you. There is no one else but you, Greta."

Her skin cooled. Was it the air or the silence behind his words? His hands stilled, then deliberately he drew away from her, the tip of another cigarette glowing red in the blackness engulfing them. "However..."

"Hm?" He studied the stars again, the glittering sky mocking her.

"I feel like there is more you were about to say." She yanked at the tie of her robe, hoping the knot was capable of keeping her together when everything else around her was crumbling.

His hand rubbed across his face. "I'm exhausted, Greta. Let's go back inside."

She placed her hand in his. He held it tightly, but did not hurt her. They crept through the house, Tony's snoring had grown louder, helping to muffle their footsteps. Inside the room, Jimmy undid Greta's robe. Without another word, he scooped her up into his arms and laid them both on the bed. Then covered them up with a quilt.

They lay together in silence. The tick of the clock signaled the passage of time, but neither could sleep. Nor could they talk. The sky began to lighten. Magenta and golden light peeked through the window.

"Oh God, Greta! How am I going to survive this?"

She tilted her head, watching as his face scrunched, wanting to erase the pain they both felt. "You will. As I will. We have both been through so much already, this is another bump in the road. But we will be together again."

"How can you be so certain?" His breathing was ragged.

"Because I know it. Like I know how the sun will rise every morning. The brightness of spring always chases away the darkest days of winter. We will be together again, because it's our destiny."

He didn't answer. Instead, he let his mouth, his hands explain what he was feeling. In a matter of seconds, they were both stripped bare, his need for her closeness consuming her. She never had felt such a desperate need to have him, to join as one.

She arched into him, as his mouth descended upon her sumptuous breast, her fingers gripping his hair, holding him to her. His stubbled chin scratched across her chest, as he sought her other nipple. Nipping the bud, he slid his tongue around, swirling, savoring each of her moans. Lower, he circled his tongue over the belly, running it around the flat of her stomach, her navel, down to the junction of her thighs. He parted her damp folds, and with a long stroke of his tongue, savored her salty, sweet essence.

"Oh, Greta, you taste better than honey." He dipped his tongue through her parted folds, his finger finding her aching bud. He stroked and licked her to climax. The waves of ecstasy building within and crashing in a thunderous explosion of pleasure. She screamed his name as the tremors overtook her. Holding her as she came down, he muttered sweet nothings into her ear.

She smiled wickedly at him. "Now it is your turn." Shifting on top of him, she straddled his waist between her thighs. She placed kisses along his jaw, down his throat pausing to press her tongue against the pulse in his throat. She raked her nails through the thick mat of curls on his chest, along his taut abdomen, down to his aching hardness. Raising her eyes to his, her lips curved in a sultry smile as she licked the wetness at the tip of his manhood. Jimmy shuddered and groaned, trying to shift positions, to claim her entirely.

"Not yet," she uttered, her voice lowering by an octave, her hand gripping his hardened length and gliding over the silky skin. Becoming bolder, she slid her mouth over the tip and down the length of him.

Jimmy gripped the sheets in his fists. His hips rose off the bed as she drew her head up and down in a perfect rhythm. Reaching out, he grabbed her by the shoulders and flipped her underneath him. "No more," he breathed as he wedged his knee between her legs. "Together now," he declared as he impaled himself fully inside of her, both releasing a long moan of pleasure.

He held steady, as he tucked her hair behind her ear. "Look at me, Greta," he commanded. She turned her face to his, blue-green meeting brown. And then he began to drive himself deeper and deeper, sliding back and forth, their eyes locked together as they moved in perfect rhythm. Each thrust brought them closer and closer to the edge. His pace quickened, as she wrapped her legs around him, helping to reach the perfect spot inside. Their eyes continued to hold each other's gaze as the climax overcame them both. "Greta, I love you," Jimmy shouted as he spilled himself inside of her.

As her tremors subsided, he laid his head down next to hers, his thumbs wiping away the falling tears. Greta hadn't realized she even started crying. The utter heartbreak in his eyes overwhelmed her. She collapsed into the mattress, holding his chest in a fit of sobs. He wrapped her protectively in his arms as he muttered softly and stroked her hair.

"Jimmy, I love you so much."

The rest of the day continued, wavering from rapturous abandon to utter despair. Jimmy poured his very soul into each caress, each look, each moment of blissful surrender. They never left the room. Instead, they stayed together, cherishing these last few days together, as there was no certainty for when they would next be together. He committed every piece of her to memory: every sigh, sound, every inch of her beautiful face.

He wrapped himself around her, wanting to pull her inside of him, to keep her physically a part of him, as much as she already owned his very essence. How could he leave her? How could he leave his soul behind?

CHAPTER THIRTY-FOUR

"Well, this is it, Greta." Jimmy stood before her, in his perfectly pressed uniform, his face cleanly shaved, his hair cropped short. Gone was the carefree man of the past several weeks. He was replaced by the statue standing rigid before the love of his life. And this was it, their final goodbye. He was trying to build a wall to protect what would remain of his heart once he stepped onto the vehicle, leaving her behind. There were so many words he still wanted to say, but what was the point? Why make this harder, but he knew there was no way to make it easier.

"Jimmy, I want to thank you for everything." Greta reached out to entwine her fingers with his. "You saved my life, you gave me the strength to survive. I don't know where Ezra and I would have been without you."

"You saved my life, in more ways than you could know." He fought the desire to fall to his knee and demand she marry him, then and there. Who cared about the law, about what his government said? What right did they have to declare this woman in front of him an enemy? She had been abandoned by her own country, stripped of her citizenship, and sent to a concentration camp. Yet now she was not allowed to leave. A woman without a home. It was beyond unfair. Ruth and Ezra could find a fresh start. Jimmy and Tony could return home. But Greta had to stay. "Anything you need, write to me. I will make sure you are taken care of."

"I will, I promise. And please..." She hitched herself closer to him. He reluctantly wrapped his arms around her. The pain of holding her this last time constricted his chest so tightly he thought his heart would shatter like glass. "Please write to me and let me know if you are safe?"

"I will." He leaned down to give her one last kiss. A kiss to last a lifetime. He poured every last bit of his soul into her, his hands moving over her back, her face, holding her to him, desperate to memorize each line, each mark. He never wanted this to end, this final moment. He could taste the salty tears flowing from both his eyes and hers.

"Jimmy, I will always love you." Her voice shook, as she reached into her pocket, extracting an envelope. "I wrote you a letter, something to keep you company on your journey home. And inside is a surprise."

He took the envelope from her, their fingers brushing. As he tucked it into his breast pocket, he caught the faint hint of lilacs. Forever lilacs.

His world was crumbling around them. The injustice of this all. He survived the accident, the war... and now was left with nothing, just unending heartache. He felt whole in her arms, felt himself becoming the man he knew he could be, the man whose soul was lost on a deserted road in Pennsylvania all those years before. He had purpose, and now, it was being ripped away.

"And I..." He hesitated, swallowing back the pain, the pain of knowing he would never feel like this again. "I love you, too." He lifted her chin with both hands, kissing her with languid reverence.

The major cleared his throat. They had to leave now. Jimmy held her one last time and boarded the transport. *I've died,* Jimmy thought as the vehicle drove away and he caught his last glimpse of Greta. *Not on some distant battlefield, but here, in this moment, I've died, and I will never be again.*

As the transport drove away, he watched as she disappeared over the horizon. His precious Greta. Long after she vanished from sight, he continued to stare out the back of the vehicle.

He reached into his pocket and retrieved the envelope. Holding it to his nose, he breathed in the sweet, powdery scent. With his finger, he broke open the flap. As he extracted the sky-blue sheet of paper, something fluttered onto his lap. It was a picture of the two of them, sitting in the clearing. She gazed adoringly at him, while he smiled for the camera. He remembered the day so well, the picnic and bottle of wine. Would he ever be happy again?

He ran his fingers over the edges of the photograph, feeling himself transported to the picnic in the woods. Tony nudged his shoulder. "Whatcha got there, Captain?"

Jimmy turned the photograph toward his friend. "Ever see this?"

"Was that from the picnic? What a rainstorm and the two of you were soaked." He let out a low whistle. "Greta is a real dish, Captain."

He tucked the photograph back into his pocket; he didn't want the others to see. Unfolding the letter, he began to read through her sharply slanted handwriting. The letters were such a unique shape, a faint mimic of the woman he loved. It took him a moment to decipher the words, but when he did, his heart raced.

My dearest Jimmy,

I am writing this while I watch you sleeping so soundly in our bed. I have a little confession, I often would lay awake at night watching you sleep. How could I be so lucky to have found you? What did I do to deserve such a beautiful gift from God? My heart beats only for you, Jimmy. No matter how many miles separate us or how much the fates are determined to keep us apart, my heart will forever belong to you. Continue to cherish it. On lonely nights, when you feel all is without hope, look to the moon. Know I too will be watching the same sky and thinking of you. Our love is timeless, Jimmy. Whether in this life or the next, we will be united again. Promise to keep a piece of your heart for me? You have mine completely, I belong only to you.

Forever yours,

Greta

GRETA STOOD ON HER TOES, as she watched the transport carrying the love of her life fade into the horizon. *So that's it.* The past several weeks with Jimmy had been the most incredible of her life. Glorious, every moment together was a gift she would always cherish, memories that were hers and his alone.

She closed her eyes and covered her face with her hands, picturing him lying in their bed. Inhaling deeply, she could still smell the lingering scent of him on her clothes. The heady mixture of musk, bay rum, and cloves. The aroma caused her stomach to flutter and goose pimples to erupt over her arms. *I wonder if I could bottle it, spray it over my pillow at night?*

She sighed heavily and turned around. It was time to head home, but she was not ready to be there yet. Being there without him felt crushing, like the emptiness would close in around her. Ruth and Ezra had decided to stay behind at the cottage. Earlier, Ruth admitted she was not capable of saying goodbye to Tony.

"I'm a coward, Greta. If I watch him get onto the transport and drive off, it will be too much for me." Her head bent as she looked away from Greta. "It will be too much like watching Daniel be taken away all over again and far too heart-wrenching for Ezra."

"And what does Tony say about it?"

"I explained my feelings to him last night. He understood. Told me it wasn't a goodbye anyway, since I will be leaving as well in a few days." She laughed lightly. "Forever the optimist."

Greta had to see Jimmy off, in fact, she didn't even sleep the night before. Instead, she spent every possible moment she could watching him, touching him, savoring their final hours together.

And yet, as she walked home, she did not feel like this was the end. How could it be? After everything they had done for one another, how close they had become, how could it end like this? It seemed a preordained destiny they would find their way back to each other again. Somehow they would meet one day – be it five months from now or fifty years in the future, she knew their story was not finished.

These thoughts gave her the strength to keep walking, to anticipate the rising sun. Each new day brought them closer to the day of their reunion. Yet, there was a voice of niggling doubt weighing heavily today. It was the reason she could not return home.

She could not watch Ruth pack. She and Ezra would be leaving soon and with them would leave the last connection she had to Jimmy. She could not walk through the door and be reminded of him, not yet. She kept walking and found herself in a familiar place. The red and yellow curtains smiled a soft greeting as she rapped gently on the heavy wooden door.

It opened and the softly lined face she had come to love like a mother greeted her. "Oh, Greta. My darling girl. Come in." Warm, fleshy arms wrapped around her. She felt a soft, motherly kiss on her forehead. "You come inside and let Liesel make it all better." The smell of fresh coffee and cake sweetened the air. Liesel would help and perhaps, Greta could find a new path, determine her new future. One that would, hopefully, tie the fated strings of Greta and Jimmy together forever.

CHAPTER THIRTY-FIVE

Liesel's arms rested on Greta's shoulders. The steps felt heavier than before, as if she no longer had the strength to move forward. Somehow she managed to make it to the worn sofa and fell with a plop. Liesel smoothed her hair and muttered calming platitudes into her ear.

"So your American, he's gone?" One solemn nod was her answer. Liesel continued to chatter away. "Now, chin up. This is no time for despair. Let fate be your guide, and if it is meant to be, you will be together again."

Greta slumped against the sofa. "Do you really believe so?"

"Do I believe in fate? My dear child, after everything you have been through in the past few years, how could you not believe that the universe has plans for us all?" She walked towards the kitchen. "What we need is lots of coffee and cake."

"So, he left today?" Fritz leaned against the door jamb, his face heavy with concern.

Greta bit her lip to keep it from trembling and nodded. Fritz pushed off from the door and sank onto the sofa next to her. He placed her hand in his, enveloping it in tender warmth.

"My offer still stands, Greta. I've never stopped loving you and would happily marry you."

"Oh, Fritz." She tried to pull back her hand, but he held it in a steady grip. She cupped his cheek in her hand and kissed the tip of his nose. "My darling friend. I am no longer the woman you fell in love with." He started to speak, but she placed a finger over his firm lips. "And my heart will always belong to another."

Why did this feel as painful as saying goodbye to Jimmy? She did not know, but the tightness in her chest threatened to squeeze what tiny bit of control she had remaining. Fritz was her first love, but Jimmy was her true love. In a different time, Fritz and Greta would have been happy together, content. It never would have been the consuming passion she felt for Jimmy; and had she never known of such feelings, the life with Fritz would have been enough. But now she could never be happy settling, even knowing how utterly adored she would be. No, there was only one person she was meant to love and to be loved by.

"Then you will understand if I find someone else to marry? I want children, a wife." His eyes, once bright like a summer sky, now held such sorrow.

"Yes, and I pray you find someone who makes your very soul soar to the heavens. Who becomes a part of you, and you a part of her. It's what you deserve, Fritz, and nothing less."

He smiled, though it did not quite reach his eyes. "All that?"

"And more." She patted his knee with friendly affection. "One day you will understand what I mean, and you will thank me for saying no."

Liesel returned to the room, carrying a tray laden with coffee and cakes. Fritz helped his aunt set it on the coffee table. "That lovely Tony gifted me some coffee before he left, so I thought we would enjoy it together." She poured three cups and settled onto the sofa across from Greta and Fritz.

"I've been thinking of my mother and wondering what may have happened to her." Greta refused the cake with a wave of her hand. Liesel shot her a disapproving look. "Nerves," she explained, and Liesel clicked her tongue in understanding.

Fritz took a large bite of the honey-sweetened cake. "Perhaps it is time you return home, see what you might find."

Liesel nodded approvingly. "Yes, a perfect suggestion! Time to find answers, instead of wallowing in your own misery."

"And perhaps another solution will present itself," Fritz added, biting into a second piece of cake. His lean body was starting to fill in, his muscles becoming firm and defined. "There are more Americans in Berlin, more people who might be able to unite you and Jimmy."

"Or perhaps, it is time to move forward and let the memories keep me company on lonely nights," Greta said.

Liesel quirked a brow and studied Greta's face skeptically. "Perhaps. But now, we shall try to find your mother. A daughter needs her mother."

And she did. Since Jimmy had left, the one person she longed to see was her mother. To wrap herself in her mother's healing embrace. To hear the songs and stories of her childhood. To be worried and fussed over, as only a mother could do. There was no one she wanted, nay needed more than her mother.

"Yes, let's go. All of us." Greta clasped her hands together with excitement. It was all she could do to keep herself from bolting through the door and running all the way to Berlin.

Fritz shook his head. "No. I need to stay behind and work here on the farm."

"I'll go. Perhaps convince my brother-in-law, Stefan, to

relocate back home and help out. Plenty of room here." Liesel wandered around the living room, muttering. "Anything to get my family away from the damn Soviets."

A few days later and after a tearful goodbye with Ruth and Ezra, Greta found herself back in the city of her birth. She and Liesel were exhausted from the arduous journey north. They walked for miles. Hitched rides on horse-drawn carts. Traveling over broken roadways and bridges, they encountered a strange assortment of defeated people, refugees, and conquerors.

The overwhelming devastation had been the hardest to bear. Berlin was a pile of rubble. The Kaiser Wilhelm Memorial Church - now only a bombed-out bell tower. The Quadriga - the once-mighty symbol of Prussia, now destroyed with only one horse remaining intact. And the zoo - nearly all the animals were dead. Oh, why weren't the poor creatures protected from the bombings and ravages of war?

Traversing the city was a test of memory, as nothing remained of familiar landmarks and street signs. Meandering through the streets, they walked around piles of rubble being sorted and neatly stacked by the Trümmerfrauen. Later, these materials would be used to rebuild, but hardly any remained of the once thriving and beautiful metropolis. Yet, Greta felt no anger toward the Allies, the people of Germany brought this destruction on themselves for tolerating such evil.

Greta's heart raced with anticipation. What of her childhood home? Each step brought them closer and closer. Mostly skeletal remains of houses remained in neighborhoods. But she hoped something of her home would be there, some clues telling her how her family survived, anything to give Greta hope of reuniting with her mother. Finally, they arrived at her street, recognizing the emerald-green door of the house at the corner.

She hurried along the cleared pathway, her feet racing along with her heart. Anticipation. And there it was, the steps she skipped up and down as a child! It was where she had first met Fritz when they were six years old. Where her best friend from childhood announced she was getting married and then later that she was pregnant. Her home. Five steps up to the heavy oak door, the last place she had seen her mother. And now, it was all that remained. Five steps and a crater.

"Oh, Greta. I'm so sorry." Liesel gripped her shoulders, held her steady. "Perhaps, they were not home? Maybe they were in a shelter?"

Yet, Greta feared she would never see her mother again. She felt hollow. No tears came. She had no more left to cry. Greta cleared her throat, flicking the wrinkles from her skirt. "Where is your brother-in-law, Stefan, staying? Perhaps we can rest and then be on our way back home to Bavaria."

"Greta Müller? Is that you?" A stout woman with braided hair twisted into a crown on her head ran up the steps.

"Katja?" She hardly recognized her childhood friend. She had grown rounder, her cheeks fuller.

"Yes! It is you! I can hardly believe it!" She threw her arms around Greta, swaying back and forth in an embrace. "I haven't seen you since your engagement party and so much has happened since then. Come, come, please. I live down the street."

Greta's feet were mired to the ground. "I just discovered my home was destroyed."

Katja stopped yanking on her arm, then tilted her head to the side in question. "You didn't know? Didn't your mother tell you?"

"My mother?" Was there hope, was she still alive?

"Surely your mother wrote to you in Bavaria." Greta shook her head. "Oh. Well, the mail has been such a mess for the past few months, maybe the letter was lost. She and your father have been staying with us since the bomb hit their home. That night, they were visiting with friends in Potsdam. We all lucked out."

Liesel looped her arm into Greta's as they followed behind Katja. She whispered in her ear. "Are you prepared to see your father again?"

"I think so. Stay with me."

"Of course, my dear. I'm always here for you." Liesel's loving embrace gave her the courage she needed to move forward.

A short walk later, they arrived at the front of a three-story brick building. Evidence of the bombings and Soviet invasion blanketed the city. Bullet holes scarred the facade, a few windows were boarded over, and piles of rubble littered the front sidewalk.

"We have the first-floor apartment. My darling Karl-Heinz secured the house for us shortly before..." Katja paused, cleared her throat. "Before he was sent East again."

"He was injured at Stalingrad, correct?" Greta rested her hand on Katja's shoulder, who leaned against her friend for a brief moment.

"Yes," she breathed out softly. "He finally healed, just in time to be sent back to the front lines. He died in a field in Poland."

"Oh, Katja. I'm so sorry. You loved your husband dearly. Karl-Heinz was a good man." A mezuzah on the door frame caught Greta's eye. She placed her fingers over the object and whispered a silent prayer for the former residents.

They entered the spacious living room. The opulent room boasted silk-striped sofas of yellow and cerulean, heavy velvet curtains, and a grand piano. Liesel's rounded eyes surveyed the room, as she nudged an elbow into Greta's side. "Katja, your home is splendid." They exchanged a knowing look with each other.

"Thank you! I couldn't believe it was abandoned. Karl-Heinz had a friend in the Gestapo who alerted us to this place, and we took the opportunity to up residence. Furnished to boot." She picked up a few scattered toys from the floor and motioned for them to sit down. "Your mother is in the kitchen making lunch, I'll go get her."

Liesel leaned over to Greta. "You know this place was not abandoned?"

"It makes me sick sitting here. Like we are criminals returning to the scene of a crime."

Liesel patted her hands. "I've been praying for those poor people the moment we stepped foot into their home."

"Me, too." Greta couldn't hold back the overwhelming feeling of despair as she took in the opulent apartment. There was no doubt the former residents had long since perished, victims of the Nazi regime.

Greta heard Katja calling for her mother. "Margaretha, you'll never believe who's here!"

From the back of the apartment, they heard a pan clatter to the floor. Through the hallway ran her mother. Wisps of light gray hair escaped her perfectly coiled braids. Her white apron was spotted with flour and a little grease, but her lavender dress was spotless. In a moment, she wrapped Greta into her arms and sobbed her name over and over again. "You are alive!" she cried, her arms shaking.

Her mother's face had more lines than she remembered, but her eyes were the same sparkling azure blue. Greta's own eyes were one half her mother's, the other half her father's, the perfect blend of azure and jade. "So are you, Mama." It felt so wonderful to be held in these arms again. If only Jimmy could be here too, to share in this joyful moment.

"Liesel, it is so good to see you too!" She held Greta's face in her hands. "So you were in Bavaria! Your father told me he sent you there, but I didn't believe him, but he must have sent you if you were with Liesel. As pretty as always. My beautiful daughter!"

Greta's heart sank. Her father had lied to his mother all this time. How could she explain her father's betrayal? "I've been in Bavaria for most of the time." She felt Liesel's hand on her shoulder, the pressure telling her silently not to continue.

"Yes, she stayed at my farm. I was so happy to take her in." Not wanting to say more, Liesel changed the subject. "You look well, Margaretha."

Her mother blushed faintly. "A little older, but thank you, Liesel." They moved to sit down on the sofas. "And what of Fritz? After you left, I did not know what to tell him and I worried about him. His parents said he was wounded." Her mother stacked their hands together on her lap.

"He's well, Mama."

"So, when will you marry?" her mother asked hopefully. "It is about time now."

"Oh, Mama. There is so much to tell you, but not yet. Right now, we will be happy to be together again." She was hesitant to ask, but wanted to know how long she could stay before her father would return. "When will Papa be here?"

Katja returned to the room, her daughter resting on her hip. The plump toddler rubbed sleepy eyes, her chestnut-colored hair in disarray. "He and Heinrich should be here any moment. They had a meeting to attend."

Greta's skin prickled in warning, and Liesel shot her a questioning glance. *Heinrich?* No, the name had to be a mere coincidence, there is no way it could be that Heinrich.

She set her daughter on the floor, who sleepily wandered over to Greta's mother. Lifting her arms into the air, she grunted until Margaretha picked her up and snuggled her against her shoulder. "Your mother has been such a blessing to us and little Sofie here. Almost like an Oma."

"Such a dear child, how could I not love her like a grandmother would." Margaretha kissed the mess of curls covering Sofie's head.

Liesel's curiosity helped her ask the question Greta was dreading. "Katja, who's Heinrich?"

"Oh, Greta! You won't believe it." She dramatically fell into the chair across from Greta and her mother. "After Karl-Heinz died, I was distraught."

"Naturally," said Liesel and Greta in unison.

"Shortly after I received the notification, I started receiving flowers and notes from none other than Heinrich Braunfeld." Her smile was wide and bright.

Greta felt the floor move beneath her and her world slipped away. "Fritz's cousin? But you hated him." She ran her hands over her face in agitation, holding back the urge to flee immediately.

"Oh, silly Greta! You were always so mean to him, but I know the truth. He told me how you used to flirt with him, teasing him to make his cousin jealous."

Bile rose, she felt hot and faint. "I have to go."

Liesel stood up and agreed. "Oh, yes. We have a very important meeting. Can't be missed. We will come by again soon." She ushered Greta to the door, her mother protesting.

"But no, you just got here." Sadness wrapped around each word.

"I know, Mama, but we will come again."

Liesel muttered under her breath, "With a Division of Americans."

At the same time, she heard Katja exclaim, "I knew you

would be jealous. Well, he chose me, Greta. You can have your silly Fritz; I much prefer his dreamy cousin."

Greta wanted to laugh at Katja's obliviousness, Liesel's weak attempt at humor, but the need to flee was too great. But before they could make their escape, the door opened and the two men she never wanted to see again blocked the way out.

"Greta?" her father asked.

The corner of Heinrich's lip turned up in a sneer, his eyes wide with surprise. "Why, Greta, it is nice to see you looking so well."

"Sickly is more like it," she heard her once best friend utter behind her.

"Now, Katja, darling. Greta's had a rough go of things, best we be kind." He reached out to Greta. She flinched as if she had been burned. Liesel held on tighter. "And, Aunt Liesel, what an absolute surprise. Did you miss your favorite nephew?"

"No, he's living with me in Bavaria." She tilted her chin up and glared over at Heinrich, who laughed in response. His hand brushed against Greta's breast as he leaned across to buss his aunt's cheek. Greta could hear Liesel's jaw pop, as she gritted her teeth. "We best be off." They tried to pass through the door, but to their surprise, Greta's father stopped them.

"Please, I just arrived. Let me see my daughter."

"Your daughter?" Liesel half laughed, half cried. It was Greta's turn to ease her friend's nerves with a placating hand.

His jade eyes pleaded with Greta, and she relented. "For a few more moments."

Her father's hand trembled as he reached for her arm and placed it in the crook of his elbow. Her sleeve slipped down, revealing the tattoo for a brief moment, before she managed to tug it into place. She was uncertain if he saw it. Did he even know what it meant? He leaned over and whispered in her ear.

"I was so wrong to trust him, my dear Greta. Please, let us talk."

She nodded, feeling completely unsure of herself. What did her father mean and who was he wrong to trust? It all felt so muddled, she allowed him to lead her through the room. Her mother began to protest. "Give us a moment, dear," he called back to her.

He led them down the hall to a bedroom. He motioned for her to sit down in a wingback chair, while he sat on the edge of the bed. The almost two years since she last saw her father had aged him greatly. His hair was mostly gone, a few white wisps left at his temples. His face was lined and edged with worry. As he sat, his back was no longer ramrod straight, but curved. The ugly schmisse was more prominent on his papery skin.

Finally, he spoke, his voice wavering. "That night, Heinrich came to me with a story. My dearest daughter, it seemed, had decided to throw herself at another man on the very night of her engagement." Greta began to speak, but he held up a hand, begging to continue.

"When I entered the room, he had an explanation for everything. Why it appeared as if you had been beaten and why he had bruises to his hands and face. I was angry and confused. He convinced me he was going to send you away to Liesel's. I thought it was best, especially..." He swallowed hard, his eyes not meeting hers. "If there might be a child. She could protect you and then I could make sense of what happened."

"When did you find out he lied?"

"It was shortly after you went away. Fritz kept stopping by, wondering where you were, demanding answers. Then, I wrote to Liesel, asking after you, but she was confused by my letters. She had no idea where you were, and that's when I knew. Heinrich lied. He's done nothing but lie. I'm so ashamed I trusted him, how I believed him."

"But why are you living in his house?" Greta's head spun. Was any of this real? Oh, she wanted to believe him, wanted so desperately to believe her father didn't willingly send her to that place.

"We had no place to go after the bomb. And truthfully, I wanted to keep an eye on Katja. She was your friend and had no one left to protect her. He's beaten her before, but since we are living here, he has been kinder."

"Oh, Papa." She knelt before him stroking his hand. She did not have any words yet and felt the acceptance of his story sticking in her throat.

His fingers covered the tattoo on her forearm, only this time she did not flinch or pull away. "I know what this means, and I have a million questions, but not today." She nodded, biting her quivering lip. She could not cry now. "I do not deserve your forgiveness; I will not ask for it."

She threw her arms around his neck and sobbed. Was there no end to Heinrich's villainy? She was eternally grateful for this moment, for the catharsis. Her father felt he was protecting her in his own way. He had no idea the lengths Heinrich would go to in order to bury his dirty secret. How many women had he hurt? And now poor Katja.

"I forgive you, Papa." He started to protest. "It is mine to give as I wish, and I forgive you. Him?" She gestured to the door. "I will never forgive. But you, it was a mistake of trusting the wrong man and not believing me."

"I love you, my darling girl."

There was a soft knock at the door, and Greta's mother entered the room. "May I join this happy reunion?"

Greta reached out to her mother, who joined their embrace. She wondered if Jimmy was having a similar joyous reunion with his family. As her mother fussed over her appearance and demanded she eat something, she sighed wistfully.

Hopefully, though a continent apart, Jimmy was experiencing the same warmth and love as she was.

Before crawling into bed, Greta composed her first letter.

Dearest Jimmy,

You will never believe the events of the past few days. After much difficulty, Liesel and I arrived in Berlin. The city I loved so much is nothing but a shell of its former self. But I was most sad to see my childhood home had been destroyed, as I would have dearly loved for you to have seen it. Fortunately, my family survived as they were visiting friends. By mere happenstance, I found them both again. And my father was not the man I thought he was. I have so much to tell you! But for now, I am hoping you are well. How was your reunion with your family? I hope it was filled with happy tears and much love.

With all my heart,

Greta

CHAPTER THIRTY-SIX

Jimmy stood before the door, the very one he walked through thousands of times. The emerald-green paint around the handle and hinges had chipped away, but the glass was spotless, and the golden lettering declared to all that it was O'Brien's Tobacco Shop. His hand trembled as he reached for the brass knob, worn smooth from decades of use. Jimmy flexed his hand, cleared his throat, and reached out again. Why was it so hard to simply open the door? A twist and a push. Yet his hand would not obey the command.

He set his bag on the ground and pulled a cigarette from his breast pocket. Cupping his hands together he lit it and took a long and soothing drag. The street was quiet as it was still too early for people to be shopping. He straightened his uniform, ran a hand through his hair, and debated what to do next.

He should want to walk through the doors, see his mother and father again. His sister, Erin, with her mess of auburn curls piled on her head. But the moment he boarded the ship to head back home, he felt like a fog had descended over him and he was walking through a nightmare with no end. Nothing felt right, sounded right, smelled right.

Jimmy felt bitter and angry. Shouldn't he be happy he was heading home? Shouldn't he be happy his injuries kept him from continuing to fight? Tony understood. They would stay up late on the ship, after everyone had gone to bed. Mostly they smoked and stared out into the night sky. Sometimes Tony would talk about their time in the little house. He would speak of Ezra and Ruth, but never Greta. He understood the pain eating away at what remained of Jimmy's heart.

Once the ship docked, he was separated again from the one person who could understand everything hidden within Jimmy's silence. Tony was still on active duty and Jimmy had been relieved. And so, after all the years of fighting, he came home to a place more foreign than familiar.

He knew his parents would be disappointed that he denied them the chance to greet his train, but Jimmy didn't want a public welcome. He wanted to slip in unnoticed. It was the only thing making each day bearable. They would forgive him, of course. One crooked smile and his mother would throw herself into his arms.

He crushed out his cigarette and took a steadying breath. Down the road, he caught a glimpse of buttery blonde hair and his heart accelerated. Then it crashed to a halt when the woman turned in his direction. Would this torment ever cease? He saw her everywhere he turned. One of the nurses on board the ship wore a lilac-scented powder. It drove him mad. He discovered the jar one day and stole it. Dusting it over his pillow at night, he would fall asleep dreaming of her, his Greta. He woke each morning to the heavenly aroma, a brief moment of bliss, followed all too shortly by the crushing reality that she was not there. That she would never be in his arms again.

More people were moving through the streets, a few giving

him a long stare or a polite nod. It was time. He picked up his bag and straightened his uniform. Time to force his despair aside, paste on a smile, and pretend this moment was the happiest of his life. *Think of how your mother will feel. Be happy for her sake, she deserves it.*

Those thoughts gave him strength, the trembling subsided, and he was able to grip the handle and push the door open. The tinkling bell signaled his return. The familiar smell of tobacco hit his chest like a speeding bullet. For a moment, he forgot how to move and breathe. Home. Tears blurred his vision. But he heard her approach. Saw her auburn hair in disarray. *Erin!* God, he missed her. She would understand the most, she would help him mend his aching heart.

"Jimmy!" she cried, throwing herself into his unsteady arms. "It's you! I can't believe it's you!" She gripped him tightly, her tears soaking through the collar of his shirt.

He held onto her with everything he possessed. He needed this moment, needed to feel the forgiving embrace of his cherished sister. He longed for a pair of arms to hold him again, to help chase away the sadness. Several long minutes passed before he loosened his grip and she spoke again.

"Ma is going to kill you! Why didn't you tell us you were coming home?"

He reached out and tugged on an auburn lock escaping the mass of pins trying in vain to keep them corralled. "You know me, I wanted to surprise you."

Her hazel eyes flicked up and down. "Something's wrong."

He sighed. "Why do you think something's wrong? I'm home. I'm happy."

"You are home, but you're not happy. Something's wrong, James Patrick O'Brien, and you will tell me." She poked him in the chest to emphasize the last words.

He shook his head. Erin was the only person who could see

him clearly. She may be his younger, bratty sister, but she could see through any facade he put in place.

She grabbed his hand and yanked him over to the smoker's lounge near the rear of the store. "Wait here."

He heard her rustle around the counter, the tinkle of the bell, and then she returned. She sank into a leather-covered chair and propped her feet up onto the table. She motioned for Jimmy to do the same.

"I think I should go upstairs. Say hi to mom and dad." He proceeded to the doorway at the back of the store.

"They're not here."

"What do you mean they're not here? They're always here!"

His sister shrugged a thin shoulder. "Aunt Maureen had surgery. Mom went to help out for a week. Dad left this morning to pick her up."

"I can't believe they aren't here." He slouched into his favorite of the leather chairs. Its tall back was the perfect height for resting his head and it had the perfect amount of wear to have softened the leather to an almost butter-like texture.

"Well, if someone," she pointed a long finger in his direction, "had mentioned he was coming home, they would probably be here."

"I surrender."

"Good, tell me what's wrong." She leaned forward, resting a freckled hand on his knee. He looked away; he wasn't ready to share this with anyone. "Please, Jimmy. I know something's wrong. I can feel it."

"You and your witchy ways."

"You sound exactly like Grandma." She tsked but kept her hand in place. The hand burned through his resolve. "My stoic brother does not cry. My ornery brother does not hold onto his sister like he's afraid she'll let go. Please, Jimmy. Trust me." It was his last measure of defense and she had broken through.

"I met someone."

"Where?" She leaned back, her hands resting along the armrests.

"In Germany," he stretched his legs in front of him, crossing at the ankles.

"A German, really, Jimmy. Was it her dashing Nazi uniform that did it for you?" She made a noise with her throat. Was it disapproval?

"She's not like them." His voice hardened.

"I'm teasing. Honestly, Jimmy, you should know me better. I'm not going to judge you." She edged closer to the end of the chair.

"I need a drink." He jumped up and stalked over to the bar along the wall of the lounge. He pulled out a glass and his father's 20-year-old scotch. Erin's slender hand covered the top of the glass just before he poured.

"Jimmy?" Her voice shook. "I thought you stopped drinking after the accident with Hugh?" Her freckled face tightened as she struggled with unnamed emotions.

"Well, it's about time I had one, don't you think?"

She gripped the glass tighter, the unstoppered bottle suspended in the air above. "No, Jimmy. I don't. Tell me about her."

"Let go, Erin. Please." She withdrew her hand from the glass. She hugged her arms around her middle as she watched him pour and take a long swallow of the amber liquid. "I need to be numb for a while."

He filled his glass again and sat down in the same comfortable chair. Erin lowered herself onto the table before him, she reached out, her hands resting on his knee. "What was her name?" Her voice soothed the ache in his chest.

"Greta. Her name is Greta, and she is the most spectacular woman I have ever known." He rested his weary head against the back of the chair.

"Why didn't you marry her?"

"Couldn't, it wasn't allowed."

Erin crinkled her pixie nose. "Wasn't allowed? Jonas, from down the street, married a French girl. Why couldn't you marry Greta?"

"The French were Allies, the Germans were not."

She scoffed. "The French were Allies, ha! That's not what I hear about this girl. First, she dated a German, then when they were losing, she sank her claws into Jonas."

Jimmy released a small laugh. "You only say that because you've had a crush on Jonas since the third grade."

She swatted Jimmy's hand. "Oh, you think you know me so well?" Her head tilted to the side, as she looked over Jimmy again. "Do you love her?"

He swallowed hard. "More than I could comprehend. She is stunningly beautiful and so sweet. Strong, she went through so much, you have no idea." Erin's thumbs continued to trace along the veins covering the back of his hands. The motion encouraged him to reveal more. "You would never believe what she survived. She was at one of the camps and escaped."

Erin's eyes rounded. "Seriously? How?" Her last question was a whisper.

"I'll tell you the story later. But she helped a little boy escape. She saved my life. I could go on and on, but..." She patted his hand.

"So there's no future there? What about her immigrating or you going back for her once the war in the Pacific is over?" Jimmy shook his head. "Don't lose hope, dear brother. I can feel this as much as I can feel your hand. Fate has more in store for you."

He started to withdraw. He didn't want to hear more about fate. He didn't believe in it, not now. Not after everything he had gone through, everything he survived, only to have to leave Greta. To leave behind the one person who made sense. The one person who made him whole. But Erin's grip would not break; it grew painful. "Trust me, Jimmy. You know I can see these things." She pressed harder, his knuckles crushed together. "Trust me."

The bell above the door jingled. "Erin, why in Heaven's name is there a sign on the door that says closed? You had better have..." The roughened voice of his father stopped abruptly. The keys slipped from his fingers and clattered on the floor. His father was shaken to his core. "Jimmy," he mouthed. Then with a clearing of his throat, he called to his wife, "Letty, put the sign back on the door!"

Hands like his own reached out to Jimmy and clutched him to his chest. "My God, Son! As I live and breathe." He patted Jimmy's back.

Jimmy studied his father's face. A few more lines framed his eyes, but still the same rich brown as Jimmy. Gray now dusted his sable hair.

"Why in the world would you close up shop today?" He heard his mother scolding as she walked through the shop. "Jimmy!" She stopped next to his father, her head even with his broad shoulders. Her bespeckled face played a series of emotions: annoyance, confusion, shock, and then devastating joy.

He had to brace himself for impact. He felt his tiny mother yank him into her plump arms and squeeze so tightly he thought he stopped breathing for a moment. Her words were an incoherent blubber as she ran her lovingly soft hands over his face, his shoulders, his wrists. Finally, her words grew clearer. "My son is home, my son is home."

"Yeah, Ma. I'm home." He cupped her cheek in his palm, his thumb wiped away a few tears. Her sparkling hazel eyes glowed with total adoration.

"Haven't they been feeding you?" She gripped his waist and tsked. "You have lost weight! You are skin and bones."

"Ma, leave him alone." Erin chided affectionately.

"What would you like to eat? I will make you anything you want. I've got corned beef. Maybe the butcher has a roast. We've been saving our ration cards for when you came home."

"Anything would be fine, Ma." His stomach rumbled at the thought of his mother's home-cooked meal. Her dinners were legendary feasts. And as his thoughts often did, they drifted to Greta and how she never seemed to have enough to eat. If she were there, with him now, how his mother would insist she was much too skinny. He could picture her at the dinner table, which would be covered in a mountain of dishes. His beautiful Greta and his mother chiding her to eat more, then Ma would glow with satisfaction when Greta's plate was finally empty. He cleared his throat. "Maybe some Wiener Schnitzel, Ma."

"Developed a taste for German food, did ya?" She pinched his cheek. He heard Erin cough. He glared at his sister, who was trying unsuccessfully to smother a laugh behind her hand.

"As I live and breathe, Son." His dad's watery gaze looked him over. "Here, after all this time." He went to the back of the room, then eyed the empty glass on the table. Pointing to it, he tilted his head in question, but Jimmy merely answered with a nonchalant shrug. Frank O'Brien nodded his head, picked it up, and headed to the bar. There he filled four scotches, handing them around. "I think a toast is in order."

Erin picked up her glass and held it high. "To the death of the bastard Hitler!"

"Erin Ariadne O'Brien, watch your mouth!"

His mother shook her finger at Erin, while his father shouted: "And the other bastard Tojo!"

"I'll drink to that!" Jimmy lifted his glass.

His mother harrumphed and took a long drink. "To Jimmy and his safe return."

"To Jimmy and his Greta," Erin quietly cheered.

No one but Jimmy heard the last toast. Tony may know his story; Erin, however, would understand the pain. In this moment, his confounding, annoying baby sister showed she was the one who could help him heal. He kissed the wild curls on top of her head. "Thanks, Brat."

She nudged him with her shoulder. The nickname had grown from teasing to a term of endearment long ago. "Any time," she paused, a wicked grin spreading across her face, "Boo." He groaned, it was the nickname she gave him when she was a toddler and couldn't say brother. It stuck, much to his everlasting chagrin.

As his family shuffled up the back stairs to their apartment above the store, the fog descended again. He was home. The light and warmth of his childhood home was duller; however, he could finally catch his breath. The ache in his chest was still strong, still hurting as it did the moment he said goodbye to Greta.

Home. He ran his fingers along the floral wallpaper in the living room, along the chair rail leading through the hallway to his bedroom. He stood before the wooden door and took a deep breath. The ache subsided for the briefest of moments, then accelerated as he twisted the brass knob. Silence greeted him like an old friend. His room had recently been cleaned, the curtains tied back to let in the afternoon sun. Shelves were covered with old mementos and photographs. He was a stranger in his own room, these memories no longer belonged to him. His home was once a citadel of comfort and belonging was as foreign to him as distant shores.

From his bag, he retrieved the stolen jar. He dusted the fine powder on his pillow and held it to his face, breathing in the sweet scent. He lay on his bed, burying his face in the memories. And it all came crashing down, the thin thread holding his weakening composure snapped and the monsoon of tears flowed freely. He railed against the injustice of it all. Punched his bed, headboard, wall until his knuckles bled. But the ache persisted.

Long hours later he awoke to the moonlight streaming across the room. His temples throbbed, his eyelids scratched over dry eyes. A soft snoring was the only sound. Across his chest lay a thin, bespeckled arm, the hand resting over his heart. He covered the hand with his own. The ache lessened.

"Erin?" She mumbled sleepily in response to her name. "Why are you here?"

She rested her head over his heart. "My big brother needed me."

He choked back an answer and enfolded her in his arms. The fog faded. He could breathe. This was where his new world began, a world built on uncertainty.

"Jimmy?"

"Hm?" he replied. His mind was blissfully empty.

"You have one week to mourn. Then you need to put yourself back together." She met his hardened stare. "Trust me on this. If you give in to the sadness, it will consume you. I know all too well." A look of longing flashed behind her eyes.

He tugged on a curl. "So you're the expert now, Brat?"

"I'm an expert on everything." She tweaked his nose. "But in all honesty, you will be no good to her or yourself if you do not pull yourself together. I'll be here for the moments when it all seems so unbearable. But the past is the past, and now it is time to think of the future."

"And what of the future, Erin?" That was the question haunting his dreams. How could there be a future without Greta? What life would be worth living, without the love of his life at his side?

"In time, it will fall into place, and you will know your path. For now, it is about finding the little joys."

Sometime later she drifted off to sleep again. But sleep evaded Jimmy. The ache in his chest grew, squeezing unbearably tight. The only way to calm the madness was to put it away, bury it behind a wall. As the next day broke, he continued to build the wall inside, locking away the memories. The ache dulled, reason ruled. He would not need the week. Nothing remained of his once beating heart. All that endured was stone and mortar. Lilacs, music, moonlight, and endless blue-green were smothered underneath. He rose from his bed and grabbed the jar. Into the trash it went. Followed by a letter she had written. A drawing of Ezra's. The bullet she removed. Then finally, the picture of the two of them laughing. He shoved it all into the wastepaper basket.

The ache left. The sadness left. Only a dull fog and nothingness persisted. This was his future, the world without Greta.

CHAPTER THIRTY-SEVEN

The time had come for Greta to say goodbye to her parents before she and Liesel took on another adventure. A chance encounter with an old acquaintance of Liesel's helped Greta secure a job for which she would be perfect — reuniting families who had been separated during the war. The position was in the city of Nuremberg in the state of Bavaria. She could hardly wait to share her wonderful news with her parents.

She returned to Katja's apartment and knocked on the door. The evening before, she had agreed to visit, but arrived a bit earlier than expected. When no one answered, she tried to open the door. It was unlocked. "Hello?" she called out, but there was no answer. She walked towards the hallway which led to her parents' bedroom. That was when she heard the door click and a bolt slide in place.

In an instant, she could feel *him*, her heart thudding in panic. The hair on the back of her neck prickled. She could smell him, stale cigarettes oozing from his pores. No one else was home, she was certain now.

Then he spoke, his condescending tone sent waves of nausea roiling through her stomach. "Greta, I never thought I would see you again. And there you were in my home. After all this time." He stalked closer to her. She counted, steeling her composure. "And now, you are back. Hoping to find me, I assume?"

"Heinrich," she spat out. Balling her fists at her side, she readied herself for the inevitable attack. She was sick of cowering, sick of being a victim to men. "I would never want you."

"Too bad, I have been searching for you. Craving you since the night I had you. You are still so beautiful, but I prefer you in something silky, not these rags." He reached out to the sleeve, running the fraying hem between his fingers.

She wrenched back from his touch, but he followed her movement, closing the distance. "Seems I haven't had time to worry about my appearance. But at least I don't smell like a barnyard. My, my Heinrich. What have you done with yourself?"

Her jab landed as she hoped. He always prided himself on his appearance, but it was obvious he had been unable to find proper clothing. "Ah, my sweet dumpling. I know you've missed me." His grip tightened on her wrist.

"There is nothing in this world I have missed less than you. My only thoughts of you have been wishing for your very slow and painful death."

"I'm so sorry to disappoint you." His sinister laugh echoed around her. "Did you not like where I sent you? I was there for a while, and I thought it wasn't so bad."

He towered over her, as he pressed his hardening length against her belly. She breathed in deeply, Jimmy's instructions playing through her mind. She shifted her feet, settling her weight on her back foot. She waited for him to strike.

"I've had so many women since you, but none fulfilled me

like you did." He licked his lips, spittle gathering at the corners of his chapped mouth. His eyes raked up and down her body making her feel cheap and used.

"And why Katja? Why did you marry her?" This was the most puzzling of his actions. Why would he marry a widow with a young daughter?

"She has everything I need. A massive bank account and connections in South America." He patted his shirt pocket. "I received my new identification papers today. And you can be my farewell gift."

Her lips curled. "I'm to be your parting gift. Oh, Heinrich, how fitting."

For a moment, a flicker of doubt shone in his eyes, but then he did exactly what she wanted. He lunged, grabbing her, and forcing his tongue into her mouth. She didn't panic. The moves Jimmy had taught her flooded through her muscles as she swung her fist, connecting with his ear.

Heinrich reeled back, holding it. "You bitch," he hissed. Drawing his hand away from the side of his face, he saw blood. He pounced on her again, but she was prepared; a wickedly irrepressible smile spread across her face.

She brought her knee straight up, kneeing him in his bladder. Instantly, urine soaked his front. He doubled over, clutching his groin. "How dare you!" Deadly rage colored his face.

Her laughter echoed hauntingly off the papered walls. "Oh, Heinrich," she mocked, "did you have an accident?"

He grabbed her, twisting her arms. Her hands and arms burned. He breathed in her ear, "I am going to enjoy this so much more than our last time." He squeezed her tighter. She knew she had won, her victory would be impossibly sweet. Time seemed to slow, seconds turning to long minutes. Her head dropped to her chin, she relaxed for a moment, breathing in a full breath. Then, without hesitation, she flung her head against his face, smashing his nose.

His hold broke. But she was not finished. She turned and faced her tormentor, screaming: "This is the end of you!" She shoved into him with every ounce of strength she had. He fell backward on the ground with a sickening thump. "I was there for 65 nights, 65 nights of hell and torture. And now it is my turn for payback. This is for the night of my engagement." She kicked him in his stomach. "This is for my tattoo," kicking his knees. "This is for my first night in hell," landing another kick on his shoulder.

Someone grabbed her, hauling her backward. It was her father. "Greta! What are you doing here?" His grip dug into her arm; he was shaking. "You should have never come alone."

"Oh, Papa, I wanted to say goodbye. I didn't realize you wouldn't be home."

He pushed her behind him. "No time for that, my Gretel. Please go." Hearing her childhood nickname again caused a flicker of anguish, she would never be that innocent youth again and the man responsible for the end of that innocence lay bleeding on the floor. Her rage boiled over.

Heinrich pushed himself off the floor and stood on wobbly legs. "You both will pay for this."

Her father revealed a Luger pistol from behind his back. "Papa, no!" she screamed.

"Yes, Gretel, it is time for his reign of terror to end. No one will care that I shot him. Not even Katja. He deserves to pay for what he has done."

Heinrich looked annoyed and undeterred by the gun pointed at his chest. His eyes terrified Greta, as much as the bloodlust she saw in her father. "This is not the way, Papa. We will turn him over to the Americans."

"Who do you think gave me my new papers? Americans

will do anything for the right amount of money." Heinrich smoothed his shirt.

"He hurt you, Gretel. He took you away from us and left you to die. He deserves to die." The gun remained trained on Heinrich's heart.

"Please, Papa. Lower the gun." She stretched out her palm. She couldn't have her father kill anyone for her, even if it was Heinrich. "Look at him. He's not going anywhere with wet pants." Her father smirked. The gun pointed down and Heinrich lunged forward.

Bang! The room spun. A high-pitched ringing assailed her ears. A heavy body weighed her down. Acrid gun smoke filled her nostrils. Blood, sticky and warm, pooled around her. In the distance she heard her name being called over and over again. A face swam before her eyes, a flash of jade green eyes. Then it was gone.

Warm breath whispered in her ear, "It's all right now. Everything will be fine. Let me take care of things." She heard footsteps in the hallway, loud bangs echoed through the apartment. Her father's arms lifted her from the ground, helping her back to her parents' bedroom. "Now, you stay hidden. Don't come out until I tell you to." He closed the door behind him.

She lay down on the bed, curling up with her hands pressing against her belly. If only Jimmy was here, he would make things right. She had seen the warrior in him before, during the fight with the German soldier. Never in her life had she felt so safe as she did whenever he was near. Jimmy's lessons were successful; she managed to get the upper hand against Heinrich. When she first hit Heinrich, first saw the blood, she swore she heard Jimmy exclaim, "Attagirl, Greta!" Knowing how proud he would be energized Greta. Each time her hits connected with Heinrich, the vindication was glorious.

But then her father showed up and it all changed so

quickly. She gripped her queasy stomach tighter. Was Heinrich dead? She bit her hand to stifle a sob. If her father killed Heinrich, what would the authorities think? What would happen to him? She had to know more. On unsteady legs, she rose and crept to the door. Opening it slightly, she pressed her ear to the gap.

There were several different male voices. She could hear the low timbre of her father's voice. There was another German voice belonging to a man she did not recognize. Then there were two others, Americans she believed. One spoke only in English, the other seemed to be acting as an interpreter. It was difficult to discern the specifics of the conversation, but she was able to understand key words.

Her father spoke. "Came home... on the floor."

The German, presumably speaking to the Americans, "... appears to be self-inflicted... angle of the gun..."

The words hit Greta with a blinding force. Heinrich was dead, somehow in the struggle for the gun, he had been shot. And her father was covering up the earlier fight. She peeked through the crack in the door. The hall was empty. She snuck down the hallway to the back entrance. Quickly, she headed down the stairs to the street below.

Several curious onlookers were watching the building. A few American soldiers closed off the entrance. Keeping her head down and moving with purpose, Greta wove her way through the crowd until something snagged her sleeve. A long-fingered white hand gripped her arm.

Katja hissed in Greta's ear. "Come with me." She dragged Greta around the corner and through a doorway of an abandoned building, out of sight of the pedestrians on the street. "What happened? Why are you sneaking down the back steps like a common criminal?"

Greta did not want to tell her what had happened; Katja

would never understand. It had become increasingly clear that the Katja she knew from childhood had turned cynical and bitter. Greta empathized with her friend; they had experienced such loss and devastation, had circumstances been different, Greta may very well have ended on the same path. Katja had lost her first husband, the true love of her life and was now widowed again. Though her second husband had married her for connections and money, she was nevertheless a widow for the second time before the age of 23.

"I know you are somehow involved. Be honest with me. Are you the reason Heinrich stole my money?" Katja's grip softened, a glimmer of her friend reappeared.

"Why did you marry him?" Greta leaned against the doorframe, and Katja released her grip.

"I needed protection. Both of my parents were gone, and I had a young child. He promised me. He claimed he would take care of us both. It seemed like the perfect solution, until he started to reveal his true self." She looked at the ground and shuffled her feet.

"What happened?" She wanted to keep Katja talking, to find out her true feelings for Heinrich before revealing the incident in the apartment.

"At first, he would get mad at me for only the slightest provocation. Then it would escalate. He would call me names, hit me. Then..." She stared off into the distance, searching for the way to continue. "He started to force himself on me."

Greta moved closer to her, but Katja put up one hand. "I need to say this. Your parents have been an absolute godsend. They saw what was happening and were able to intervene. Heinrich became nicer for a while. Then today, your mother told me about what actually happened to you. Oh, Greta." She sobbed. "I had no idea. I wanted to hate you. All he did was talk about you and how perfect you were. He compared me to you every single day. How much prettier you were. Cleverer. Wittier. It was awful. I started to hate you."

Finally, she allowed Greta to wrap her arms around her and hold her while she cried. "I am so sorry, Katja. Truly I am. I wish there was a way I could have warned you, but I've been hiding. For so long I lived with the fear of being discovered and sent back to that place."

Katja nodded against her shoulder. "Sometime, I want you to tell me how you survived, but now I want to know what happened. Did he hurt you again?"

"Yes, but he won't hurt any of us ever again." She held onto Katja's shoulders and pleaded with her to understand. "He was planning on leaving you. He showed me his travel documents. He attacked, but I hit him back."

"You did!" Katja's eyes lit. "You must show me how."

Her lips turned in a slight grin. "I will be happy to teach you one day. But there's more." She dreaded this moment, but she had to continue. "My father came into the room." Katja stared with a puzzled expression. "He had a Luger and threatened Heinrich. And I don't know what happened exactly, there was a struggle, and the gun went off."

Katja took a step back, her face not revealing much. "And Heinrich?"

"He's dead, Katja. My father was talking to the authorities when I snuck out."

"Dead?" She turned away, repeating the word a few more times. Each time, her tone altered. Finally, she laughed, her back to Greta. "I'm free! Truly free of him." She spun around smiling. "This is going to be so hard, to go back there and act sad. But the man was truly a monster. I am well rid of him." Suddenly, her face fell. "But your father? Will he be arrested?"

"I don't believe so, when I left I heard the men in the room talking about suicide."

She nodded her head. "I must get back. I need to help corroborate his story. Let them know how depressed he has been lately. And also see if he has my money."

"What money?"

"It is where your mother and I were this morning. I had a note from the bank stating how I was overdrawn. It was impossible. When we arrived, they showed us that all the money I had inherited had been withdrawn two days ago by Heinrich." She stomped her foot, her anger returning.

"Liesel and I are leaving today. I was only stopping by to say goodbye, when…" She waved her hands. "When this happened. But I really must leave."

Katja gripped her hand. "I understand. I will tell your parents your goodbye. Take care of yourself, dear friend." They hugged and parted ways at the street corner.

As Greta worked her way through the maze of streets, she composed another letter for Jimmy. She could scarcely believe the events of the day and could constantly hear Jimmy's voice in her head. She missed his praise, the warmth of his arms. Whenever he was near, her confidence soared. And perhaps, what she missed most was his affection. He would work on the tension in her neck, his lips would press against the tender spot on the back of her head. He would worry over the little bruises and the ringing in her ears. With those thoughts, a lone tear escaped, and she began her letter.

My Dearest Jimmy,

It seems almost every day something unexpected happens. I wish it was as simple as coming home to your arms to tell you about these events, but I guess we both have to be happy with a simple letter. Heinrich tried to hurt me again, but you would be so proud of me, Jimmy. I did everything you told me and was able to hurt him back. I could almost hear Tony and Ruth cheering me on. More happened, but the details are not important at the moment. I will say that I never have to worry about him again. Liesel and I head for Nuremberg. As soon as I am settled, I will write and send you my new address. I long to hear from you. I hope you are well.

All my love,
Greta

CHAPTER THIRTY-EIGHT

Another day of complete exhaustion. In the few short months since Jimmy's return, he worked himself from sunrise to late in the night. His father's shop had never been more organized and efficient. He, on the other hand, was a walking disaster. In order to compensate for the long hours, he filled his body with cups of coffee and cigarettes. At night, in order to clear his mind of all thoughts of Greta, he would drink until he would pass out. The days blended into the next, all a blur.

His mother thought his problem was loneliness. She convinced every mostly eligible young woman in a five-mile radius to visit the shop and flirt with Jimmy. But he was having none of that and had managed to chase them all away. Well, except for Carla Hepplewhite, who seemed to have found Jimmy a particular challenge and visited the store every day for the past two weeks. She would bat her eyelashes and laugh uproariously at whatever he said. Then she would drop something, say oops, and lean down provocatively to pick it up. The nauseating sight was so cringeworthy, Jimmy paid a local kid to keep watch for her. He would signal Jimmy so he could make his escape. Then he roped Erin in to cover for him. It was childish to hide from Carla, but being blunt got him nowhere.

In his room, he poured two fingers of scotch and added a splash of water. He kicked off his shoes and lounged in his brown armchair. Last night it took three glasses before his mind was numb. Hopefully, tonight's oblivion would come more quickly. He swallowed the amber liquid in two gulps, the burning sensation in his chest signaling the magical inebriation would soon take over.

Everywhere he looked, he was still reminded of her. The ache it left behind was unbearable. He needed an escape, but all he could manage was work and blissful intoxication. At one point he thought he could find relief in the arms of any woman. He had gone out with a few friends, met a beautiful brunette and went back to her place. They were both sotted. He tried to make a move, leaning in for a kiss. But seeing her lips so close to his made his skin crawl. He ran to the bathroom and emptied the contents of his stomach. She passed out on the sofa. It was the last time he tried to use a woman to get over Greta. No, his heart would forever remain hers and hers alone.

A soft rap on the door drew him out of his stupor. "Come in," he growled. It could only be one person, his meddlesome sister Erin.

"Drunk again, I see."

He raised his glass. "Sorry to disappoint, only one glass in. But stick around, Brat, I'm sure it won't be long now." He refilled his glass, three fingers this time and no water.

"Don't call me that." She crossed her arms and glared over at him.

"Why not? I've always called you Brat and you never minded before?"

Her eyebrow arched perfectly. "That was my sweet older brother and his term of endearment. I don't know what you are, but you aren't him. When you say it, you sound mean."

He had no energy for this discussion. He was hoping this would be the last of the scotch he would need to drink tonight. He could feel his ears growing warm, it was only a matter of time. "What do you want, Erin?"

She knelt in front of him and reached out for his hand. He recoiled from her touch. She sighed heavily and patted his knee. "We need to talk, you cannot go on like this. Your liver cannot go on like this."

"Why not? I seem to be doing just fine." He could feel the numbness settle over his head, clouding his thoughts. A few more minutes.

"Ha, look at you! You can't even keep your eyes open." He opened one eye. "Both eyes, Jimmy."

He growled, prying both eyes open with his fingers. "Better?"

"Not really. Why don't you read her letters? She has sent so many of them." In her hand was a neat stack of unopened envelopes.

"No, we agreed this wouldn't work out. We had to end things." Even he didn't believe the words as he said them.

"But what if she needs you?"

His chest tightened. What if she did need him? He shook his head. No, she had others. There was Liesel and Fritz. He clutched his hand thinking of her former fiancée, imagining her kissing Fritz, kissing any other man. He stood and paced the room. "She doesn't need me."

"How could you be so certain?"

He glared over at his sister. "You know something, tell me."

She shook her head. "If she has something to say to you, it is in these letters. Preventing yourself from reading them is not helping you. You must find a way forward." She waved the stack at him.

"And what do you know of broken hearts, Erin? Why are you so concerned with solving this impossible situation?"

"I understand the pain of lost love more than you could ever understand, James Patrick O'Brien." He drew back from the anger in her voice. "You do not know half of what I have been through. So for once, you arrogant ass, listen to your sister." She threw the stack of letters at him. "There is hope for you yet, assuming you don't jump behind the wheel of a car again."

He threw the glass at the wall behind him. "You went too far, Erin. You know it." They could hear their parents stirring in the next room. They both lowered their voices.

She walked over to him and cupped his face with her hands. "It was uncalled for. I apologize. But I cannot sit idly by and watch you throw your life away. You love her and even if you can never be together again, you can at least read each other's words. A part of her in your hands."

A shaky whimper escaped before he swallowed back the rest of the tears threatening to overwhelm him. "I miss her so much. It feels like the entire world is crushing my soul."

"I know. Don't give in, dear brother. Please come back to us. And I will help you mend your aching heart."

She laid her hand against his chest and hummed in his ear. He held onto his sister. "Erin, one day you will tell me the name of this unknown heartbreaker. After I am done rearranging all of his internal organs, he will make things right with you."

She chuckled. "Ah, there's a glimpse of the brother I love so well. Welcome back, Jimmy."

He placed a brotherly kiss on her head. She stopped at the door and reissued her command. "Please, read them. At least you can see how she is doing. I know you are worried about her." She left him alone.

Stripping out of his clothes, he lay down on his bed and picked up a letter. He held it to his nose. After all this distance it still smelled of lilacs. Instantly, he felt his length hardening, demanding to feel her again. He ignored his tightening body and slid his finger along the edge of the envelope. A single piece of paper with her slanted handwriting greeted him. As he read, he could hear her voice.

∼

My dearest love,

It breaks my heart that I still have not heard from you and am desperate to know you have returned safely. I heard from Ruth yesterday. She and Ezra are happily settled in Texas. He plays baseball with the neighborhood kids and seems to have adopted Tony's accent. She is blissfully happy.

Liesel and I have moved to Nuremberg. I started my new job and love the experience. Seeing the joy when families reunite brings me such happiness. It gives me hope that one day we too will be united. Until then, my love, know I am faithfully yours.

Love always,

Your Greta

JIMMY PICKED up the letter and kissed her name over and over. He tucked it under his pillow, then picked the rest off of the floor. He found a shoe box and dumped them inside, then shoved the box under his bed. Erin was wrong. Reading the letter made the pain more real. He could not continue like this, the wall he built was beginning to crumble, and his resolve weakening. No, the only way forward was to leave the past behind. He closed his eyes and drifted off to sleep. He dreamed of a little house and a field of lilacs.

CHAPTER THIRTY-NINE

The bell above the tobacco shop door jingled. Jimmy turned to see who could be stopping by at such a late hour. He was busy counting inventory, too busy to spend time chatting with a customer. He did this to forget, drowning himself in mounds of paperwork and bottles of scotch. Anything he could do to dull the pain and drive away the memories of her. So far his father's store was thriving, he had discovered the perfect cure for a hangover, and he was utterly miserable. She was everywhere. A faint scent in the air, a smile on another woman, the color of the sky reminding him of her eyes, a distant laugh. Then there were his dreams, nightly erotic fantasies driving a stake through his heart. He wanted to forget, he needed to forget, but he could only remember, and it was driving him mad.

"May I help you?" he called out, making his voice as unwelcoming as he could muster. He walked through the doorway from the backroom and was greeted by a shocking sight.

Leaning heavily on a wooden cane was his childhood friend. He still smiled the same smile, the one which charmed young girls and teachers alike. Helping them escape innumerable hours of detention. Persuading Father Matthew it wasn't the two of them who placed frogs in the baptismal font at church, even though their clothes were stained with muddy pond water. Convincing Jimmy's mother it was Erin's idea to eat all three apple pies for the bake sale, when they had to bribe Erin to be quiet with the third pie they were saving.

"Hugh!" he exclaimed. "What are you doing here?"

Jimmy extended his hand, which Hugh accepted with a firm shake. During the last few years, they had changed much from the young, naive university boys to the men they were today. Both had journeyed through a lifetime of experiences. Whereas Hugh's body had never fully recovered from the accident, his face still soft with youth. Jimmy's, however, was the hardened face of a man who had seen and done far too much. The youthful mischievous sparkle had left his eyes, replaced by bitterness and cynicism. Too much exposure to the outside elements had weathered his skin, leaving it perpetually bronzed.

Jimmy motioned to the lounge. He locked the door and joined Hugh in his favorite of the well-worn leather chairs. "Would you care for a drink?"

"Sure, whatever you're having." Hugh sat with a small grunt and leaned his cane against the arm of the chair.

Jimmy poured them both two fingers of whiskey with a splash of water. "It's good to see you again." He propped his booted foot up on the table in front of him and motioned for Hugh to do the same.

"You as well." He saluted with his drink. "To victory."

Jimmy returned the toast and threw back the contents of the glass. The amber liquid burned, but he relished its numbing effect. After a few moments of silence, Jimmy asked again why Hugh had come. "It isn't that I don't want to see you, I know you too well. You were not one for idle conversation."

A reluctant smile tugged at the corner of Hugh's mouth. "No, I never enjoyed senseless chatter. Unless it was to talk someone out of punishment or apple pie." He winked, then picked a piece of lint off of his pants leg. "Your sister came to see me."

Jimmy asked sardonically. "Really? And why does my darling, meddlesome sister think she needs to see you?" It really bothered Jimmy how his family tried so desperately to get him to talk. They were constantly nagging him to share stories of the war, and Erin was the worst of them. She knew far too much about Greta and begged him to answer the letters. Didn't they all understand how he needed to forget? How he had no choice but to forget in order to survive?

"I've been asked to help with the trials being held in Germany. I am one of a group of lawyers being sent over to help the prosecution. These war tribunals will be making history, as the Allies hold the Germans responsible for their crimes against humanity."

"I've read about them, one is starting very soon. They will be monumental. But, what does that have to do with me? I never finished law school?" Jimmy studied his friend. He really seemed so much the same, even after all of these years. Same clothes, same gestures, same old Hugh.

"I want you to come with me. No, I need you to come with me. You may not have finished law school, but you know the ins and outs of the laws of the Geneva Convention better than anyone I know. Not to mention you were there. I am a great lawyer, Jimmy, but I need the help of someone I can trust and someone who understands what happened, someone who actually saw evidence of these crimes." Hugh leaned forward, his brown eyes pleading and wide.

"I can't, I just can't go back there." Jimmy was certain it would be enough of an excuse. Naturally, Hugh would assume Jimmy's reluctance stemmed from the experiences from the war. Reopening old wounds. However, Jimmy couldn't go back. Not knowing he would be so close to Greta, and not have her in his arms.

"Jimmy, there is no one I trust like you. You owe me."

Jimmy set his drink down, coolly assessing his friend. "How does helping you with this trial make us even? I nearly took away your ability to walk."

Hugh broke the tension with a disgruntled laugh. "Do you honestly think that accident was your fault? Good God, man, I am not sure which one of us idiots was more drunk. Truth was, had you not been there to pick me up and carry me to help, I would have died on a lonely country road. And I can walk. I learned while you were away." He sighed heavily in frustration. "Jimmy, because of you, I am here."

"Because of me, you almost died!" Jimmy jumped to his feet, his leg protesting the quick movement and causing him to stumble.

"Look at you, same as me. Can't hardly walk." Hugh hobbled over to the whiskey and poured another finger's width into his glass. "Two different versions of the same story. I don't care what you think or how you've spent all this time blaming yourself. Truth is, the accident made me into the man you see before you. A man, I might add, that I am damn proud to be."

Jimmy wanted to protest, but he couldn't argue with his logic. He could never debate Hugh successfully. Not with the way he understood all sides of an argument, twisting around words and phrases until one couldn't help but inevitably agree. It was what made him such an excellent lawyer. "You really feel that way?"

"Because of your cock up, I ended up with a very successful career and a rather happy life. Yeah, I would say it worked out for the best." He peered over at his friend. "Well, almost the best. Jimmy, I missed out. I couldn't fight because of my bum legs, but I can do something now. Please, come with me?"

"And what if it is too painful?" Jimmy needed to stop the infernal ache from building in his chest.

"Seeing Germany again?" Hugh gave a meaningful pause. "Or that you might see her?"

Jimmy swung his eyes to Hugh. "What do you mean — her?" Now he was wondering how much Erin told his old friend. First, it was Ruth writing letters, begging for him to answer Greta. Then came Tony's phone calls. And now, it seems she recruited Hugh. Erin really was pulling out all the stops. He would be impressed if he weren't so damned determined to bury all of his feelings.

"Jimmy, you are the bravest man I know, but only a woman could keep you from doing what I know you were meant to do. You love the law, and this is the chance of a lifetime. To make those who deserve it most, pay."

"And what do you know of her?" Jimmy's agitation with his sister magnified.

"Greta? I know as much as Erin told me, which is probably more than you actually told Erin. From what I understand, she's been writing to Greta all this time."

Jimmy shrugged but couldn't suppress his grin. "How like Erin to go behind my explicit demand to leave all things alone and write to Greta on her own."

"She's worried about you, Jimmy. We all are." Hugh laid a firm hand on his shoulder. "Come with me, help me do some good, and while you are there, see if there is something remaining between you and this Greta."

"It wouldn't matter if there was. We come from two different worlds."

"It's a lame excuse and we both know it." Hugh's tone gentled. "There is no reason not to try and rekindle your feelings."

"Why do you want me to go? Honestly, why me?"

"God, you're obtuse." Hugh gripped Jimmy's shoulder tightly for a brief moment. "Because, you idiot. You love her and you are a completely useless mess. Go to Germany with me, find her, then marry her. Honestly, the rest of us are getting tired of the moping." Hugh picked up his cane and worked his way to the door. "Go, stay, it's up to you. But honestly, from what Erin says, there is more to this story, and you need to go back and find out what it is."

Jimmy's heart raced. "What exactly does that mean? That there's more?"

"I'm not sure. Your sister is keeping quiet for once, and no one is getting the whole truth from her. Be ready to leave in a week." Hugh gave a brief salute and walked out the door.

Jimmy locked the door behind him and rushed up the back stairs to see Erin. Why she had hidden letters from Greta was beyond comprehension. She was the only person he trusted with the whole story, the only one who knew his true feelings. Not even Tony understood the full depth of his attachment.

Sailing past his parents, who were chuckling at the antics on *The George Burns and Gracie Allen Show* playing on the radio, he burst into Erin's room, the door banging against the wall. Without turning around, Erin set down her copy of *Look* magazine and glared pointedly into the mirror on the wall. "Yes? Care to explain the barbaric display of masculinity?"

"Don't play games, Erin." Jimmy closed the door and grabbed the wooden desk chair. He straddled the seat with his arms resting on its back. "I saw Hugh." He waited for her to say something, anything.

She raised her brows and smoothed the pages of the magazine. "And how's Hugh?" Her voice was deceptively nonchalant.

"He said some interesting things to me, mainly hinting about letters to Greta. Letters you sent." He gripped the chair harder, hoping to steady his shaking hands.

"I see. Well, maybe I have." She idly flipped through the pages.

Jimmy exploded, sending the chair flying to the floor. "Give them to me, Erin."

"No." She glared daggers at her brother. She knew his act was nothing but sheer bravado and he could do little to intimidate her. His jaw twitched. She was playing a game she was determined to win. "Jimmy, the letters are between her and me. I would be happy to tell you some of what she said, but it would betray her trust if I shared them with you."

"What are you? Best friends? What type of relationship could possibly exist between two people who've never met?" He was incredulous.

"Well, I am hoping we will be sisters, but it entirely depends on you, doesn't it?" She poked his chest with her finger.

Her statement caused him to stumble. Righting the chair, he slumped down. "Sisters? You mean there's hope?"

"Yes, Jimmy. Go with Hugh, it is the perfect excuse. Find her, bring her home." She leaned over her bed and rooted around for an old shoe box. Rummaging around the contents, she found an envelope and handed it to Jimmy. "There's her address. Notice where she lives now?"

"Nuremberg." It was the city where the tribunals were

being held. He traced over her delicate writing, circling her name. He held the envelope to his nose. Lilacs, forever lilacs.

"It's fate, don't you think?"

"What did you say?" His heart stopped for a moment, his entire world spinning around him.

"It's fate, you and Hugh going to the exact city where she is now." She propped the pillows behind her, picking up her magazine.

"Fate." He couldn't argue with her. Fate was calling him back to Germany, back to find Greta. If only she would have him, if only this time he would propose, if only this time she would say yes.

"Oh, Jimmy." Thinking she was going to say something sly, he turned prepared to sting her with a brotherly retort. But what he saw changed his intentions. "There's more, I can't tell you now, don't be angry with her."

He wanted to know all of it, wanted to squeeze the truth from his sister, but he shook his head and left. Inside the envelope was a single piece of paper. Thinking his sister accidentally left a letter behind, he pulled it out without letting her know. To his surprise, the paper was addressed to him.

Dearest Jimmy,

I told Erin to give you this if you ever talked about coming for me. After months of never receiving a reply to my letters, I understand now what you couldn't tell me before. It's best we part as the friends we were. Know you are forever in my heart, my dreams, my very soul. I wish we had met in a thousand other ways or in a different time, but that wasn't the case. As it is, as it was, you will always be the love of my life. Let's part as we did, allowing the memories to keep us warm on lonely nights. I love you Jimmy, but this is what's for the best.

Yours forever and always,
Greta

JIMMY TRACED the words over and over again. Oh, how wrong he had been. She loved him and he loved her. He wondered how soon he could leave for the trial. A week was a lifetime away.

CHAPTER FORTY

September 1946

The wind played havoc with Greta's clothing, whipping her skirt relentlessly around her legs. She clutched at her hat in desperation, hoping to keep it from flying away. Then came the raindrops, thick and heavy, sliding down the sleeve of her coat as she ran to the nearest shelter on the street. A coffee shop, a perfect place to seek refuge from the deluge outside. Nodding to the proprietor, Greta looked for a place to sit. The café was mostly empty, only a few patrons engaged in soft conversations. Sitting down near the window, she tugged off her drenched coat and set her hat on the corner of the table to dry.

Across from her sat two men, bent over a stack of papers with a few empty plates occupying the rest of the table. They were deeply engrossed in discussion. There was something so familiar about the taller of the two men. His face was bent and turned away from her, but his bearing and gestures caused her heart to flutter with hopeful recognition. She shook her head to clear it and ordered a piece of cake with her coffee.

After all this time, she still saw Jimmy everywhere. The butcher had his eyes, her boss was the same height and similar build, even the postman smiled the same half-crooked smile of Jimmy's. They say time heals all things, but that was anything but true. Time made them feel raw, causing old wounds to fester.

The men continued to attract her attention as she glanced covertly in their direction. She sipped her coffee and ate a bit of cake, wishing there was a mirror or something she could use to see the face of the man with his back to her. Her eyes wandered over to the table again. Sensing they were being watched, both men turned. And that was when she felt the earth tilt on its axis, throwing her entire world off balance.

"Jimmy," she stammered as she cowardly ran back out into the pouring rain, leaving her hat behind.

"Greta! Wait!" Jimmy was out the door and reached her in ten quick steps, twisting her around to face him. "Just wait," he pleaded, gripping her, afraid to let her go.

The rain poured over them, leaving no spot devoid of the river of water. Despite the weather, they stood facing one another, a gulf of silence between them. "Why?" she asked faintly.

Jimmy brushed his thumb along her jaw. "Why am I here?" Greta tilted her head slightly and wiped the drops from her eyes. "For you, Greta."

A sob escaped, Greta's hands flying to her mouth to stifle any more sound. Wrapping his arms around her, Jimmy laid her against his chest, resting his chin on the crown of her head. And when her tears flowed. Nothing could hold back the pain she had felt all those long and lonely months of separation, the sorrow of losing him, the joy of being in his arms once again.

They were impervious to the stares from people on the street, to the cold, hard rain. She clutched the back of his coat, her hands fisting in the material, desperate to never let go, desperate to hold on in fear that this was a cruel illusion. That she would awaken in her bed, his touch a distant memory. He cradled her against his chest, using his body to shield her as much as he could.

Once the tears were under control, Greta turned up to him. She shoved back the sopping curls from her face. "My apartment is not far from here, I think, perhaps, we might need to talk."

"All right, lead the way."

They twisted and turned through a few streets, walking over piles of rubble. They passed by bombed-out buildings and structures being cleared away in order to rebuild. Onward they walked until they came to a four-story building. Its top floor was missing most of the roof and it still showed signs of fire damage. She led him up two flights of stairs to a scarred old door. It opened with a creak.

Inside was a small, tidy room with a table and a few chairs. Lace curtains framed the only window in the room, with a worn-out sofa underneath. On the opposite wall was a kitchenette with a cabinet and stove.

"Let me get you a towel." Greta pointed for him to take a seat. In the bathroom, she squeezed what water she could from her hair, untied her shoes, and hung the coat over the bathtub to drip dry. Then she returned to Jimmy, handing him a towel.

"Here, dry off as best you can. I'll be right back." She hurried into the bedroom and took off the rest of her soaked clothing, choosing to wear a plain burgundy dress with a wrapped skirt and robe. She returned to him. He was awkwardly sitting on the edge of the chair, trying not to make a puddle on the furniture. He had removed his shoes and coat but remained completely soaked through. "Oh, Jimmy, you are like a drowned puppy!"

He graced her with one of his heart-stopping smiles. "Thanks for not saying I looked like a drowned rat." He rubbed the towel over his hair, leaving it standing at awkward angles. Meeting her quizzical expression, he continued. "The saying in America is that someone looks like a drowned rat."

What a horrid expression. No, never, you're far too striking." She tugged nervously at the belt of her robe, biting her lower lip. "We need to get you dry. What should we do about your wet things?"

He lamented the pathetic state of his clothing. "Not much hope here. Do you have an extra robe?"

"No, but here." She undid the garment and handed it to him. He began to unbutton his shirt. "Jimmy, not in here!"

"Greta, you've seen me with a lot less clothing than this."

"I know, but that was before, and things are – well, things are not what they were. Besides," she added, waving her hand towards the floor where he was standing, "you are dripping all over my clean floors."

He raised a thick brow and bowed in assent. "As you command."

With Jimmy in the bathroom, Greta wrapped the blanket from her bed around her shoulders. She sat on the sofa, cocooned, but feeling no warmth. Jimmy returned, standing in front of her, a disgruntled poodle in pink ruffles.

"I look ridiculous!" he exclaimed.

Greta stifled a laugh. The pink silk robe with its ruffled collar went just past his knees and gaped widely across his wide chest, revealing the mat of dark brown curls. His hair was disheveled, a wet lock curled above his right brow. The longer she stared, the harder it was for Greta to resist standing up to brush away the irritant lock. He was ridiculous, ridiculously handsome, and a danger to Greta's peace of mind.

"Sit," she croaked out. Clearing her throat and motioning for the sofa, she tried again. "Sit, please."

He sat on the opposite end, facing the door, his legs spread slightly, the robe gaping further. Greta felt her cheeks burn as she peeked at his now revealed thigh, remembering how deliciously toasty they felt when they were wrapped around her. His eyes followed hers, a knowing smile creeping across his face. "Missed me?" His velvety voice sent rippling waves of desire coursing through her.

Dazed, she found herself nodding, then shook her head to clear her thoughts. Her tone was flatter as she continued the conversation from earlier. "Why are you here, Jimmy?"

"Well, officially, I am here helping with the Nuremberg Trials." He stretched his arm across the back of the sofa, his fingers inching closer to Greta.

"But the actual reason?" She held her breath.

"I told you." He turned to look directly at her, his chocolatey brown eyes breaking down the barriers she tried to maintain. "I came back for you." His hand captured hers, lacing their fingers together. "Greta, I haven't stopped thinking of you since the day I left. There were things I wanted to tell you, things I wanted to show you. I tried to forget you, but each day was a painful reminder of what I once had but had no longer." He cupped his hand around Greta's cheek, rubbing his thumb along the side of her face. "I love you, Greta, I will always love you. This thing we had isn't meant to be over." He paused, drinking in the sight of her. "I need you." He leaned forward, his lips tender against hers.

Greta lifted her chin, enticed by his gentle caresses, the smooth pass of his lips against hers. Their kisses were languid, savoring the feel of their lips mingling. Jimmy drew her closer, moving his hands around her waist, his tongue prying her mouth open. There was a knock at the door and it creaked open.

"Greta, bist du zu Hause? Es tut mir Leid, aber Jens hat Hunger." The pleasantly rounded woman was in her mid-fifties, with graying hair. In her arms was a baby, babbling excitedly. Her mouth gaped as she took in the sight of Greta and Jimmy. She stood frozen at the door. Awkwardly, she turned left and right, as if trying to figure out if she should flee or stay put.

"Um, Jimmy, you remember Liesel."

He gave her a two-finger wave.

Greta spoke to Liesel in German. "Don't worry. Everything is fine. I'll take Jens now, thanks for your help." Greta gave an embarrassed smile as she took the baby from her arms.

Liesel's eyes narrowed. "Humph, so now you're here." She motioned to Greta. "The baby needs a new diaper. I would like to say something to Jimmy. Alone."

Greta began to protest, but the frown on Liesel's face abruptly ended any further debate. Reluctantly, she went into the bedroom, closing the door gently behind her.

Jimmy tugged at the ruffled collar of the pink robe, trying to maintain some semblance of modesty, but the garment was entirely too small for his tall frame. Liesel dragged a kitchen chair over to sit down in front of him. For a long moment, she looked him over, saying nothing.

"She was devastated when she did not hear from you." Her voice was strangely even, but the heat burning through her cornflower eyes revealed her true feelings. Not only was it a matter of assuring the woman he loved of his intentions, but he also needed to regain the trust of the people closest to her.

"Liesel, there really is no excuse for my behavior. I could explain everything to you, but it would sound like a justification. Like I was trying to gain sympathy. In the simplest of terms, I lost faith and thought what was best was severing all connections."

"You thought wrong."

He started to speak but was cut off as she held up her hand and continued.

"You hurt her in a way I am not sure deserves forgiving. It is not my place to tell her what to do or what to say. But I will tell you here and now, you do anything like that again, and your life will not be worth living."

"I assure you my intentions are honorable, and I will not leave her again."

"See you don't. You plan on giving her an honest recounting of what happened during all this time?"

"A complete and honest recounting."

"Be truthful with me. Did you have someone else waiting for you? Is that why you did not write back to her?"

Jimmy blanched. He expected people to think the worst of him, how could they think anything less? "No, there was no one. I would explain more, but I haven't yet told her everything. She deserves to hear it all first."

Liesel moved the chair back to the table. "You are correct. She's the daughter I never had, and I only want her to have the happiness I was lucky enough to find."

Jimmy extended a hand. "Truce?"

She debated for a moment, considering her answer. "Truce. Auf wiedersehen."

"Liesel." She paused at the door. "Who is the baby?"

She smiled for the first time since entering the room. "A beautiful blessing. So delightful, he reminds me so much of my Johann at that age. Same sweet disposition."

"But whose baby is it?"

She looked fondly toward the bedroom, where Greta was

currently changing the baby's diaper, then back at Jimmy. "I hope to see you again soon." She shut the door behind her.

The bedroom door creaked open, and Greta peered around the corner. "Did Liesel leave?" She untangled the baby's fist from her hair.

"Yes." The baby began to fuss, sucking loudly on his plump fist. Jimmy walked over to Greta, who was nervously rocking the babe back and forth. "Who is Jens?"

"Jimmy," she corrected, but he misunderstood.

"Yes? Who is Jens?" It was all he could do not to rail at Greta. The betrayal. A child. Whose child was it? It couldn't possibly be Jimmy's, could it?

"No, his name is Jimmy. Liesel calls him Jens, says it's more of an appropriate German name." She placed the baby on her shoulder as she unbuttoned the top of her dress.

"Jimmy," he said quietly, reaching out a hand to touch the little wisps of dark brown hair covering the back of his head. "Whose baby is he, Greta?" His voice was rough with an array of conflicting emotions.

"Yours, Jimmy. He is your baby." The baby let out a wail of protest and began to cry in earnest. "I'm sorry, Jimmy. I have to feed him." Greta returned to the sofa, placing the baby to her breast, who latched hungrily.

Jimmy remained as he was, dumbfounded. Greta and a baby. A baby. His baby. This is what Erin was trying to tell him about. This is why Greta had sent letter after letter. The ones he never answered. His stomach flipped. He wanted to be sick. But there she was, beautiful as always. At her breast was the dark-haired babe, happily suckling. His baby.

He raked his hands through his hair, wiped them across his face. He could not speak, he did not trust his voice, his words. He wanted to flee and wanted to stay. He felt like weeping and screaming, he wanted to rage against the injustice of it all, but mostly, he wanted to gather his son into his arms and never let go.

Without moving forward, he finally spoke. His fists clenching and unclenching. Greta jumped at the sound. "Why did you not tell me?"

"Not tell you? Jimmy, I tried to tell you." She transferred the baby to her shoulder, gently patting his back. Little Jimmy let out a healthy burp and nestled his face against her shoulder.

"No, you didn't." He ran his hand across his face, trying to come to grips with this unexpected turn.

"Yes, I did!" she shouted. It was the first time she raised her voice. Little Jimmy protested and Greta shifted him to her other breast. "Yes, I did," she repeated quietly. "But you never once answered my letters. Erin finally wrote to me, and I found out you weren't bothering to open and read what I wrote to you."

He felt like the world's biggest jackass. "I did. Oh, God. Greta, I didn't read them." He grabbed a chair, falling onto it. "I tried so hard to forget you, I didn't want to read your letters. I couldn't read your letters. I thought you would talk about how wonderfully life was going for you or about the past. I couldn't bear to read your words, not without being with you. And I was terrified you might tell me you had found someone else and no longer felt the same as I did for you." He buried his head in his hands. "I am such an utter fool."

Greta continued to nurse their son. "I tried everything I could think of to get you to read the letters, to learn you had left something behind."

"That's why you wrote to my sister." He finally looked up at her, his eyes filled with anguish. "Greta, I am so sorry."

"You didn't know." The baby finished eating and now slumbered peacefully in his mother's arms. "I didn't even know when you left. I figured things out long after you had gone, long after Ruth had left."

He approached her, kneeling in front of her. "You had no one."

"My parents have sent money when they can. Liesel watches little Jimmy while I work. And Fritz has been able to send extra food and money our way whenever he can."

Jimmy bristled at the thought of Fritz lending help, instead of himself. He swallowed hard. "Are you in love with Fritz?"

She let out a slight laugh. "Are you jealous?"

He groaned, resting his arm on his knee. "Yes! Of course I am jealous. Devastated. A complete and utter wreck. Another man has been a father to my son. The woman I love has had my child and I was not there for her. I don't think there are enough words to capture how I truly feel."

She reached out to him, cupping his cheek in her hand. "Fritz married four months ago, Jimmy. To a delightful woman, who has generously allowed our friendship to continue." She emphasized the word friendship as she reached over to stroke his cheek.

He leaned into her caress. "You know my sister has been hounding me for months. She finally convinced Hugh to bring me to Germany with him, to help him with the trials. I've been obtuse." He reached his arm around her waist. "I've been hunting for you since I got here."

"I am so glad you are here."

Jimmy sat down next to Greta. "Can I hold my son?"

She laid the sleeping babe into the crook of his arm. Gingerly, Jimmy ran his index finger over his teeny face, touching his nose, his chin. He lifted the baby's tiny fist and held it in his hand, so soft in his rough hands. He smelled the sweet, milky breath as his son dozed so contentedly in his arms. In an instant, he fell in love, his son. A tear tracked down his cheek as he said the words again. "My son."

"He looks so much like you," Greta said, admiring both the child and the father.

"Poor kid." Jimmy laughed, tears filling his eyes. He placed a soft kiss on his son's pink forehead, then drew Greta to his side. "There is no way I am leaving again without the both of you."

"So what does that mean exactly?" Her blue-green eyes melted his heart. They were awash with the hurt he had caused. If only he could take it all back, so she would never doubt him again.

"Greta, when I saw you in the coffee shop today, it felt like my whole world began to make sense again. I have been in Germany for months, hoping to find you. Then, out of nowhere, you appear."

"We've had to move a few times." She reached up to stroke his face.

"So I've gathered." He sighed, shifting the baby to his other arm.

"Here, let me put him down in his crib. Then we can talk easier."

Jimmy looked at her reluctantly. "I've only just met him."

She smiled knowingly. "Yes, but I promise you can be the one to change his diaper when he wakes up in four hours. Besides, he will sleep better in his crib without us talking next to him."

Jimmy released his hold but helped Greta put the baby to bed. They returned to the sofa, Jimmy stretching out along the length of it, gathering Greta into his arms. "The moment I saw you again, I wanted to ask you to marry me." He searched her cherished face. "I was a fool for so long, afraid we would never be together. I didn't trust in fate like you did, that somehow we would be together again. I drowned myself in work, bottles of scotch, and shuttered my heart from the memories of you."

She listened to all the words he needed to say with bated breath, her heartbeat accelerating with anticipation of hearing what she longed for the most

"I hurt you. I hurt my son, without ever knowing he existed. And most of all I hurt myself. By not reading your letters, by not holding onto us, I nearly destroyed the one chance we had for true happiness. Can you forgive me?" He held her hands against his chest, pressing them against his aching heart.

Tenderly, her lips brushed against his. "I know too well how easy it is to lose faith, to build up walls you believe protect you, but instead only cause you pain. I actually believed my father betrayed me, but he was fooled as well. I forgave you the moment I realized it was you sitting in the cafe. That you came back."

"Why did you run away from me?" He held onto her tightly, never wanting to let go again.

"I was terrified. I didn't know why you were there, and I was worried you wouldn't even recognize me."

"Not recognize you? When the very picture of you is forever burned in my memory. No, there was no chance." A beam of moonlight filtered through the clouds, the rain finally stopped, and night fell. The warmth from their bodies enveloped them, the moment filled not with arousal, but with total and complete love for each other. She lay cradled against his chest, listening to the steady beat of his heart. "I love you."

She felt the words as much as she heard them, filling her completely. "And I love you."

"Then will you marry me?" He held his breath, as he waited for the answer he prayed for since returning. Nothing would be complete without his Greta.

She saw all the love and the hope she felt deep within his penetrating gaze. Cupping his face, feeling the coarse stubble against her palms, she let the words flow freely. "Yes, Jimmy. I'll marry you."

He crushed his mouth to hers, each desperate touch speaking the thousands of words he wished he had said, wished he had written to her. He longed for her touch, the feeling of her with him. Now he had the rest of his life to worship her, to make right all the time they had spent apart. "I love you, Greta. We are as we were always meant to be, together at last." With those words, he drew her down to him, showing her all the ways he felt with his body and showering her with all the words he should have said in all the letters he should have written. At last, she was finally his. His Greta. His love.

EPILOGUE

July 1948

The white clapboard house stood a short distance from the road, its green lawn dotted with an array of blooming flowers. Laundry hung on a wash line, baby diapers, blankets, and gingham rompers all waiting anxiously for the new arrival. The windows, framed by evergreen shutters, were open. The lace curtains swayed in the humid summer breeze. Greta waddled out to collect the clothing from the line, but Jimmy caught her. "You can't be leaning over. You are about to drop the baby any moment now."

She laughed. "This isn't our first!" She lovingly ran her hand over her swollen belly, feeling the baby stretching and moving.

"No, but the last thing I want to do is be the one to deliver it." He kissed her forehead and then brought the washing in for her. "What time do they arrive?"

"I can't remember, the telegram is next to the phone." She

waved to the phone stand in the hall as she struggled to sit down. Finally, she leaned back, allowing gravity to take over, and plopped onto the overstuffed chair. She brought her feet up to rest on the ottoman. "Jimmy?"

"Yes, my Angel?"

"Can you get me some water? I really don't want to get up again. I just got comfortable." She stuck out her lip in a mock pout.

He brought her a cup and made sure she was content. He knelt beside her, rubbing his hand proudly over the wide expanse of her belly. He tickled the tiny foot pressed against her navel and laughed as it kicked him in response. "Hello, baby number two." He leaned in and kissed her stomach and then moved to her lips. "I love you."

She gifted him a brilliant smile. "And I love you." They stared adoringly into each other's eyes. "Jimmy, when are they arriving?" They were both excited for their visitors.

"The telegram said four o'clock, so any time now." He stood up, walking into the kitchen to get another glass of water for his wife.

Jimmy couldn't believe his luck. After finding Greta, Hugh promptly declared the hotel room was 'too small' and suggested Jimmy live with Greta. It gave them the opportunity to fall madly in love again and become a family of three. Jimmy was amazed such a precious little being could capture his heart so completely. He adored being a father, finally finding what he never knew he was missing.

When the first trial ended in October, Jimmy and Hugh stayed in Nuremberg to continue preparation for the subsequent trials. In December, Jimmy and Greta finally got the news they had been praying for; the American ban on marriages to Germans was lifted. They could finally marry.

Their ceremony at the registry office was intimate; attended by her parents, with Hugh and Liesel serving as witnesses.

They stayed in the country for a few more months as Greta's visa application wound its way through the bureaucratic process. She sat for numerous, arduous interviews digging into her family history and character. The exhausting process seemed to last forever, but she was finally approved and could emigrate to her new home in America. Before leaving, they took one last trip to visit her parents in Berlin. While heartbroken that their grandson would be moving so far away, they were happy for their daughter's future.

Upon Greta and Jimmy's return to Pennsylvania, Erin quickly determined that not only was Greta her new sister-in-law, but also her best friend. His parents were thrilled to meet their grandson and were adapting to the idea of having a German daughter-in-law. He suspected his mother was far more pleased with his wife than she let on.

A few months later they purchased a small house, thanks to the generous terms of loans being given to veterans and began to put together the final part of their plan they talked about in Germany. In a month, he would be opening a tobacco shop with his father's help in State College, Pennsylvania. They planned on expanding the family business to other areas in the state and possibly bringing Tony in to help. Tony was more than receptive to the idea; he had a few loose ends to settle in Texas before moving North.

Greta started to rise from her chair, trying to shift her weight to give her the correct momentum. "Sit," he scolded. "She is coming to help you."

"I thought they were coming to help you open the new store?"

"That too, however," he nudged her back down, "the store

doesn't open for another month. You, on the other hand, will pop any day now."

"It is unfair to push a pregnant woman back into a seat when she has gotten herself halfway out of it," she growled at him.

He laughed at her. "Sometimes I like you better pregnant, I can make sure you actually take it easy. Rest, wife! For God's sake, take it easy."

The doorbell rang. "Oh my goodness, they are here. Help me up," she demanded, throwing her arms up for him to leverage her out of the chair.

He backed away. "Stay put, woman!" he chided and ran to the door.

His mother burst into the entry. She kissed his cheek, handed him her bag, and demanded to know: "Where is my grandson?"

Jimmy hugged her and she patted his back. "Nice to see you too, Ma."

"Yes, yes. Important things first. I have a grandson to spoil."

"He's asleep, so you'll have to wait. Aren't you going to say hello to Greta?"

His mother eyed him. "Of course." Greta inched her way forward on the chair. She had managed to push herself up when Letty threw her arms around her daughter-in-law. The force of the hug pushed her back into the chair. She glared over Letty's shoulder at Jimmy, who smiled triumphantly.

"Darling daughter. You are positively glowing. How's the little one?" She patted Greta's stomach lightly.

"She dropped a few days ago." Greta shifted uncomfortably.

"She is it, hmm?" The family had been taking bets on when the new arrival would come and if the baby would be a girl or boy. "So any day now? We are just in time." Letty fussed over her daughter-in-law, fetching her an extra pillow for her back.

Erin was next to enter the house. His father was slowly meandering from the car to the house, stopping every few feet to inspect the lawn or garden or whatever captured his attention. She threw her arms around her brother, affectionately pecking his cheek.

"It is so good to see you, Erin. I need your help preventing Greta from doing all the housework."

She raised a haughty brow. "Hmph, Erin, do this. Erin, do that. You know I only came so I could spoil my nephew."

"Erin..."

"What?" Her eyes glittered with mischief.

He groaned; she was trying to rile him. "Where's Da?"

"Outside, inspecting your garden." Jimmy went to the door, but her words stopped him cold. "He says you have snails."

"Oh, no." Jimmy shook his head. His father had long considered himself a gardening specialist. If he didn't stop him now, half of his flowers would be torn up before the week was over. "Help Greta, please."

"You know I will. I like her far more than I do you." She stuck out her tongue and shooed him through the door. "I see Da with the pruning shears. You better run."

Letty had Greta's feet elevated on the ottoman, a blanket draped over her legs, and was insisting she needed a sandwich. Letty began preparing a mountain of food.

"Ma, she's fine." Erin rolled her eyes. "You will smother the poor woman."

Letty was about to challenge her daughter when a small commotion upstairs interrupted them. "My little Jimmy!" Letty exclaimed. Placing a plate with a sandwich on her belly, she patted Greta's hand. "You rest now, I've got him." She flew up the stairs, taking two at a time. "Grandma's coming, little Jimmy!"

Erin laughed. "She's positively gaga over that boy." She waved a finger, pointing it at Greta's belly. "Don't you know what causes this particular problem? Already giving her another grandbaby, before her daughter is married. I shall never forgive you, Greta."

"Has it been so bad?"

"It was a three-hour car ride, and all I heard the entire time was - Jimmy's gotten married. Jimmy and Greta have a baby and another one on the way. Jimmy is starting his own business. They bought a house. When are you getting married, Erin? I'm not going to live forever, I would like to see my daughter married before I'm dead and buried." She slouched in the chair and released a world-weary sigh, blowing a long auburn tendril off her forehead.

"Thank God, we haven't moved to Vermont or another state hundreds of miles away."

Erin gasped, horrified. "No, don't you even think about it! I could never survive for so long in a car with the two of them. My dad pointing out all of the different crops and discussing inane topics like gardening. And my mother, Lord! She would be lamenting how I will never marry. Three hours is all the distance you can have, Greta."

She smiled at her sister-in-law. "I'm only teasing. We just got settled here."

"And what a lovely place it is." Erin took the plate from Greta's lap. "And how are you, dear sister?"

Greta sighed. "I'm so happy, I feel like I could burst."

Erin eyed her swollen belly. "I would rather you didn't."

"Oh, Erin. You always make me laugh! Would you believe your brother told me I waddle?"

"What! I shall kill him. He didn't?"

"What didn't I do?" Jimmy queried as he entered the room, walking over to Greta's side. He leaned down to kiss her head and rub her stomach.

"Where's Da?"

"He got a shovel and is digging a drainage ditch. I gave in trying to convince him to come inside." He lifted Greta's chin and smiled adoringly at her.

"Ugh, you two." Erin made a gagging sound. "You make a nauseating sight."

Jimmy's gaze never left his wife's. "One day, you will feel this way too, Erin."

He could sense her sticking out her tongue behind his back. "Well, whoever he is, he better not compare me to a duck when I'm pregnant."

Jimmy grimaced. "Not my finest moment. Thanks for bringing it up, Erin."

"Always happy to help." She straightened the seam in the leg of her pants. "So what are you going to name this baby if it is a girl? Erin, I presume?" Greta let out a labored groan. "It's not that bad of a name."

Greta shook her head. "No, Erin, it's not that."

Jimmy's eyes widened in fear. "What's wrong?"

"A small contraction, I'm fine." She held his hand in hers. "It's the second one this hour. Nothing to worry about."

"Today then?" His chocolatey brown eyes met hers, his face alight with excitement and anticipation.

"Probably. But it will be a long time yet. Little Jimmy took thirteen hours. So for now, a few distractions." His hand rested softly on her belly, rubbing small circles. "Tell me how much you love me?"

"There are not enough hours left in my lifetime to tell you how much I love you, Greta." He leaned forward to kiss her and felt her belly tighten underneath his palm. "You are my everything."

"And you are mine, Jimmy O'Brien. My heart, my soul." Their foreheads rested together as they counted the minutes between contractions. Any time now, he would become a father for the second time. He had never been so nervous and excited about anything in his entire life. Would this child be a girl or another boy? Would his children know how much he loved them? Would they know how close he had come to losing his heart? But he didn't. His heart sat in the middle of the living room, gazing up at him with all the love she had. His perfect Greta.

Several hours later, Jimmy cradled a baby girl in his arms. A soft pink blanket, one her grandmother knitted, swaddled the tiny bundle. Her lips pressed together, then relaxed as she opened her bright eyes and stared with wonder at her father. She yawned and fell back into blissful slumber with a tender coo.

Greta's sweet voice called out to him, "What should we name her?"

Jimmy sat down on the bed next to his enchanting wife. The room was bathed only in the light of the moon. "What name do you like?"

Greta brushed a featherlight kiss on the baby's forehead. "Rose, she is such a precious darling."

"I thought we could name her after my mother, Elisabeth." Jimmy laid the baby across her lap, her tiny head nestling in the crook of Greta's elbow. Then he wrapped the two of them into his arms, holding them both in his loving embrace.

"Rose Elisabeth, I think it's perfect. She has your chin." She gently touched the dimple. "I wonder, do you think her eyes will be brown like yours and little Jimmy's?"

"I think they will be like yours, Greta. They are already such a bright shade of blue." His wife and daughter drifted asleep resting against him, their breathing slow and even. The moonlight cast the room in a silvery glow.

In his arms he held half of his world; the other half was fast asleep down the hall, weary after a day spent digging in the garden with his grandpa. How close Jimmy had come to losing it all, because of his stubborn refusal to accept Greta as his future. And now, she was well and truly his. *Mine*, he thought, kissing both of their heads. Greta sighed and snuggled closer to his warmth.

Fate had brought them together, had tied their destinies so perfectly, that to be apart would mean they were broken. Together they would become whole, strong, and unyielding. His Greta. Her Jimmy.

ABOUT THE AUTHOR

After a rambling past, Stacia Kaywood currently resides in Kansas City, the Missouri side naturally, enjoying copious amounts of BBQ, Mexican food, and the greatest Austrian cuisine this side of Vienna. A teacher by day and author by night, her life consists of hauling children to band rehearsals, baking, and filling notebooks with newly discovered words and fresh ideas for stories. Her own world wouldn't be complete without her fantastic husband, amazing children, and two furry cats (who provide unsolicited editorial commentary while sitting on the keyboard). As a lover of languages and a student of history, she finds inspiration in the oddest places, using past human experiences as her guide for creating the characters she adores.

To learn more about Stacia Kaywood and discover more Next Chapter authors, visit our website at www.nextchapter.pub.

Bathed In Moonlight
ISBN: 978-4-82415-628-0

Published by
Next Chapter
2-5-6 SANNO
SANNO BRIDGE
143-0023 Ota-Ku, Tokyo
+818035793528

10th November 2022

Printed in the USA
CPSIA information can be obtained
at www.ICGtesting.com
CBHW030329060524
8039CB00002B/10